"GAYL̶̶̶̶̶̶̶̶̶̶̶̶̶̶̶̶̶̶̶̶̶̶̶̶
DAZZLIN̶̶̶̶̶̶̶̶̶̶̶̶̶̶̶̶̶̶̶̶̶̶̶̶ER

The prodigal return . . .

It's an absolute scandal when Captain Matthew Leland arrives at Madingley Court. Presumed dead in battle, his sudden appearance gives the *ton* quite the shock. But no one is more surprised than Matthew, because waiting for him at home is a bewitching, blue-eyed beauty—and she claims to be his wife!

Miss Emily Grey was alone in the world when a knight in shining armor came to her rescue, claimed her heart, and then disappeared. But now her little white lie, a desperate act of self-preservation, has come back to haunt her. Her husband, once a far-off fantasy, is now a flesh-and-blood man who insists she share his bed. . .

Matthew has no memory of any marriage to this scheming seductress, and he's determined to expose her in every way. But a life with the exquisite Emily will prove irresistible . . . and a marriage of deception will become a marriage of sweet, sweet surrender.

Romances by **Gayle Callen**

NEVER MARRY A STRANGER
NEVER DARE A DUKE
NEVER TRUST A SCOUNDREL
THE VISCOUNT IN HER BEDROOM
THE DUKE IN DISGUISE
THE LORD NEXT DOOR
A WOMAN'S INNOCENCE
THE BEAUTY AND THE SPY
NO ORDINARY GROOM
HIS BRIDE
HIS SCANDAL
HIS BETROTHED
MY LADY'S GUARDIAN
A KNIGHT'S VOW
THE DARKEST KNIGHT

GAYLE CALLEN

Never Marry A Stranger

AVON

An Imprint of HarperCollinsPublishers

This is a work of fiction. Names, characters, places, and incidents are products of the author's imagination or are used fictitiously and are not to be construed as real. Any resemblance to actual events, locales, organizations, or persons, living or dead, is entirely coincidental.

AVON BOOKS
An Imprint of HarperCollins*Publishers*
10 East 53rd Street
New York, New York 10022-5299

Copyright © 2009 by Gayle Kloecker Callen
ISBN 978-0-06-123507-8
www.avonromance.com

First Avon Books paperback printing: September 2009

Avon Trademark Reg. U.S. Pat. Off. and in Other Countries, Marca Registrada, Hecho en U.S.A.
HarperCollins® is a registered trademark of HarperCollins Publishers.

Printed in the U.S.A.

10 9 8 7 6 5 4 3 2 1

To my agent, Eileen Fallon: We've been together for fourteen years, through twenty-two books, and our working relationship keeps getting better—as does our friendship. Thank you for your excellent brainstorming, and your thoughtful advice which has enhanced my career.

Never Marry A Stranger

Chapter 1

Cambridgeshire, England, 1845

Captain Matthew Leland didn't usually knock on the front door of his ancestral family home, but when one was returning from the dead, it seemed the proper thing to do.

When he'd heard that the army had mistakenly informed his family that he was dead, he rushed home from India, knowing he could reach his parents as quickly as a letter could.

At his side, Lieutenant Reginald Lawton sent him an encouraging grin. Matthew and Reggie had been friends since they'd left England; they'd fought side by side, saved each other's lives countless times. Though Matthew had insisted he didn't need his friend's help as he reunited with his grieving family, part of him was glad for Reggie's presence.

Reggie whistled in disbelief as they both tilted their heads to look up at Madingley Court, the palace of the Duke of Madingley, Matthew's cousin.

It rose imposingly above them, all turrets and sprawling wings that seemed to stretch on forever, windows gleaming to light the growing darkness of evening.

"I still can't believe you were raised here," Reggie said, shaking his head. "You never seemed so fine to me."

Matthew grinned. "My mother was the daughter of a duke, after all. My cousin now carries the title and owns the property. But still . . . this is home."

Madingley Court was the place he'd lived much of each year. Lady Rosa, raised at the pinnacle of Society, conducted her life accordingly. But being born into the Cabot family had come with a price— even a curse, as Matthew had once thought it.

Cabots were notoriously scandalous, their names on every tongue, their deeds the stuff of infamous legend.

And his parents had been no different. His father, Randolph Leland, was an anatomy professor whom his mother, Lady Rosa Cabot, had fallen in love with, regardless of Society's scorn. Her own father, guilty of neglecting his children as he rebuilt the family name, gave in to whomever his daughters wanted to marry. Lady Rosa, in her pride, had thought her choice—her good sense—infallible. And then her husband dragged her into scandal.

An anatomist, Matthew's father had been paying men to purchase the bodies of criminals condemned to death, which was allowed by the law. His studies consumed him. But when he needed a female corpse, which was harder to find, his employees had dug up the graves of the newly dead. The professor was caught in the scandal of it all, and although his work was legitimate and he was innocent of the crime, he could not escape the notoriety of buying female corpses.

Matthew had only been a little boy at this time, but even he could see the strain between his parents. Lady Rosa had disregarded Society to marry a commoner, and was furious and humiliated by his actions. Each was hurt by the other's mistrust, and they'd gone to the very brink of divorce, scandalizing London for months. After being the subject of condemning newspaper stories and caricatured in cartoons, they pulled back for the sake of their family and called off divorce proceedings. On the face of it, many thought they'd healed their marriage. But Matthew and his sisters knew it was all a facade. The Lelands loved their children—but not each other.

And Matthew somehow felt guilty, for even as a boy, he had fought his natural inclinations to do whatever he wished. Trouble seemed to find him, with the help of his cousins, Christopher and Daniel. Matthew continued to resist his very nature, unable to forget the stark hurt on Lady Rosa's face whenever she was reminded of the scandal of her near-divorce. Marriage had only seemed painful to him, for although his parents tried to follow the rules and repair their relationship, they were never the same. To him, such pain didn't seem worth it.

As an adult, he'd found it harder and harder to be the proper son. His cousin Christopher had given up his wild ways when he took on the responsibility of his title at eighteen, determined to save the family by being the perfect duke. Daniel had gone the other way, invoking one scandal after another, doing as he wished. When Matthew's envy of Daniel's freedom became too much, he knew that something drastic had to change, or *he* would be the one humiliating his mother.

So he'd bought a commission in the army four years ago. His parents were shocked but did not protest. After all, it wasn't as if he would inherit a title and vast wealth, along with all the management responsibilities. Matthew had never even shown an interest in the investments Professor Leland made. And the army was a perfectly respectable choice for a gentleman.

After two years stationed in England, he was at last shipped to India—and to freedom. No one knew his name or his family history; nothing but duty and loyalty were expected of him. He could do as he wished, give in to the wildness he'd spent his whole life resisting.

And it had been exhilarating. He'd fought battles

with such ferocity and recklessness that he found himself promoted for bravery. An unintended consequence, but he accepted it with gusto. He had thought himself a new man—a free man—but with recklessness came arrogance, and he'd gone too far.

He shoved the painful memory away, feeling barely a twinge of emotion; he'd become good at ignoring what he wanted to.

Regardless of what had happened in India, he was home now—and he was different. He couldn't go back to repressing every inclination. He had to be himself, to do as he wished. Perhaps his parents would want to think the change in him was due to serving his country, but Matthew knew he would be a coward if he let them believe that. The army had freed him, had allowed him to become the man he'd always wanted to be—a man who no longer lived by Society's unwritten rules. He did as he pleased, as long as no one was hurt. His parents would someday understand that, for at least he'd always known he had their love.

At last the front door opened and Hamilton, the family butler since Matthew's childhood, gave an imposing stare down his patrician nose, first at Reggie, then at Matthew. He opened his mouth—and then his jaw seemed to drop to his chest.

Matthew smiled. "Good day, Hamilton."

"M-Master Matthew?" the man sputtered, his face going white.

Matthew winced as Reggie's elbow hit him in the side, because of the name the servants used to call him during his boyhood. But if the unflappable butler was stunned, Matthew knew that his arrival was going to give his parents apoplexy.

"I know it's a shock, but yes, it's me, back from the dead. Except I never really died."

Blood finally rushed back into Hamilton's cheeks, and he tried to use a proper expression to mask his grin. "Captain Leland, it is good to see you. It is not my place to ask about this miracle, so I will only say that your parents will be beyond grateful."

"Then they're here?" he asked, feeling a rush of anticipation and pleasure. He was relieved to at last bring them out of their grief, and to begin the journey of letting them know his real self, the one he'd been hiding for so long.

The butler hastily stepped back. "Goodness, yes, they are! Please do come inside." He glanced at Reggie.

"Forgive me, Hamilton," Matthew said. "This is my friend, Lieutenant Lawton. He'll be staying with us for a while."

As Matthew crossed the threshold, Hamilton took his portmanteau from him, and Reggie set his just inside the door.

"Do you have more luggage, Captain?" the butler asked.

"Yes, we each have another trunk in the coach outside."

"I'll see to it after I've taken you to Lady Rosa and Professor Leland."

Matthew put a hand on his shoulder. "Thank you."

The marble statues in their recessed alcoves almost seemed to greet him as something familiar from childhood. Reggie openly gaped up at them. The doors to the great hall were open, and Matthew could see the shields and swords on the walls representing the Madingley past, but Hamilton continued walking by. The butler gave him an uncharacteristic grin as he reached the closed doors to the drawing room, and Matthew shared his excitement.

Speaking over his shoulder, Hamilton said, "Her ladyship, the professor, and your wife are spending the evening in the drawing room. If I may admit to such boldness, I cannot wait to see their faces."

Matthew exchanged a perplexed frown with Reggie. Whose wife? But before he could question the servant, the door was thrown open and he saw three people sitting near the main hearth.

His father, Professor Randolph Leland, had Matthew's auburn hair, but tinged with gray. It was disheveled, as if he'd recently run his hands through it, a habit Matthew remembered since childhood. His mother, Lady Rosa Leland, looked more gaunt than he recalled, her face deeply lined—because of his supposed death, of course, and not just the passage of time. Matthew wanted to wince with guilt. With them was a strange woman who completed a cozy tableau. While the professor read the newspaper, Lady Rosa and the woman sewed, their heads together as if in discussion. They all looked up when Hamilton cleared his throat.

And something inside Matthew went still in relief, in gladness, knowing that he could bring them renewed happiness. He was so glad to be home after a long journey halfway around the world.

"Excuse the interruption, Professor Leland and Lady Rosa." The old butler's voice was husky, as if with emotion. "I bring good news."

The newspaper sagged in his father's lap, and Lady Rosa gave a sound halfway between a gasp and a cry, her sewing falling to the floor as she rose. The unfamiliar woman remained silent and still, but her face blanched.

"Matthew?" Lady Rosa spoke his name faintly, then clutched her husband's arm as if she would fall.

He rushed forward. "Yes, Mother, it's me, but please don't swoon. There was a terrible mistake made, and when I discovered you'd been sent news of my death, I rushed home as quickly as I could."

It was his parents' turn to rush, and they met him halfway across the room, tears streaming down their faces. Matthew's throat tightened at their display. Much as he'd distanced himself from Professor Leland's scandal, just as his mother had—albeit for vastly different reasons—he'd never forgotten how much they loved him.

He hugged them both at once, then let Lady Rosa sob against his chest, holding her as he grinned at his father.

"How did this happen, son?" the professor asked in bewilderment, using a handkerchief to wipe away tears.

To Matthew's surprise, Professor Leland gently patted Lady Rosa's back, as if to ease her heightened emotions. What had happened to the distance kept so carefully between them, like the earthen walls thrown up to protect a soldier? Much of his childhood involved him walking very carefully between their respective encampments, where they stood like two enemies under cease-fire.

Laughing and crying, Lady Rosa at last looked up at him, staying within the circle of his arms. "Yes, tell us what happened, please!"

"I was injured," he explained, "and my regiment had to leave me behind."

As he spoke, Matthew found himself looking beyond them at the woman who still stared at them. She seemed frozen, her sewing neglected in her lap, her hand clutching the arm of the sofa, leaving her knuckles white. Her pale blond hair was piled in random curls on top of her head, reminding him of champagne bubbles. She was classically lovely, with elegant cheekbones, a slender nose, and full lips that were now parted in shock. She seemed oddly . . . familiar.

The lure of his curiosity was such that he almost couldn't remember what he'd been talking about. He turned back to Lady Rosa. "After I recuperated and transferred to another regiment, somehow my first post thought I'd died from my injuries. I learned too late that they'd sent a letter of condolence to you."

"Oh, Matthew!" she cried again. "I cannot tell you how we grieved your loss."

She was shaking now, and he felt as guilty as if he'd deliberately misled her himself. Her dark brown hair had gone mostly gray, and she seemed frail.

At last Lady Rosa saw him look over her head at the woman.

"Oh my goodness!" she cried. "Your beloved Emily deserves the happiness of your reunion!"

Beloved Emily?

He blinked at the woman, even as his parents took both his arms and led him forward. The woman— Emily—seemed unnaturally stiff, as if fighting the inclination to lean away from him.

Lady Rose went to her, guiding her to her feet. "He isn't a dream, Emily dear," she said softly, with a gentleness born of love.

And then Emily was urged toward him, and he could see that the elegance of her form continued down her body, with delicate curves perfectly proportioned, high breasts, narrow waist, and a flare at her hips. But it was her eyes that drew him, wide and brilliant blue as china—especially against her skin, so pale as to have no color at all.

"Matthew," Lady Rosa said in a chiding voice. "Have you nothing to say to your wife?"

And then at last Matthew had to accept what his brain hadn't wanted to believe—this woman had told his family that she was his wife.

He pressed his lips together to keep a burst of laughter at bay. *His wife?*

But his parents believed it, believed her, he realized with incredulity. For some unknown reason, this woman had deceived them with her lies—and gotten away with it.

He should be angry, incensed. But instead he felt a reluctant sense of admiration at her daring, and at her success.

He glanced quickly at Reggie, but with a soldier's control, the man gave away no reaction, only awaited Matthew's response.

Matthew knew there could very well be a wider conspiracy; after all, this woman might be swindling his family. But Professor Leland was no fool, and although he might seem focused on his research, he would have known if thievery were taking place.

And there had been love in Lady Rosa's voice, and this woman couldn't have earned that very easily.

She'd claimed to be his *wife*? When the truth was revealed, it would be the biggest scandal his scandal-prone family might ever have seen. And he, having created his own scandals in India, now faced a new one erupting right in the middle of his family. Thank God he'd finally accepted the fact that scandal followed him wherever he went.

"Matthew?" Lady Rosa said hesitantly, staring between the two of them with confusion.

She held Emily's arm, but the other woman didn't even seem to be trembling. Where were her excuses, her attempts to explain what she surely thought he was about to disclose? He was eager to hear them, to see how her mind worked. But she remained silent, waiting. Somehow he had to encourage her participation in this comedy.

Matthew gave his father a confused smile. "I— forgive me, but my wounds were rather grievous. They said I almost died."

Lady Rosa gasped, one hand clutching Emily's arm, the other reaching for her husband's support. Matthew watched in astonishment as the professor gave it. But he couldn't focus on his parents, not when this situation needed careful cunning to match Emily's.

And then the answer came to him, so shocking and yet appropriate that he wanted to laugh. There was only one way to discover Emily's secrets without having her interrogated by a constable. And though it was only a temporary halt to the inevitable scandal when this story hit the newspapers, he gave in to his impulses, so long denied.

"Some parts of my memory are vague, and I thought they would be minor, but"—he gave Emily a chagrined smile—"I don't remember being married."

There was a strained moment of silence where his parents gaped at him. Matthew watched Emily, eager for her response in the battle he'd just initiated.

And then her eyes rolled back in her head and she began to collapse.

Chapter 2

Matthew scooped Emily up before she hit the floor, enjoying the soft curves of her limp body as he gathered her against his chest.

"Oh dear!" Lady Rosa cried, putting her palm gently on Emily's forehead. "The shock must have been too much for her. She has grieved for you so, especially after your six wonderful months together in India."

Reggie gave a sudden cough, then cut if off.

"She was ill when she first arrived last year," Lady Rosa continued, "just after we'd heard of your death. Poor thing. She herself hadn't even heard the news, for she was on an earlier ship."

Lady Rosa gave him a worried smile, but returned her concern to his "wife." So Emily had not just claimed theirs was a rushed marriage, but said they'd spent time together. That was incredibly risky. So what had she been doing—and trying to hide— while they were supposed to be together in India?

"She only came to you *after* you heard the news?"

he asked. Emily had obviously targeted him because she discovered that he was conveniently dead. Why would she need the protection of a man's name?

"It doesn't matter, son," Professor Leland said in a husky voice. "Good Lord, your health is more important than anything else. You've lost parts of your memory. Shall we send for the physician immediately?"

The twinge of guilt was too easily ignored. "The army took care of all that, Father. And nothing can be done except hope that time will heal my memories. I am not in any pain or discomfort."

The professor seemed to force himself to relax, his gaze falling on Emily, still unconscious in Matthew's arms. "Is she not heavy, son? You could place her on the chaise. I'm certain she'll revive quickly."

Matthew wondered if she'd portrayed herself as fragile, coming to them supposedly ill. He wanted to question her, but not in front of his parents.

He gave his father a tired smile. "Though I can't remember our marriage, I imagine I don't mind holding her."

Lady Rosa rolled her eyes even as she blushed, while the professor chuckled.

Matthew looked down at Emily's still face, adjusting her so that her head rested on his shoulder where he could see her. Her sweet-smelling breath fell softly on his neck; her closed eyelids looked bluish with fragility.

"This must be a shock for you as well, son," Professor Leland said quietly. "Memories are all we have of the past, and to lose them, especially one so important . . . " His voice trailed off for a moment, then strengthened. "But this is minor, something that will ease with time. The most important thing is that you're home with us, that you're alive. We can all make new memories together."

"Oh, your sisters will be so thrilled!" Lady Rosa cried, clapping her hands with delight. "They had already retired to their rooms. We can send for them and celebrate!"

But Matthew was too eager to begin the dance of wits with Emily. "Mother, would you mind if I take . . . Emily up to our suite? Peace and quiet will help ease her shock. And I do find myself exhausted. I only spent a brief night in London, then came directly here."

"Of course, of course," the professor said. "We'll tell the girls when they awaken in the morning, so they won't shock you with their hysteria."

"Shall I have a tray sent to you for dinner?" Lady Rosa asked.

"No, we stopped for a meal several hours ago. I'll just be glad to sleep."

His parents turned and came up short when they encountered Reggie, who clicked his heels together and bowed to them.

Matthew shook his head with suppressed amusement. "With all the excitement, I forgot the intro-ductions. Professor Leland and Lady Rosa, allow me to present my friend, Lieutenant Reginald Lawton. We traveled together from India."

While his father nodded politely, Lady Rosa took her worried gaze from Emily and gave Reggie a frank look of interest. "I will be so happy to talk with you, Lieutenant. Were you with Matthew during his marriage to Emily?"

Matthew didn't worry about Reggie's response.

"No, my lady," the other man said promptly. "I guess I'll get to know her right along with Matthew."

Matthew used a wince to hide his amusement. "Hamilton will find you a room, Reggie. I'll see you in the morning."

As his parents accompanied him through the cor-ridors, Matthew found himself nodding and smiling at the various servants who'd come to gape at him in astonishment. Some he didn't recognize, but of the ones he did, many were wiping their teary eyes with handkerchiefs. He was strangely moved.

Yet what impressed him was how many looked at his "wife" with true concern. Apparently, Emily had made herself at home in his household, and turned even the servants into her admirers.

He wondered if she was faking a swoon to delay his inevitable questions until they were alone. That would be a good tactic. Her angelic demeanor and delicate body made it easy to forget what she'd done. He had been celibate since last year, so he could be excused for his inability to look away from the woman in his arms.

Lady Rosa opened the door to his suite.

The chit had been living in his rooms, of course, he thought with amusement. To his surprise, she'd changed nothing of the masculine decor of dark wood, nor added feminine frills.

He placed the woman gently on his bed. At last, his parents left them alone, after lighting lamps to combat the growing gloom of the evening. A servant had already lit the coal in the hearth to chase away the coolness of the autumn night. He was glad of that, for after the heat of India, England seemed far too cold. Absently, he rubbed his scarred arm where the skin had pulled tight over his elbow as he'd carried her. Not exactly painful but . . . uncomfortable, and a constant reminder of his mistake in battle.

Matthew stood beside the four-poster bed, staring down at Emily—or whatever her name really was—for several long minutes. She didn't stir. Long brown lashes lay on her porcelain cheeks; pink lips were parted softly with her breathing. Though he leaned close, still she remained unmoving. If she was pretending unconsciousness, she was doing a masterful job of it.

He searched the wardrobe in the dressing room and found serviceable clothing, nothing indecently expensive or flamboyant, several gowns a variety of black or gray. But of course she would have just emerged from mourning only months ago, he thought, smiling, wondering if she was the sort to miss lovely gowns.

Back in his bedroom, he went to the dressing table, which had once housed his razor, shaving brush, and cup, but now held a woman's matching comb, brush, and hand mirror set, as well as glass bottles of perfume. He went through the chest of drawers, but found no hidden jewelry, nothing that incriminated her in any way. He was relieved.

But in the desk, several papers were gathered in a leather folio. He stared in surprise at a marriage license with his own signature on it. *Had* his injury made him forget something so monumental? But no, he could remember everything he'd done, every moment of his time in India. He peered more closely at the document, and realized that although the signature would pass cursory inspection, someone had carefully copied his own to forge it, to provide a way into a celebrated family.

Not someone: Emily Grey. Unless that was a false name she'd written on the license.

But even her name struck a chord within him. Had he met her before? Was that why she'd chosen his family?

The town listed on the license was Southampton, where his ship had departed England, the wedding date only two days before he'd left the country. She knew much about him and his movements before he'd deployed. But she'd been clever enough to pass them off as a love-at-first-sight couple. What— or who—had induced her into this mad scheme? His parents said she hadn't come to them until last year, just after they discovered his supposed death. Obviously she had chosen him from the list of the deceased.

He put the license back where he'd found it. He would have to exercise the ultimate patience, even as he played the befuddled husband. He shouldn't be enjoying this so much, he knew, but couldn't seem to help himself.

Husband, he thought again, looking down at her.

Off the top of his head he'd claimed amnesia where she was concerned. But if he were pretending to believe all of her lies, was he supposed to treat her as a wife in truth?

Even share this bed?

Something wicked stirred to life inside him.

Matthew shook his head and looked away, rallying his control. He'd spent his life mastering his every impulse; he would take things slowly as he figured out Emily Grey. How bad could she be if his parents already loved her?

Her eyes blinked several times, then opened, showing him the captivating blue, as well as her confusion.

And then she saw him and gasped.

"Hello, Emily," he said softly, smiling. "Your husband is home."

Emily opened her eyes, thinking groggily that she was supposed to be in the drawing room. Instead she was lying on her back, beneath the canopy of a bed—in her husband's bedroom.

It all came to her suddenly, and her wary gaze found the man who'd brought her here, who now watched her after his pleasant greeting.

The dead man she'd *claimed* as her husband.

She'd thought she had become a strong woman, but his entrance into the drawing room stunned her so that she'd been speechless, unable to think about what to do. She'd fully expected to find herself tossed from the house.

But he hadn't denounced her. When he said he'd lost part of his memory, her relief had been so absolute she must have fainted. How appallingly weak of her. Weakness was a liability; only her strength and her wits would see her through this now.

She found herself studying Captain Matthew Leland, trying to remember the man she'd known for only a few hours not quite two years ago, the man whose death she'd used for her own convenience.

But he wasn't dead. He was very much alive, and alone with her in the bedroom they were supposed to share as husband and wife.

But he wasn't her husband.

She wouldn't panic. This rare illness of his had given her the chance to continue playing the role of his wife. She was strong now, and had learned she was capable of doing terrible things in order to survive. And she would survive this.

"Matthew?" His name came out in a feigned whisper of disbelief.

Casually, he leaned against the bedpost, arms folded across his chest, and a small smile turned up his lips.

He was a handsome man, as she'd thought from the first moment she saw him on a boat in the stormy English Channel. He had dark, auburn hair that glistened by lamplight. His amused eyes were hazel, but the more she looked at him, not just one color, but changeable. When she first met him, she'd thought his eyes intense, as if he would focus only on her whenever they spoke together. With a classically square jaw and thin lips, he was the picture of what a handsome man should look like. He was still broad with muscle, perhaps even more so since serving as a soldier in India. His coat almost seemed too tight across his shoulders, as if he hadn't had time to purchase a new one since he'd been back.

Well, of course he hadn't. He'd rushed straight from the ship to tell his parents that he was alive—only to find a wife he didn't remember.

What would his wife do?

Without a second thought, she flung herself from

the bed and into his arms. He didn't even stagger, so strong was he. She thought he hesitated, but at last his arms came around her and she was enveloped by warmth—but not security. She would never delude herself. She'd grown up thinking that marriage meant security, but had found it herself, without needing an actual husband. She'd learned never to rely on anyone else.

At last she leaned back to look up at him, smiling with happiness, forcing tears to glisten in her eyes. "Matthew!" She repeated his name with gladness and joy.

He was smiling down at her, which gave her some ease, but he studied her face closely. Should she kiss him, distract him from thinking too deeply? She was fully prepared to do what was necessary, but . . . something stopped her.

"They called you Emily," he said slowly, as if testing out her name on his tongue, his voice a deep rumble of masculinity.

She grinned as her hands stroked down his shoulders. "I *was* Emily Grey, but you made me a Leland." She let her smile fade. "But now I don't know what to do. I want to show my happiness for your safe return, and cry at the same time. Do you truly remember nothing?"

He shook his head. "A fine homecoming for a wife who hadn't allowed herself to hope I would return."

His hands slid down her back slowly, coming to rest on her waist. She'd wanted to distract him, but strangely, just his touch was distracting her. And she knew she could not risk such a mental failing.

"How could I hope?" she asked, fingering his lapels. "They said you were dead. I was ill when your mother told me. Even now I remember how lost I felt. But to you, I am just a newly introduced stranger." As a tear fell from her lashes, she was grateful for such a mask behind which to hide. Though she was playing with fire, she reached to touch his cheek, feeling the warmth of his skin and roughness of stubble.

Suddenly, his hands tightened on her waist, pulling her even more intimately against him. His gaze was centered on her mouth.

He thought she was his wife. He could claim his marital rights.

She found she couldn't breathe, her breasts rising and falling against the hard wall of his chest. Though he was not an exceptionally tall man like his cousin the duke, he still leaned over her, powerful and intimidating. If he ever remembered everything—

He bent even closer, his mouth just above hers. She felt his breath, knew an intense ache that she couldn't identify. To her surprise, at the last second he turned his head and pressed his warm lips to her cheek. He let her go so quickly that she stumbled back against the bed.

He caught her arm, his smile charmingly distressed. "I need . . . time to get to know you again, almost as if we are starting over. I know that isn't fair to you—"

"Of course it's fair," she said, almost too hastily. She was supposed to be distraught and sad—but she could also be an understanding wife. She took a deep breath, then patted his hand where it still gripped her upper arm. "This is all a shock to me, too."

He nodded.

"We have not seen each other in over a year," she continued, feeling calmer, stronger. "I find myself wondering how you've changed, wondering what you've seen and done while in the army."

He let her go and stepped back. "My parents said you'd spent six months with me in India."

"Until you thought I would be in too much danger if I stayed with you. Do you remember any of that?"

He slowly shook his head.

"By the time I returned to England to meet your family, it was only to hear that they'd already had word that you were—dead." She looked away, inspired to fumble for the handkerchief on her bedside table. She blew her nose.

When she looked back at him, he was walking toward the desk.

"I found our marriage license," he said.

Her breath halted in her lungs as she waited for him to continue.

"It's dated only two days before I left for India. I remember some of the preparations in London, the train journey to Southampton, but not how long I spent there."

"Two weeks. It is where we met. I am from a nearby village, where my father was a country squire."

"Was?" He sat on the edge of the desk, watching her.

Was he deliberately keeping his distance? What a shock he must be feeling, faced with a woman he thought intimately connected to him. But she could not let herself feel sorry for him, or feel sorry about what she was doing.

"My father and brothers perished in a boating accident on the Channel," she said.

Even now the memories of the wind rising up, the waves crashing over the bow, haunted her, distracted her. In her nightmares she could still see her oldest brother swept over the side, vanishing from sight. She did not have to fake these emotions; they pierced her stomach with such sorrow that she'd been unable to come up with a lie for Matthew's family.

"I was sailing with my father and brothers when the boat tore apart in the storm. As I clung to the wreckage, I thought for certain I would die. Then I heard the sound of the ship's bell and saw the schooner emerging from the mist. Yours was the first face I saw as you leaned out over the water above me, like an archangel come for me. I thought you were—fearless, so brave." She looked away, swallowing. "You only smiled at me with encouragement, though I clung to your hand so tightly I could have dragged you under with me."

She risked a glance at him, but he still watched her with intent.

Calmly, he asked, "You had no other family?"

"No one close. My mother died when I was a child. I thought my brothers would care for me no matter what."

"How old were you?"

"Twenty."

"And there was no man in your life before me?"

She shook her head. "I spent most of my time in our small village. I just . . . assumed I would marry one of the gentleman farmers, a man of my father's class, but I never found anyone. And then I met you. You were so caring, so concerned about me, making sure I had a place to stay with fellow parishioners. You stood by me at my family's funeral, came to visit me every day. Talking to you made me remember that Father would want me to go on with my life. To distract me, you told me stories of your family, the cousins who were like brothers to you, the sisters you doted on. Hearing about another family helped me remember the good times with my own."

He cocked his head, his expression interested. "And what stories did I tell as I courted you?"

She smiled playfully, taking a chance that he would respond to flirting. "There were so many. We even spent our nights on the steamship to India talking under the stars as we related our childhoods. But one story I remember was how you played the big brother when your cousin Daniel was teasing your sister about her obsession with painting. If I remember correctly, Daniel ended up with paint all over him, and you were Susanna's hero."

A half smile quirked his mouth.

In a softer voice, she added, "As we spent time together, I came to see what kind of man you were, so close to your family, yet wanting to serve your country. I admired that."

He looked away then. Was flattery going too far?

She walked slowly toward him. "I know it happened quickly, but somehow we fell in love." The lies came out of her so easily now. "I was alone in the world, and I worried that I was clinging to you, my rescuer, but you did not agree. You thought . . . you thought we were perfect together."

"I wasn't looking for a wife," he said.

"You said as much, even then. But what we had . . . you didn't want it to end. So you proposed marriage, and wanted to take me with you to India."

"And you didn't mind becoming an officer's wife, following the drum?"

She shook her head. "There was nothing in Southampton for me. A distant cousin inherited our family manor, but I did not want to live with strangers. You were all I thought I would ever need."

"And we married so quickly that I did not even have my family join us?"

"You were scheduled to leave. There was no time."

Emily held her breath, hoping he wouldn't ask when they'd notified his family of the marriage. Because then she would have to mention the letter that loomed large in her mind, containing a secret that could destroy this fake marriage and her life. For Matthew *had* written his parents about a marriage—but she wasn't the bride.

Lady Rosa had mentioned it to her when she was still ill, and Emily remembered feeling dull and resigned, thinking her masquerade was finished. In the letter, Matthew wrote that he had married, but gave no other news, not even his wife's name, promising to explain everything when he had more time.

But he never had. The Leland family simply assumed he'd been preparing his family for Emily, making them even more willing to accept her. And all along, the worry lurked in the back of her mind that another Mrs. Matthew Leland would return.

What had happened to his *real* wife, and why

wasn't she with him? For this was the one woman who could spoil everything she had worked so hard for.

It was so easy to study her, Matthew thought as he watched his "wife." Emily Grey had not only beauty, but true poise—and an answer for every question. She'd leapt into his arms as if he truly were her long-lost husband. She even cried on command.

She'd gone to a lot of trouble to build a life for herself here; his memory loss played right into her hands.

But not every word was a lie, for her story made him remember the boating accident. The local Southampton authorities had begged for any soldiers willing to sail out into the storm to help mount a rescue.

"Matthew?"

She stood close to him, put her hand tenderly on his arm. He could inhale her sweet scent, stare into the lovely blue of her eyes. A woman of such beauty surely knew how she affected the male of the species. Did she think she could sway him so easily? He looked forward to matching his intellect against hers.

He remained seated on the edge of the desk, which almost put them at eye level. He gave her a tired smile. "I'm sorry, my mind must have wandered. It is so damn frustrating to know something happened, but be unable to conjure up even one memory. How could I forget *you*?"

She blushed and looked away, pink highlighting the perfection of her skin.

"So you spent six months with me?"

She nodded.

"And there wasn't a child?"

She shook her head, then whispered, "But how I wished for one when I thought you dead."

It was his turn to nod, his deepest concern satisfied. At least there would not be a child hurt by what she'd done. "I am sure I'll have many more questions, but not tonight. I am exhausted."

"Oh, of course you are," she said swiftly, her forehead creased with worry. "Can I do anything to ease you?"

He tilted his head and smiled, even as her blush deepened. He held her eyes for a moment, and she stared at him. He won this small contest when she lowered her gaze. The devil inside him wanted to ask what she was offering tonight. Her lips would taste sweet; her body would ease his tired soul and let him truly forget.

But would she surrender willingly, while inside some part of her retreated?

He didn't want to use her like that, even though this situation was of her own making.

"Go to sleep, Emily," he said at last, straightening up and brushing past her. "Is anyone in the adjoining bedroom?"

She shook her head, then spoke with obvious incredulity. "But this is *your* bedroom."

"But you have been using it. I'll use that one for now. Don't most couples have separate lives, separate beds?" he asked casually. "Or were we so very different?"

She hesitated, then softly said, "We were good together."

He gave her a half smile. "I'm glad to hear that. I would hate to think I left you with sad memories." He walked to the door leading to the dressing room connecting the two bedrooms.

"Remember, Matthew, we can make new memories," she called. "Good night."

He wished her the same.

When he was alone, he stripped the cravat from around his neck then looked at it too long as it dangled from his fingers.

His mind was racing, and he wasn't going to be able to sleep for a long time. Silently, he crossed to the door leading into the hall and left his suite.

Chapter 3

It was easy enough to find Reggie, who would be housed in the bachelor wing.

Matthew knocked on the door of the first guest chamber. From the other side he heard, "I've already poured you a brandy."

He entered the room to find Reggie sunk low in a wing-back chair before the hearth, his head leaning against the back, his eyes twinkling. A tumbler of brandy was cradled between his hands, while another waited on a small table beside him.

Matthew grinned, took his glass, then with a sigh, stretched out in the next chair. Reggie continued to eye him lazily, waiting.

Matthew lifted his glass. "To my wife."

His chuckle merged with Reggie's laugh, and they clinked glasses before drinking deeply.

"How you kept a straight face is beyond me," Reggie said, his shoulders still shaking. "Good thing no one was looking at me, because I probably would have given the whole thing away."

"No, you wouldn't have. You would have taken it for the opportunity it was."

"And was it?"

"Was it what?"

"An opportunity?"

Matthew hesitated. "I guess it was—is."

"And how did you leave this new wife?"

"Shh," he said, smiling even as he glanced at the door. He knew his family was far away, yet there were always servants about to see to a guest's comforts.

"Well?" Reggie demanded, sitting up a bit to focus his stare on Matthew.

"I left her alone. And no, I didn't take advantage."

Reggie's mouth dropped open for a moment. "So she was *willing*? And awake?"

Matthew rolled his eyes and took another sip of his brandy. "Of course she was awake. But it didn't feel right to press it."

"Right? She's claiming to be your *wife*!" Reggie said with disbelief. "She's *asking* for your attention."

"No, she thought I was dead," he mused. "She's obviously here for some other reason."

"And you couldn't get it out of her?"

"No, she's very good. I'm vastly impressed."

"You mean you're vastly besotted. She's as scandalous as you spent your life longing to be. Your cousin Daniel will be no match for you now."

"Oh, please, who knows what trouble he's gotten into since I've been gone? And you know too much about me," Matthew grumbled good-naturedly.

"I should. I've known you since we were green officers together in Southampton, waiting for a ship to take us around the world."

"Apparently, that's where I married Emily. Were you my best man?"

If he were outside, Reggie's constantly gaping mouth would have drawn flies. *"That's* what she's claiming?"

"I did meet her there, you know. Remember the family killed in the boating accident?"

"You've mentioned it a time or two."

"She's the girl I rescued."

"In more ways than one, obviously."

Matthew lifted his glass again. "Obviously." He wouldn't say it aloud, but there *had* been a connection between them, and he still felt drawn to her. The protective instinct was too deep in him, had gotten him in trouble before—and obviously had again.

"So she met you . . . " Reggie urged.

"And then she must have decided to use me, once my name turned up on the casualty list. A lot of the facts are real, of course; her description of the accident, and the way I spent time with her, was correct—to a point."

"You must have been very impressive."

Matthew winced. "Hardly. We talked, that was all. She was a frightened, bedraggled kitten of a girl, whose family had all just died tragically. I felt sorry for her." He remembered her lost amidst the damp towels, too shocked to even grieve at first. How could he not have pitied her?

"Keep talking."

He shot a distracted glance of amusement at his friend. "Very well, it was more than pity on my part. I could have just given her money and left. Instead I found her a hotel room, ordered her hot food and maid service, and came back the next morning to see how she'd fared. Even in her grief she'd been sweetly charming, for she hadn't wanted to burden me, tried to pretend that everything would be all right."

"And you got involved."

Bemused, he murmured, "I did the one thing that led her directly to my family. I gave her a letter of introduction to them, including both their London address as well as the one here in Cambridgeshire. I told her if she ever needed help, to go to my family in my name and ask."

"By the devil, you really did ask for this."

Matthew shrugged. "Do you think—" he began, then broke off for a moment. "In her terrible grief, could Emily have fantasized more to my kindness than there had been?"

Reggie peered at him over his glass. "You mean is she touched in the head?"

"She said she had no close family left. Could she have convinced herself we really had married?"

"Out of desperation, do you mean? Don't you think someone that daft would have given herself away in a year's time? I don't imagine your family are all that foolish."

"You're right, of course," Matthew said, shaking his head. "If she had fantasized the marriage, she would have gone to my parents immediately. Instead, six months passed—and someone had forged a marriage license for her. I'll have to study it again, and see the name of the man who supposedly performed the ceremony."

"Now isn't that interesting," Reggie said. "You don't think she did the forgery herself?"

"She could have. With my letter, she had the opportunity to copy my signature. But she might not be alone in this. I wonder if she brought someone into the household with her?"

"Or if there is someone nearby, at her beck and call, just waiting. What will you do if that's the truth?"

"Take it as it comes," Matthew said, letting a smile widen his mouth. "It's just so curious why she wouldn't simply ask for my family's help, as I gave her permission to do."

Reggie rolled his head back and forth against the chair, sighing. "I recognize that lame grin of yours. You're enjoying yourself."

"What's not to enjoy? I have a beautiful woman doing her best to please me."

"And a little danger to make it exciting," Reggie added. "And here we thought England would be boring after India."

"I have learned my lesson, you know. Though scandal is pleasurable, nothing real can come of it. I'll enjoy unmasking Emily, but that will be all." He'd had enough of entanglements to last a lifetime. It was time for some fun.

After finishing off his drink with Reggie, Matthew said good-night and returned to the family wing. In his new bedroom in his old suite, he stripped off his clothes and fell into bed. Still, he lay awake too long, imagining his "wife" in the next room, asleep in his bed.

As he looked at the ceiling, he heard an unusual sound in the corridor. He came instantly alert. In that moment it occurred to him that Emily might actually try to escape.

He pulled on his trousers and peered out the door, but saw no one. Though a lamp at each end of the corridor provided faint lighting, he saw no shadows, heard no sound. Swiftly, he went back through his room and the dressing room, then leaned his ear against Emily's bedroom door. Nothing.

He told himself that she would not flee in the middle of the night. He'd found nothing hidden in her room that would help her escape, no money, no jewels.

But then he imagined his parents' faces if she were gone in the morning, if he had to explain what she'd done—what he'd done in response. No, he wouldn't let it end like this, not until he knew everything. Very carefully, he eased her door open.

Faint moonlight came through the windows, highlighting where it touched, deepening the shadows where it didn't. Though it had been several years, he knew the room well, was able to skirt the desk chair and the chest at the foot of the bed.

And then he saw her.

She was asleep in his bed, her expression as serene as an innocent. The counterpane was pulled up to her waist, letting him see her nightgown, plain and unadorned, but so fine that it outlined each curve of her body, from the delicate bones of her shoulders to the tips of her breasts. Her lips, softly parted with her breathing, were made for a man's kisses.

He stood staring for far too long, until at last he shook himself out of his lust-filled stupor. He'd assured himself of her whereabouts. Of course she hadn't fled from him. Whatever her motive was, she had gone through too much to back down now, especially when he'd given her the perfect reason to stay. It was time for him to find his rest at last.

But back in his new room, he still tossed and turned, for he now had the sleeping image of her in his head.

Arthur Stanwood, prosperous Southampton innkeeper, was prosperous no more. His creditors had at last come calling, and they weren't the sort to give one a bloody note of debt and wait for an honorable response. No, they would kill him soon and take all that he had left, if he didn't come up with the money he'd gambled away. Over his breakfast, as he read the *Times*, he found his solution.

Captain Matthew Leland, cousin to the Duke of Madingley, had returned from the dead.

Emily Grey had tried to tell him she'd married the bloke before he went off to India. She, a country girl, wed into a duke's family? He hadn't believed it, knew that she'd only been using the dead man.

With the old vicar dead, Stanwood had thought for certain that he had her completely under his control. But she'd disappeared. He'd been too careless, he realized. He stewed for months over her escape, searching his brain for the name she'd given him, which was his only clue.

And now here it was in the bloody *Times*, the answer to his desperation. The article mentioned that the captain had returned to his young, grieving widow—Mrs. Emily Leland.

It was time for him to pay a call on the lovely

"Mrs. Leland," and see how she and he could help each other. Stanwood glanced at his pocket watch. If he took the train, he would be able to reach Cambridge that afternoon.

When Matthew awoke, he lay still, mind empty, not certain he remembered the last time he'd slept in so comfortable a bed. On the steamship, his berth had been made of hard wood with a too-thin mattress on top. And during his travels in India, luxury was the leaf of a dining table propped on three cane chairs.

After assuring himself of Emily's whereabouts, he'd been dead to the world, not even remembering his dreams. But now the sun was peering through his draperies; he'd slept later than he meant to. The house was so quiet.

As usual, he was stiff as he sat up, the scars from his burns stretching tight across bone. He looked around—and realized he'd never slept in this room before. Early that morning his clothes must have been unpacked and pressed in the dressing room, and now a valet he didn't recognize arrived to help him dress. Matthew sent him away. Although he wasn't embarrassed about his injuries, he didn't feel the need to have horrified servants spreading gossip.

He put a hand on the doorknob to his old bedroom, then thought better of letting himself be distracted by the lovely Emily when his sisters were waiting to see him. He went down to the breakfast room alone.

In the doorway, he came up short. They were all there, his parents, sisters, Reggie—and Emily. None of them noticed him right away. They were talking excitedly among themselves, food forgotten. His sisters, Susanna and Rebecca, sat on either side of Emily.

A softening feeling of gratitude to God moved through him, that he was able to be with them again. There was a time when he lay writhing within the fiery agony of his burns that he'd almost wished for death. He'd learned the hard way that his life and family were important to him.

Susanna, at twenty-six, was only a year younger than he was. She acted as their father's assistant in the anatomy laboratory, sketching the muscles and organs of the bodies the professor studied. She was a bluestocking of the first order, intelligent and calm, with the same auburn hair they'd both inherited from their father. Lady Rosa had long since given up on the idea that Susanna would ever exert herself enough to attract a husband, which still made Matthew sad. Even though he didn't want a wife, it surely was better for a woman to marry a man and have her own household. And his sister deserved to be happy.

For the past several years Lady Rosa had concentrated all of her matrimonial efforts on Rebecca, who was nineteen, a beauty, with dark brown hair and hazel eyes. After a childhood weakened by many illnesses, Rebecca had matured into a poised loveliness that surprised Matthew, who rather thought that in rebellion she might end up being the wild one of his family.

But of course he hadn't heard everything she'd been up to since he'd been gone. He looked forward to finding out. There had been a time, while he was recovering at the mission, when he thought he might never see his family again, so long did it take for him to heal.

To his amusement, they were all focused on Emily, the wife whose husband had returned to her. Her expression was animated as she spoke to his sisters, looking back and forth between them, gesturing with her fork. Susanna gave her a brief hug, as Rebecca giggled from the other side. How at ease they all seemed together, like real sisters.

Then Susanna saw him in the doorway. "Matthew!" Her voice was a shriek.

He gave her a fond grin. "Hello, little sister."

And then pandemonium ensued as Susanna and Rebecca rushed across the room to throw themselves at him. He staggered back against the door, an arm around each of them, grinning as he hadn't in a long time.

"No need to crush me," he said with amusement.

"Oh, dear, you've been dreadfully injured!" Susanna said, pulling back and looking up at him.

"I am fully recovered now."

"Mama said you were burned?" Rebecca's sweet voice was full of hesitation, as if she thought even talking about it would hurt him all over again.

"There was an explosion. And I was bayoneted," he said cheerfully. When they collectively gasped, he hugged them back against him. "But I've been recovered since the beginning of the year. You do not have to treat me as a fragile invalid."

"But your memory . . . " Susanna said with doubt.

Matthew looked at Emily, now standing beside his parents, her face full of sweet concern for him. She wore a gown of plain yellow, as bright as the sun. Had she wondered—and worried—if sleep had brought the return of his memories? His parents had probably wished for the same thing, without the worry.

"There is nothing I can do about my mind," he said. "The memories will return or they won't."

He found himself studying Emily, wondering how to needle her, to trip her up into revealing more about herself. He had a sudden, incredible idea. He'd claimed "holes in his memory"—why not take that even further, expand upon his memory loss? Such a weakness would allow him to stay close to her, to learn everything he could about her. If he couldn't remember how to do some of the basic things in life, then as his wife, Emily would have to teach him.

"We can tell you anything that you want to know," Rebecca said, pulling him farther into the breakfast room and giving him her chair beside Emily. She gestured with amused poise. "This is your wife, Emily."

He grinned at Emily, who grinned back as she sat down beside him.

"Rebecca," Lady Rosa said in a warning tone, "now is not the time to tease your brother."

"Mother, if I am not teased," he said, "how will I know I've returned home?"

Professor Leland gave an easy chuckle and resumed his seat near the head of the table. Even when his cousin the duke wasn't in residence, they always seemed to leave the head of the table open for him.

The servants were bringing Matthew a plate overflowing with ham and eggs and toast, his favorite breakfast. It all looked delicious, and he found himself starving.

He forced himself to hesitate over his plate, remembering the holes in his memory, hoping to attract Emily's notice.

"Matthew?" she said quietly.

He looked at his family, busy eating, as if he didn't want them to notice his dilemma.

"It is the strangest thing," he said in a low voice, meant for her ears only. "I can't remember how I like my toast."

Her expression was full of worry and compassion.

"You mean your amnesia affects even such simple things?"

"Sometimes. Other times I feel confident, to the point where I forget such a weakness even exists. But I couldn't remember some of the servants' names last night."

"Oh, but surely, after two years—"

"But I knew they'd been here my whole life!" He let some of his frustration show. "And you're my wife! How could I—"

She put a gentle hand on his arm, glancing at his oblivious parents. "Matthew, the more you give in to frustration, the worse it will be. Relax, and let it come back to you slowly."

"And if it doesn't?"

With conviction, she said, "Then you create new memories."

Create new memories with Emily. What an intriguing thought. He held her gaze, looking into those sincere blue eyes, trying to exude a vulnerability that would draw her to him—and trying not to look at her mouth with too much hunger.

He was distracted by a tug on his coat sleeve, and he turned to Susanna, on his other side.

"Obviously Mama told us of your dilemma," she said in her no-nonsense tone. "Tell me what it feels like to have 'holes' in your memory."

She must have been listening to their conversation. "Studying me like your latest project?" he asked.

She gave a faint blush. "I have simply never met anyone with your condition. When I think of you and Emily seeing each other for the first time in over a year, husband and wife yet almost strangers—"

"Susanna." Lady Rosa once again spoke in that tone of voice reserved for mothers.

"Let them ask their questions," Matthew said easily. "Maybe talking will help me. You'd want that, wouldn't you, Emily?"

"Of course."

To his family, he said, "This is surely difficult for her. We've decided to take our relationship slowly, get to know one another all over again."

Rebecca frowned. "To Emily, you are her long-lost husband, but she has to think of you as a suitor again?"

Emily put down her napkin and gave Rebecca a smile. "I do not mind at all," she said, her voice firm. "I will do whatever is necessary to make our life normal again. After everything that has happened, we cannot expect that to come about quickly. And you mustn't feel sorry for me. I am not the one without memories, who was almost killed."

Matthew noticed the fond approval in his father's gaze, the way Lady Rosa dabbed at the corners of her eyes. Even Susanna and Rebecca looked chagrined. Emily knew just the right things to say.

But how could he have expected otherwise, after seeing the household's devotion to her?

He took her hand and gave it a gentle squeeze. Her skin was warm and soft, and he had to disregard the sudden images that came to mind of her hands touching his bare skin. "We will get through this, I promise you."

Emily gave him a tremulous smile. She could even tremble on command, he thought, hiding his enjoyment.

And then he saw Reggie openly staring at him, barely masking his anticipation of the next act in this play. Matthew realized he should save his more intimate persuasion with Emily for when they were alone.

He released her as he turned back to Susanna. "As for holes in my memory, at first I didn't notice I had forgotten anything, until someone told me."

"Usually me," Reggie volunteered.

"Your help must have been comforting," Lady Rosa said.

Now Reggie looked uneasy. "I don't know how much 'help' I was."

Was his friend realizing how difficult it was going to be to lie to his family? Since Matthew had spent his whole life pretending, trying to be the person his parents expected, he was rather used to lying, at least about himself.

Reggie sent a sincere glance to both Susanna and Rebecca. "But I did my best."

Matthew wanted to roll his eyes. His friend wasn't going to be bothered by guilt for long. He noticed that although Rebecca smiled at Reggie's flirtatious look, Susanna went back to eating, as if indifferent. Had she truly given up on finding a husband for herself? Not that Reggie came from exactly the right Society, Matthew mused, at least as far as the *ton* was concerned.

Matthew returned to explaining his supposed amnesia. "Occasionally something very basic is just suddenly gone from my mind. It is . . . frustrating, to not know everything." And captivating, he thought, watching Emily.

"Let Matthew eat," the professor said.

Matthew smiled at him and dug in. For Emily, he made a show of randomly choosing peach jam for his toast. He couldn't help noticing that she ate with as much gusto as he did. Guilt certainly didn't bother her appetite.

After a while, with a young woman's impatience, Rebecca said, "Surely you've eaten enough, Matthew."

"You don't look like you've been starving," Susanna observed. "Tell us about your injury."

He smiled and held up a hand before Lady Rosa could protest. "When I first arrived in India, my regiment was assigned to General Napier, who was determined to control the Sind, the territory between India and Afghanistan. There were battles aplenty, and I was deemed a bit reckless."

"Reckless?" Susanna echoed, looking puzzled. "I would not have thought so, Matthew."

How could he explain what it was like, fighting for his country? He'd wanted to rediscover himself, and with nothing to lose except his life, he'd walked the edge of safety. It had been an incredible—if sometimes painful—experience.

"Remember, my battle skills were part of the reason I was promoted to captain," he told his sister.

"But they didn't save you from getting hurt," Rebecca said.

He grinned, for she sounded almost disappointed in him, as if he should have been invulnerable. "In the next battle, I took a bayonet wound to the side, but I thought it minor and continued on. I was told later that there was an artillery explosion, which was how I was burned, but I remember nothing of it. So perhaps holes in the memory can be a good thing."

He found himself glancing at Emily, who watched him intently but remained silent.

"You were so lucky that your face was not

touched," Rebecca said solemnly. "Did you awaken on the battlefield?"

He shook his head. "I awoke in a Christian mission. The regiment had left me behind to recover. I was there for several months." He tried not to think of those days, and where his stupidity had led him. Reggie was watching him a bit too solemnly.

Matthew smiled regretfully at his parents. "This is when the mistake of my supposed death happened. And I am so sorry for it."

Lady Rosa spoke at last. "If you were there for several months, why did you not write to us?"

"My new regiment went much farther upriver, away from English outposts. I knew any letter I wrote I would have to carry out with me, so I waited too long."

Hamilton came through the doors then, carrying a silver tray stacked with letters and the newspaper, which the professor promptly took.

After glancing at the newspaper, Professor Leland fixed Matthew with an amused gaze.

"As of today, all of England will know of your return. You made the *Times*."

He displayed the front page, and they all could read the headline: OFFICER RETURNS FROM THE DEAD!

"I was only in London for a few hours," Matthew said, amazed.

"The servants at Madingley House must have

been so excited," Lady Rosa said, clapping her hands.

"And talkative." Matthew glanced at Emily, wondering at her reaction. "I did not think I could keep my return a secret, but I've been in England less than two days. This is fast work."

Lady Rosa smiled. "Good news can travel just as swiftly as bad. Perhaps people are glad to have a reason to celebrate."

Matthew smiled at Emily, and she returned his smile. But did she seem a bit . . . distracted? What did she think of having his arrival—and her own name—splashed across England's most widely read newspaper?

Chapter 4

The eggs tasted like dry pieces of rubber going down Emily's throat. She hadn't anticipated that a duke's cousin returning from the dead would be so newsworthy. But, of course, he was an army hero—who was not quite married. If *that* got out, it would set the newspapers ablaze.

She took a deep breath to calm herself. There was nothing she could do now. She only hoped that Emily Leland would not be connected to Emily Grey.

She glanced at Lieutenant Lawton, Matthew's friend, with his curling black hair and rakish grin. His presence complicated everything. At first, thinking he would denounce her, she nearly panicked, then realized that he hadn't done so last night. If Matthew truly was married to another woman, then Lieutenant Lawton didn't seem to know her. What a confusing mystery.

Emily looked around the table, where everyone watched Matthew with the rapt attention of a loving family thrilled to have their only son back. They weren't examining his words as she was, studying his expressions and mannerisms. Perhaps that was why something rang false for her. He skimmed over months of painful recovery too easily. She decided to help him explain his poor correspondence, in hopes of eventually earning his trust.

She asked him, "Wasn't it also difficult to write a letter when you couldn't remember everything? I imagine you did not want to reveal your problem."

The two sisters gasped in unison, as if they'd been foolish not to realize that.

Matthew looked down at Emily, one brow arched in surprise. "Yes, it was difficult," he said softly.

"A wife would understand," Lady Rosa murmured with pleased satisfaction.

No, Emily thought, a woman who spent time analyzing everything she said or did would understand.

"As I mentioned," Matthew continued, "I had to be told about my duties in my first regiment. I was worried there were other, more important things I couldn't remember. And of course, there were," he said, glancing at Emily. "I didn't know what to write, and I didn't want to make you all worry if I sounded . . . wrong."

"Of course, son," the professor said. "What are

letters, when we now have the real thing? The rest of the family will be overjoyed."

"Can we discuss all of this later today, privately, Father?" Matthew asked. "I have so many questions."

"We will speak when you're ready," the professor said, happiness softening his eyes. "I do not have to be at Cambridge until tomorrow."

Emily realized that Matthew probably wanted to talk about *her*. When she'd awakened that morning, she half expected to find him there in the bedroom with her. Even in a common marriage of convenience between acquaintances there was a price for the woman to pay: physical intimacy without any love. She told herself that she was prepared to pay the price.

Rebecca began, "Matthew, what about—"

"Enough, girls." Lady Rosa rose to her feet. "Poor Matthew came home late. He has more recovering to do, so I suggest we allow him to do it at his own pace."

"Mother, I don't need to be coddled," Matthew said, giving her a wry smile. "I think the best thing for me would be to resume my old life. Surely there's a ball or two to attend."

Rebecca straightened in her chair with obvious interest. "There is a dinner tonight hosted by Lord Sydney."

The professor frowned. "Surely it is too soon."

They all looked at Matthew, not bothering to hide their surprise. Why did his request to return to a normal life seem so unusual to them?

"Not at all," Matthew said promptly. "We should go." And then he turned to Susanna. "You'll introduce me to those I can't remember?"

"Rebecca can help you," Susanna said, patting her brother's arm.

"And why would *you* not go?" he asked, wearing a faint frown.

"She's too busy in Father's laboratory," Rebecca said, giving an exaggerated sigh.

Susanna's voice was cool. "It is important work."

"Of course it is," Matthew agreed, "which means you need the occasional amusement to relax."

"You know I don't consider such events relaxing," she said.

"You used to be an excellent dancer. Why is that not relaxing?"

Susanna only shrugged as she picked at her eggs.

Their mother said, "Randolph, I wish you would make clear to your daughter that being seen in Society can only help her."

The professor's face became impassive. "We've had this discussion before, Rosa."

Emily saw Matthew look between them in resignation, as if he wasn't surprised at their disagreement. But she knew the Lelands' relationship had become stronger this past year. She herself had encouraged it, almost as if helping them eased her debt to the family. But pushing this subject now could only make things worse.

"Matthew, would you go for a walk with me in the garden before you speak with your father?" she asked.

She could feel the tension ease in the breakfast room, as Lady Rosa smiled.

"That is a lovely idea, Emily, dear."

"And you don't even need a chaperone," Rebecca said with a smile.

Matthew pushed back his chair and rose to his feet. "A walk with my wife is an excellent suggestion. Emily, I need to speak to Reggie for a moment. May I meet you on the terrace?"

She smiled. "Of course." But inside, she was already considering ways to use their time alone together to her advantage.

Matthew caught up with Reggie in the great hall, where his friend was staring up at the display of swords and axes on the walls.

"Are these all from your family, or did somebody merely decorate the walls with them?" Reggie asked skeptically.

"There have been Cabots fighting for England for hundreds of years."

"Impressive. My father was in the infantry fighting in France. Always claimed he saw Napoleon from afar. No mementoes, though."

They stood side by side for a moment, and Matthew considered the fifteenth century suit of armor he'd been forced to learn about when he was young. "So . . . what are your plans?"

"You mean now that you'll be too busy to keep me amused?" Reggie said thoughtfully.

Matthew sighed. "I'm sorry about this."

"Don't be. This is vastly entertaining." He glanced over his shoulder, then lowered his voice. "Your wife is quite composed and intelligent."

Matthew nodded slowly. "How could she not be? She's fooled everyone for almost a year."

"And lovely," Reggie continued. "I hadn't quite realized that, when she looked like death upon seeing you last night. A man could do worse."

"For a wife?"

"For—anything." Reggie straightened. "I think I'll take myself off, then. It's been a long time since I've ridden the English countryside. I imagine the park is beautiful here."

"And extensive. You'll return for luncheon?"

"Maybe not."

"Then the dinner party."

"Oh very well, if I must converse with pretty girls, then I must." Reggie grinned, even as he gave

Matthew a speculative look. "Will you be fencing Emily with words today?"

"It might feel that way."

"Then enjoy yourself."

"Oh, I intend to."

Reggie sighed. "I am quite envious."

After Reggie left for the stables, Matthew went through the drawing room and outside. Emily was waiting for him at the edge of the terrace. In yellow, she rivaled the hollyhocks lining the gravel path below them. Though it was autumn, the sun shone between puffy clouds, and she only wore a simple black shawl over her gown. Several curls escaped her chignon to flutter in the breeze. She absently pushed one behind her ear, her expression serene, as if with his return, she no longer had any cares in the world. Together, they walked down the marble steps and onto the pathway.

He took her arm, entwining it with his. She didn't try to pull away. In fact, she momentarily leaned against him, shoulder-to-shoulder, and hugged his arm to her. Was she thinking of other things a husband and wife did together? He was; his desire for her seemed heightened with the mystery of her.

"So when I sent you from India," he said, saving the conversation about their imaginary six months together for another time, "you arrived here ill. Was the sea voyage hard on you?"

She shook her head. "I have always found the sea quite invigorating."

"Ah yes, the family boat," he said with sudden remembrance. "How terrible of me to force you on another voyage so soon after the death of your family."

"I wanted to be with you," she said almost boldly.

The jolt of her deep blue eyes hit him hard. She affected him so easily, but she would learn he was not so easily manipulated.

"And then you heard that I was dead. It must have been . . . very difficult on my family—and you."

"They'd already been notified of your death before I arrived," she said quietly, tilting up her face as the sun came out from behind a cloud. "It sounds so strange to talk of such things around you. Having cheated death, you seem almost larger than life."

Flattery again? It was a good tactic to use on a man.

"We were all consumed with grief," she continued. "They are a wonderful family, and they helped me recover in ways I'll never forget."

"And by the way they dote on you, you must have helped them recover, too."

She hesitated, then let out a breath. "We all helped each other wait through . . . the length of a month."

She looked determinedly at a distant fountain.

A month, he mused—and then it dawned on him. The length of a woman's cycle.

"They thought you might be with child?" he asked, working hard to hide his amusement.

"I did not think so, due to the six week length of my voyage, but your mother was so full of hope."

He did not want to think of Lady Rosa grieving for him. "When that long wait was over, what then?" he asked. "What did you do here, in mourning?"

"I became acquainted with your family, of course," she said. "We women spent much time together sewing and painting."

"You're an artist?"

"As much as any woman taught the basic skills. I have no great talent," she admitted, "unlike your sister Susanna. Our evenings were quiet affairs, of course. The immense library here was a great consolation. After a brief leave of absence, your father went back to teaching and his research. Susanna's quiet sessions sketching at his side seemed to ease him. If only your mother had such a preoccupation."

"In mourning, she could not see to Rebecca's social calendar."

A smile tilted the corners of her mouth. "No, but since the spring, she has made up for the lack." She shot him a speculative look. "Why was your family so surprised that you wanted to go to the dinner tonight?"

He debated how to answer that, and decided on the truth. "I used to be . . . rather set in my ways."

She laughed aloud, and it was the first time he'd heard her amused. He'd read once about a woman's laughter being compared to the sweet ringing of bells, and he'd scoffed at it. No more.

"You, set in your ways," she said, when she finally collected herself. "Not the man *I* married."

"Well apparently, marrying you was the first spontaneous thing I ever did. And then India allowed me the freedom I'd never granted myself."

"You can't tell me you didn't attend parties."

"Of course not—you know my mother."

They exchanged smiles.

"But I kept myself very controlled. I think my family assumed my amnesia would make me retreat until I felt more myself, and once it probably would have. But now—no. I'm home, where I want to be, doing what I want. And a dinner party with my family will make me happy. Susanna can do as she wishes, even bury herself in her laboratory. Not me."

He felt her arm tense against his.

"Matthew, that is the wrong attitude to have toward your sister. You men can do as you please, roam the world and earn your fortune. But not we women. Don't dismiss Susanna's problems."

He smiled, but she didn't smile back. "I'm not

dismissing her problems," he said. "But she's an adult, long past starry-eyed girlhood."

"And so that means she's right?"

Her eyes held his with such seriousness, as she stopped on the path to face him.

"Right now, Susanna's life is as she wants it," Emily said. "But someday your parents will be gone, and she'll find herself either alone or a dependent in a family member's household. Everyone will have children and be living their lives, and she'll feel . . . apart."

He couldn't take his eyes from her, wondering what part of this passionate speech was real and what was just a masquerade.

"I don't think she's truly happy," Emily continued thoughtfully. "She knows her mother is disappointed, but Susanna doesn't know what *she* wants."

"I think you're challenging me to do something about it."

She blinked at him, then spoke slowly. "Maybe I am."

It seemed to him that the only way Susanna could be happy was to find companionship among the *ton*, with whom she'd be spending the rest of her life. "Very well, then. Together we'll launch her again into Society, beginning with the social events here in the country. We'll make her see that with a little effort on her part, she can make more friends and be a happier person. A happy person attracts men easily."

And while he was helping his sister, he would be able to watch Emily.

"She's always attracted men to her side," Emily was saying, "but apparently not the ones she's interested in, because she rebuffs them. But I like your idea. I can help."

"I don't doubt it." He took her arm again and they resumed their walk. "Now back to learning more about my wife. What have you been doing since coming out of mourning?"

"Well, the family had two weddings to plan, which gave us all something to do."

He came to a halt and stared at her. "Weddings?"

"Oh, I did not realize . . . well, your cousins, of course, Mr. Throckmorten and His Grace, the duke."

Stunned, he said, "We regularly corresponded before my injury. I did not even hear word that either of them was planning to court a woman, let alone marry. Of course, I could have forgotten that, too . . ."

"No, you did not," she said firmly. "Both courtships only just happened this summer, and once decided upon, the weddings were rather hastily done."

She was wearing a quirky little smile, as if she

thought the antics of his cousins amusing. He could understand Christopher's marriage—he needed a duchess, after all. But Daniel? He was a womanizer of the first order. Matthew had thought Daniel would be the last one of all the cousins, male or female, to marry.

He found himself stopping beneath a tree on high ground. Spread below was a large pond, and beyond it the ruins of the old castle, home of generations of dukes, and earls before that. Emily stepped away from him, gazing into the distance.

"I love this view," she said quietly. "The ruins are so romantic."

Then she glanced at him from beneath her lashes almost provocatively.

"Oh, do not think I mean to tease you," she continued. "For your benefit, I am trying to censor everything I say or think, but I don't always succeed."

Matthew considered her with amazement. Last night she hadn't tried to run, hadn't tried to explain what she was doing here. And with this flirting, it was apparent that she meant to stay here and be his wife—in every way? What woman dared such a thing? And why?

He lightly grasped her upper arms, then slid his hands down to clasp hers. "I understand more than you might realize. I have to censor much of what

I say, too, for my family's sake." *And yours*, he thought, wanting to smile.

"I noticed that at breakfast," she admitted.

He raised his eyebrows.

"Oh, just that you seemed to be weighing what you said," she quickly added. "You think it would be too difficult for your family to hear the truth about how you suffered."

He shrugged. "But not difficult for you?"

She lifted her chin. "I am your wife."

So brazen. He studied her, thinking about their conversation. He realized that when he'd asked her what she'd been doing since coming out of mourning, she deliberately sidetracked him into a discussion of his family. What didn't she want to discuss?

He rocked back on his heels for a moment. "Keeping quiet any suffering I experienced is not my only reason for speaking carefully. I told you at breakfast—didn't I?" he added, trying to sound concerned.

She stared up at him solemnly. "The toast, of course. And all the normal things you fear you've forgotten. How can I help you?"

A warm feeling of satisfaction moved through him. "I feel embarrassed to even ask. I don't know you—"

"But I know you," she said with earnest conviction. "Let me help."

"Then teach me." He gripped her hands even tighter as they stared at each other.

She blinked up at him in surprise. "What . . . ?"

"Teach me what I cannot remember, about our life together, and about the simple things I used to do so regularly but that have disappeared from my mind."

Her face full of compassion, she said quietly, "I would be proud to."

Proud? God, she was good at this masquerade. It was easy to believe every word she spoke. Whatever doubts she had, she'd squelched.

"What should I do?" she continued.

He gave a rueful grin. "There are so many holes in my memory that it's hard to know where to begin. I guess one of the problems, as we walk these paths, is that I cannot remember the layout of the park beyond the gardens. I should be able to see it in my head, for I explored every inch of it growing up. But it's just . . . gone." He shook his head. "It would be embarrassing if I got lost on a ride and had to be led back by a shepherd."

She smiled. "It makes an interesting image. Of course I'll be glad to ride with you until you're familiar with the park."

They stood close together, holding hands, looking out over a view she'd deemed "romantic." To his surprise, she lifted his hand to her cheek, simply holding it there. He felt unsteady, as the arousal that simmered all morning burst into flame. Her skin was so warm, so soft. An overwhelming ache of need moved through him.

He leaned down and kissed her, light as a butterfly, simply feeling the sweet softness of her lips against his. He could have deepened the kiss, he knew, but something stopped him. Her cheek was warm against his palm, and he brought his other hand up so he could cup her face. He was surprised that even though this might be the most innocent kiss of his life, he wanted it to go on.

But he lifted his head and looked down at her, seeing how flushed her face was, how her breathing was quick and uneven. Whatever the reasons for her masquerade, he did not think she was faking her response. Or did he just want to assume himself irresistible? he wondered wryly.

And then she put her arms around him and held him tight. "Oh, Matthew, this seems too wonderful to be real. Yesterday at this time I was still a widow, learning how to live my life alone, and today . . ." She gave a long sigh. ". . . I feel complete again."

He rubbed her back, amused that he almost felt awkward. He wanted to be rubbing her in other places. Her smooth hair teased his neck; her breasts, lush and well rounded, were a further torment. But he could be patient. He still had so much to learn about her.

"I should get back to the house to meet with my father," he said reluctantly. "What are you doing today?"

She lingered within the circle of his arms, looking up at him, smiling so broadly that her eyes sparkled. "I was planning to go into the village, but that was before your return."

"Perhaps we could go riding after luncheon."

"Of course, Matthew."

"Allow me to escort you back to the house."

"That would be lovely."

Looking at her smile, he felt almost dizzy, as if she were able to create a new reality for both of them just by sheer will.

When Matthew left her for Professor Leland's study, Emily stood on the terrace, watching him go. He walked with smooth control, back straight, broad shoulders squared. He was a soldier, of course, and that had shaped him for the last several years.

Could she continue to get away with this charade? Already he seemed to feel more at ease with her. And then there was the attraction between them. She wasn't going to resist it, and apparently neither was he. Would he forget the questions and doubts she glimpsed lingering in his eyes? She didn't need to love him—that wasn't important to her. Security was. Yet . . . Susanna had security, and she wasn't happy.

But Susanna had never known what it was like to have no security at all.

It would be interesting to see what Matthew thought he should do to help his sister—and how he would overcome Susanna's objections.

She remembered that moment of intimate connection with him as they'd stood above the ruins, his warm, callused palms on her face, without gloves to separate them. He'd kissed her with tenderness. For just a moment she'd let herself forget what she was. He did that to her so easily, as he tried to scale the wall she kept between herself and everyone else. And now he'd asked her to help him remember parts of his life. She almost laughed, which would have made her look crazy, standing alone on the terrace, the autumn wind tugging at her hair. She went inside and passed through the drawing room.

"Emily!" Susanna, dressed in the usual practical navy gown that she wore in the laboratory, hurried down a corridor. As she slid to a stop, she pushed her spectacles up with one finger. "Well?"

"Well what?" Emily asked.

Susanna rolled her eyes. "I did not have a chance to speak with you this morning, but I thought, with Matthew's return, already you seem so much happier."

Emily had held Matthew's sisters as distant from her as she could at first, afraid of hurting them. But gradually they'd burrowed their way into her heart, each for different reasons. Susanna was a self-educated woman, and had encouraged Emily to follow her own thirst for knowledge. Rebecca, though only a few years younger, was on a path to marriage, single-mindedly guided by her mother, yet she always made Emily feel a part of everything she was doing.

Now, Emily took Susanna's hand. "I am truly happy, my dear. Your brother is alive and returned to his family. But we are . . . starting over. I am a stranger to him, and yet to me, he is my husband."

"He will fall in love with you again," Susanna said with conviction. "How could he not?"

He *would* love her, Emily thought fiercely. She would make it happen, and then he would be bound to her. "I will have to trust in his love, I guess."

"You can help him remember the woman you are. Show him your work in the village. He will be proud of you."

Emily shrugged, feeling uncomfortable. "As I told Matthew, I cannot leave the house just yet. It would seem . . . wrong. I'll send word that I hope to be in Comberton tomorrow."

"I still think you should show him the life you've built for yourself."

"I will, I promise. But for now, I think I will remain nearby."

Susanna smiled. "In case he needs you. Oh, Emily, he will need you again, I just know it."

Emily smiled. If only she would be lucky enough for that to happen. But she kept remembering the article in the newspaper mentioning her name—and the other wife Matthew didn't remember. Right now too many things stood in her way. But she would overcome them.

Chapter 5

Since Matthew's father wasn't the master of the household, his study was in his suite of rooms in the family wing of Madingley Court. He also worked in a laboratory created for him in the servants' wing, when he wasn't lecturing or researching at Cambridge University.

Matthew knocked on the study door, and after opening it at Professor Leland's call, was surprised to find that both his parents were there. Of course, he should have expected their curiosity and eagerness to talk with him. The professor sat behind his desk, while Lady Rosa was reading in a chair near the windows. They both stood up as he entered, and the joy in their faces pleased him.

Lady Rosa took his arm and led him to a chair near hers, and Professor Leland came around the desk to join them. For a while they talked in general of the state of their large family, the new scandals, the marriages, land in which his father had invested.

Matthew brought up his new contacts in India as well as exciting investments he wanted to work on with Professor Leland. "Even the railway," he said. "There are so many opportunities, and it is an exciting time for England."

The professor blinked at him. "You've never mentioned such an interest, Matthew."

"I know, and I was wrong. I didn't really know what I wanted, and I was trying not to be a disappointment to you."

"You could never be that to us!" Lady Rosa said, looking stunned.

"Yes, I could have, but I held it all inside, feeling like I was going to burst from the pressure. Now I feel ready to do as I wish. And these new investments, these new industries, excite me."

She put a hesitant hand on his arm. "But Matthew, these enterprises are well and good for other people, but they are not exactly within the realm of a gentleman."

He patted her hand. "Mother, I promise you that I will be circumspect in my business dealings, but I cannot let myself be held back by what others think of me. Frankly, I no longer care."

Her mouth fell open, yet nothing came out.

"I know this is very different for me," he said, looking to Professor Leland for approval.

The professor only nodded. "Go on. I'm very encouraged by your interest in our future."

"I used to be so concerned with the present, with being so careful, with always doing what Society expected of me."

"And what is wrong with that?" Lady Rosa asked in a bewildered voice.

"Nothing, Mother—except it wasn't me. I was hiding everything I was inside, pleasing everyone else, but not myself. I always wanted excitement and adventure, to be free of constraints."

"But you never said any of this, son," Professor Leland said slowly.

"I know I didn't, and that's my own fault. My service in India opened my eyes to how stilted I'd been, living my life. I was trying so hard to be perfect, without scandal, just like my cousin Christopher spent his adulthood. But really . . ." He leaned forward and took both their hands, concerned about hurting them. "I wanted to be just like Daniel, to be my own man. I've become that person these last two years. I've been making my own decisions, and accepting the consequences."

For a moment he felt the pain of some of those decisions, but he let it go. It was in the past.

Lady Rosa's lips tightened. "Daniel has hurt this family's reputation since you've been gone. This past summer he made a wager with an innocent young girl, and it became very public."

"Is this the one he married?" Matthew asked, trying not to smile.

His mother sighed. "She is. And she's a wonderful girl."

"And she's been good for him," the professor added. "He's found his music again, Matthew, and all because of his wife."

"Then I guess his decisions made him happy." Matthew focused on Lady Rosa. "Can you be happy for me, Mother? Let me do as I wish, and trust me enough to know I can make everything work out?"

When she nodded, and Professor Leland gave him a grin, Matthew told himself that it was as if he now had their permission to handle this situation with Emily as he saw fit. And if that was a bit of an exaggeration, he would live with it.

They discussed the men interested in Rebecca, and when Lady Rosa noticeably avoided the subject where Susanna was concerned, Matthew spoke up.

"About Susanna," he began. "There is a dinner tonight, and she refuses to attend? Is this normal?"

"It did not used to be so," Lady Rosa said tightly, "but I guess you are not the only person who wants to do as he wishes."

He smiled. "Susanna is strong-willed. But Emily is worried about her."

"As are we all," Lady Rosa continued, "but she wants me to give up persuading her, so I have."

"I'm not ready to do that. Has anything in particular happened to make her more reclusive?"

Lady Rosa sighed. "If so, she will not tell me. But she used to at least try to socialize and be friendly, but now, more and more, she spends all her time in the laboratory."

Matthew waited for Lady Rosa to throw an accusing glance the professor's way, but to his surprise, she didn't.

"She feels like herself there," Professor Leland said quietly. "We did not want to take that away from her."

The "we" was so shocking to hear that Matthew almost forgot what they were discussing. What had brought about this thaw in his parents' relationship?

But he reminded himself that they were talking about Susanna. "I think I can help her. I want to persuade her to attend tonight's dinner with us, and to guide her into seeing that she can be herself, yet still find her future within the *ton*. Do I have your permission?"

"Permission?" Lady Rosa said, throwing her hands wide. "I would take any help you offered. Perhaps she would try to be happy, for your sake. She's missed you so."

He wondered if his "death" had been part of what harmed her, and it made him feel ill inside. He would have to make things better. Emily's challenge to him was the right thing to do.

It was amazing, he thought wryly, that a woman

whose life was based on a lie seemed to be able to make good choices—sometimes. She was an intriguing mix of contrasts.

Lady Rosa cleared her throat. "Your behavior is so normal, Matthew. It is hard to believe you're having . . . problems."

"Mental problems?" he said, grinning. "And is it all that normal to want to change everything about myself?"

"Not everything," Professor Leland said. "You are still the same good man as when you left."

If he felt a twinge at that, it was small and easily ignored.

"This must be so difficult for you," Lady Rosa said at last, reaching out to touch his arm.

"You mean Emily?" Matthew asked, looking out the window.

Professor Leland cleared his throat. "You have absolutely no memory of her?"

"None, although she says I rescued her at sea. I do remember a boating accident, but it's vague."

"Ah, such a shame to lose the memory of your first six months together," the professor continued, shaking his head. "I am so sorry, Matthew. And I have little to tell you, because poor Emily was so traumatized by your death that whenever we brought up the subject of your time in India together, she would burst into tears."

He looked between them with interest, but remained silent.

"She was so sick and thin," Lady Rosa added, wringing her hands. "For many months I truly feared for her. You see, she was robbed in Southampton when she returned from India, and without payment, her seasick maid left her. Poor Emily had been all alone for many days before arriving here."

"We did receive a letter from the vicar who married you," the professor said.

Matthew straightened with interest. "What was his name?" he asked, hoping to match it to the marriage license he'd found.

His parents glanced at each other, then both shook their heads.

"I don't remember," Professor Leland said.

"I'm sure I have the letter in my chambers," Lady Rosa added.

"What did it say?" Matthew asked.

"Only that we should expect Emily soon," she said, "that she'd married you before you left the country, and was in India with you until you feared that your assignment would prove too dangerous for her to be with you." She blushed. "I remember it so well, because I was so shocked and grateful to meet the woman you'd chosen."

"The letter said nothing else?" he asked, hoping for some kind of clue.

She shook her head. "No, my dearest. And does it really matter? You and Emily are together again."

Matthew took a deep breath, feeling a twinge of guilt. But he wasn't the one who started this charade. "Emily tells me you spent most of your time here at Madingley Court when you were in mourning. But after that?"

"The girls and I went off to London," Lady Rosa said with forced brightness. "They are young, and had their lives to live. I hope you understand . . ."

"Of course I do, Mother. Did Emily enjoy Society?" Matthew asked.

She frowned and glanced at her husband. "I had a terrible time making her leave Madingley Court. She'd never been to London for a Season, and was worried she would embarrass us. She kept calling herself a country girl. She was appalled at the abundance of clothing I wanted to buy for her, and refused everything but the barest necessary."

Professor Leland said, "She even tried to refuse the allowance we offered her, though it came from your inheritance."

"She took it at last," Lady Rosa said, "but I know she mostly uses it for her causes in the village."

So much for Emily having a monetary motive, Matthew thought with surprise. "Causes?"

"Oh, let her show you all of her good works. You'll be so proud!"

Matthew sank back in his chair, knowing that

questioning his parents further would be useless. They only had praise for Emily, and seemed to love her as a daughter. How had she succeeded in swaying his entire family? But then again, he already knew the lure of her sweet personality, the way she could make a person focus only on her.

At least he had places to begin his research, from her parish vicar to her "causes" in the village. Maybe she had another reason for spending so much time in Comberton. A lover perhaps?

Yet her sweet kiss haunted him. He realized he wanted her to be an innocent, which hardly made him objective.

Matthew couldn't find Emily.

He told himself it was a large mansion and she could be anywhere. He looked for her in all the main public rooms, from the conservatory to the library to the great hall. It wasn't until he was outside the dining room with his parents before luncheon that she arrived with Susanna.

Emily gave him a sunny smile, those blue eyes studying him as if she needed to know everything about him. Well, of course she did. And he didn't mind being studied. He enjoyed her attentions.

He asked, "And what have you been doing this morning, Emily?"

"She was with me in the laboratory," Susanna said.

Matthew glanced at his parents, who both deliberately looked away. He tried not to smile. "And do you sketch, too, Emily? I thought you told me you were not a true artist."

"Oh, she doesn't sketch," Susanna said matter-of-factly. "She studies."

He looked between them, watching the blush that suffused Emily's cheeks.

"I know it is not quite the thing for a young lady to do," Emily began slowly, "but I am fascinated with learning, and the professor's knowledge is impressive."

"*You're* studying anatomy," Matthew said.

"It's a shame Emily cannot attend university," Professor Leland said cheerfully. "She would be an excellent student."

Lady Rosa rolled her eyes. "This isn't helping, Randolph."

Matthew wasn't surprised by Emily's intellect. But he'd thought they had an agreement to help Susanna change her behavior and become a happier person.

Hamilton, the butler, rounded the corner and came to a stop as he saw the family talking outside the dining room. Behind him, Matthew saw Reggie, and a young man, tall and blond, his gaze fixed eagerly on Emily.

After a moment, Matthew recognized him: Peter Derby. He'd grown up in a neighboring manor, the youngest son of a squire, and had spent much time at Madingley Court. Peter had even been tutored with them—he and his cousins—since the Derby family could not afford more than a governess. He was intelligent, and when only his older brother had been allowed to attend Eton, Peter's disappointment made him work even harder to educate himself.

To Matthew's surprise, his parents gave him a swift, almost guilty look.

Peter grinned at Emily, who stiffened.

"Mr. Derby has arrived," Hamilton said, speaking to Matthew's parents. "Forgive me for not realizing that luncheon was being served."

"I can return at a later time," Peter said, not taking his eyes off Emily.

"But you will wish to be here, Mr. Derby," Emily said. "Did you not see the *Times* today?"

"I've been out riding."

At last he lifted his gaze to the rest of the family. When he saw Matthew, his smile disappeared as abruptly as a candle flame in a sudden wind. Matthew, being no fool, realized why. Reggie looked from one of them to the other, and frowned as he obviously controlled his amusement.

Peter had become Emily's suitor. Was he one of her "causes" in the village? Matthew felt an unfamiliar tightening in his stomach, and told himself it couldn't be possessiveness—could it?

Chapter 6

Emily looked between Mr. Derby and Matthew. She knew they'd grown up together, had been friends for many years, but now things were . . . different. She'd been politely trying to dissuade Mr. Derby's interest in her since she first emerged from mourning, but he always implied he knew what was best for her. Eager, arrogant man. He'd gone from claiming two dances at every party, to "accidentally" meeting her on a country lane, to recently calling on her—to the Leland family's surprised pleasure.

"Matthew?" Mr. Derby said, his eyes wide in his pale face.

Gradually, the man began to smile, but he wasn't quite able to conceal his . . . disappointment? But he and Matthew had been good friends.

And yet he'd been making his intentions toward her very clear, and now Matthew's presence would obviously put an end to that.

Smiling, Matthew put his arm around Emily's shoulders. "Peter, it is good to see you."

So he remembered his friend, at least. But she hadn't thought he would be the sort who needed such a masculine display.

Something within Peter seemed to ease, and his smile became more genuine. "How did this miracle occur?"

Between Rebecca and Lady Rosa, the entire story tumbled out.

"That is incredible," Peter concluded. "I will write to my family about your good news."

"Do have luncheon with us, Mr. Derby," Lady Rosa said, taking his arm and steering him into the dining room. "Are your mother and brother in London?"

Her voice and his answer faded away.

Emily was surprised by Lady Rosa's invitation, considering that Mr. Derby could no longer court her, and it might be rather awkward now that Matthew was home. But then she noticed that Susanna had gone into the dining room ahead of them, saying nothing. Did Susanna think her mother now meant to steer Mr. Derby's attention toward her?

Matthew kept his arm about her. "We'll join you in a moment, Father."

The professor, trailing his wife, gave Emily a sympathetic nod. Reggie offered a casual salute as he passed by.

When they were alone, Matthew guided her away from the open door. "So, you and Peter?"

His voice was calm, almost speculative, as he released her.

She lifted her chin. "I was a widow out of mourning; he was persistent. I did not encourage him."

"Why not? I would not fault you for that."

"Then you are an incredibly understanding husband. I guess I should have realized that, by your tight arm around my shoulder."

He continued to study her, laughter in his hazel eyes. "Sarcasm. Faint, but noticeable."

"If it's called for."

He chuckled. "I like you, Emily Leland."

"So I assumed when you married me."

His voice became deeper, rougher. "I guess marriage meant that I more than liked you."

She looked away.

"Does that hurt you?"

"No. It is simply still difficult to remember that I thought all of this"—she gestured toward him with both hands—"with you, was gone."

"So you will not mourn whatever relationship you had with Peter?"

She smiled and lowered her voice. "He tried to make it more than it was, but I felt nothing." She looked over her shoulder toward the entrance to the dining room. "It seems we will continue to see much of him."

"He is an eligible man, and my mother has two single daughters."

"But did you see Susanna's reaction to him?"

"Perhaps she is hiding an interest she doesn't know how to express. After all, Peter was here to see you—and has been seeing you. I'm not used to finding my wife being courted by another man."

"How do you know?" she teased him, hoping it was the right tactic.

His eyes seemed to sharpen, making her hold her breath, but he continued smiling. "Because I'm far too confident in my abilities to keep a wife satisfied."

The shot of heat was startling, surprising. Just his words could make her react to him? "Oh, my," she murmured, fanning her face.

His eyes widened, then crinkled with amusement. He looked past her toward the dining room and sighed. "Speaking of things you're not telling me, what is this about you and Susanna in the laboratory today, right after we discussed bringing her back into the folds of Society?"

She frowned. "I don't understand."

"I assumed we were of one mind, that she needs to give a woman's daily routine a try."

"So you do not want her to pursue the things she loves?"

He hesitated. "I was hoping to convince her to find other, more feminine pursuits."

"You didn't make that clear to me. I think painting is a very typical pursuit for a young lady."

He put his hands on his hips as he stared down at her, saying nothing.

She sighed. "Very well, painting musculature for an anatomist is not very typical. Do you really think she should give it up?" She let her voice express her doubt, but did not contradict him. How could she, in her role as his wife?

"Perhaps there are men who think it unseemly— if they even know about it."

"A few may," she mused.

"Which means they told a few more."

"I see. What would prompt Susanna to give up something she loves, for a future that might never happen?"

To her surprise, he stepped closer to her. "We can show her what a happy marriage can be like. You know, she grew up with only our parents' strained relationship to emulate."

Emily licked her suddenly dry lips, his chest so broad before her. "Our happy marriage you cannot even remember?"

He touched her chin, lifting it. "I want to remember. I *will* remember. You captivate me, Emily."

For a moment she thought he might kiss her, right in the corridor while his family waited luncheon for them. She wanted him to. She needed him to be captivated.

But she didn't want him to remember.

She smiled and touched his chest. "I am beside

myself with curiosity. Did you find answers to all your questions when you spoke to your father? Or am I still a mystery to you?"

He smiled. "My parents are very fond of you. But I hear they weren't totally surprised when you showed up on their doorstep. They said they had received a letter from your parish vicar in anticipation of your arrival last year."

Tension contracted her stomach, chasing away all the pleasurable feelings he'd inspired. "Yes, I hadn't known the dear man was sending it."

"Was he the man who married us? I could not remember his name, and neither could my parents."

"He was." She wanted to stroll to the windows, try to find air to breathe, but didn't dare give evidence of retreat. "Mr. Tillman. He's dead now," she said impassively, and she saw the flash of memory as a pillow was held over his face. She could not control her shudder.

"I am sorry to remind you of such sad tidings," Matthew said, putting his hand on her shoulder.

"You couldn't have known."

"Was I supposed to remember?"

The faint pain in his voice made her look at him again. "No, this is nothing you've forgotten. He died just before I arrived here."

He held out his arm to her. "Let's put such sadness behind us. Shall we rejoin my family?"

She nodded, hiding her relief.

*   *   *

During luncheon, Matthew found himself watching Peter Derby, who did his best to not even glance at Emily, and any time Peter looked at him, it was a tentative glance. Matthew made it a point to smile at him, to let him know that his past behavior toward Emily was understandable.

"What have you been doing with yourself these past few years, Peter?" he asked.

"The usual social engagements, of course. I accompany my mother when she needs me, and assist my brother with the management of our lands. Although right now, as I explained earlier to Lady Rosa, I am more idle than usual, as my mother and brother have gone north to visit her sick aunt. I stayed behind on my brother's behalf."

Lady Rosa inclined her head to Peter. "And so I told him he should not stay at home alone. He should spend several days here with us."

She was not very good at hiding the look she gave each of her daughters. Both of them smiled politely.

"This is very gracious of you, Lady Rosa," Peter said, his eyes bright. "Matthew, I would enjoy hearing all about your time in India."

Matthew smiled. "Of course."

Peter turned to the Leland sisters and opened his mouth as if to speak, but Rebecca interrupted.

"Did you see the abundance of mail we received

today?" she asked, too brightly, of the entire room.

Lady Rosa smiled. "Did you receive any special correspondence, Rebecca?"

She blushed. "Nothing unusual, Mama. Just an invitation to tea with Lady Brumley."

"Ah, and isn't her son handsome?"

Matthew watched his sister smile and shrug, and it could have been a coy move, but . . . it wasn't. For a brief moment he thought she seemed uninterested. Wasn't she supposed to be the sister eager for marriage? What had been going on here the last two years? he wondered with mild disbelief.

Rebecca continued, "Emily, I set your letter beside your plate."

Matthew's gaze shot to Emily, who only smiled.

"All of the newest invitations also included Matthew in the address," Rebecca added.

"Then the whirlwind has begun," the professor said dryly.

Matthew smiled at Rebecca. "Who are they from?"

She listed the invitations from various families to breakfasts, dinners, and even a ball there in the country. He recognized all the names as friends or relatives, and although he smiled and made the right responses, even frowned as if his memory failed him once or twice, he continued to watch Emily. She had received a single letter, and for a moment betrayed confusion as she looked at the name affixed to it. Did she not receive many letters? Or just not recognize the name? She didn't open it at the table.

Lady Rosa cleared her throat, and the table became silent. "To celebrate your homecoming, Matthew, I propose that we invite the entire family to come at the end of the week, and that during their visit, we host a ball for all of our neighbors."

"That sounds fine," he said. He could confide in his cousins, Daniel and Christopher. The three of them had always been able to solve a problem together.

After a long conversation about who they would invite to the ball, Lady Rosa asked, "And what are you doing this afternoon, Matthew?"

"Emily and I are going riding."

Susanna brightened. "Can I c—"

She broke off as Rebecca elbowed her.

When Lady Rosa stood up, everyone else joined her. "Mr. Derby, do send for your things. I was very serious about you joining us. You young people will have so much to do together."

"I'll journey home this afternoon, my lady," Peter said. "I have correspondence to take care of before returning."

As everyone left the dining room, Matthew didn't realize that Emily was gone until he turned around. If she was simply changing into her riding clothes, why not say so?

He caught Reggie's arm. "Did you see which way Emily went?" he asked in a low voice.

"Sorry, I thought you were keeping close tabs on your wife."

He laughed. "I don't have time right now. Susanna?" he called, seeing his sister reach the end of the corridor.

She turned back to him, and when she saw Peter going a different way, smiled and approached Matthew.

"I have something to discuss with you," he said, ignoring her reaction to Peter—for now. "Reggie, what are you doing today?" he asked as his friend moved away.

Reggie turned around but kept walking. "Obviously not riding with you," he said, and waved.

By then Susanna stood next to Matthew, who took her arm and led her into a smaller drawing room across the corridor from the dining room. Lady Rosa hesitated, her expression concerned. He smiled as he closed the door without inviting her inside.

When he turned around, Susanna's arms were folded over her chest, her chin lifted, spectacles glittering on her nose.

Matthew blinked at her. "Is something wrong?"

"It depends what you mean to say," she answered coolly.

"Very well, I'll come right to the point. I'm worried about you."

She sighed loudly and threw her arms wide. "You've been talking to Mama and Papa about my spinsterhood, haven't you?"

"You speak like it's a foregone conclusion."

"I am twenty-six years old, Matthew. Let me be. My life is as I wish it, and I am happy. Even Mama has accepted it."

"I haven't. And Emily hasn't."

Susanna looked briefly stricken. "Emily? But she and I—"

"She did not betray any confidences, let me make that clear. But she is a woman who has known what it is like to feel alone in the world. She is worried about that happening to you."

"Alone? But I have all of you, my aunts, and my cousins. How could I be alone?"

"Emily thought she had a large family to protect her, and they were all taken from her in one moment of heartbreak." He raised both hands. "I know you have extended family, and such a tragedy is highly unlikely, but we're both concerned that you will end up feeling alone, when everyone has their own family but you."

"I like being alone."

But she spoke too quickly.

"That may be. But much as we hate to consider it, someday our parents will be gone, and Rebecca and I will have our own households. I do not think your inheritance will be enough for you to live very comfortably alone."

"So I'll live with you."

"And you can do so forever. But . . . Emily and I plan to have many children." A small lie to persuade his sister.

"I can help her."

"But will it be easy to watch, knowing you'll never have any of your own?"

Susanna swallowed, saying nothing for a moment. "I will take my life as God sees fit to grant me."

"Then do me a favor. Give me the next few weeks. I want you to accompany me to every event I attend. I want to show off my accomplished little sister."

"Accomplished?" She gave an awkward laugh. "Will you hide my bluestocking ways?"

"Not hide, no," he said gently. "But I'll ask you to refrain from them for just a while. This isn't about appeasing Mother—it's about making sure there is not a man out there for you to love, one who would accept you in every way, if given a chance."

"When did you become a romantic?" she asked with suspicion, but her voice was mild.

"Perhaps Emily made me one."

"You *are* very different since your marriage."

He did not explain that marriage had had nothing to do with the way he'd changed his life. "I hope you mean that in a good way."

"You are happier, Matthew," she said softly, touching his arm. "The entire family has noticed. And if only for that reason—and my deep joy at your return—I will *briefly* acquiesce to what you're asking of me."

He smiled. "Thank you."

"It will be very difficult, do not doubt that."

"Oh, I know. We males of the species are terribly difficult to get along with. But I thank you for humoring me."

"We'll have to prepare Mama. Otherwise she will faint with shock when I willingly attend the dinner tonight."

Matthew decided not to let her know he'd already discussed her problem with his parents. As they left the drawing room side by side, he was already focusing on Emily, and the afternoon he had planned with her.

Emily couldn't return to Matthew's suite—he would certainly come upon her reading the letter, and she couldn't risk that. So she headed for the library and closed the door behind her.

Then she looked at the letter again, angry with herself for the way her hands shook. The penmanship was a man's. Who would be writing to her?

She broke the wax and unfolded the single piece of paper. Her stomach twisted with fear when she saw the initial at the bottom. Then she forced herself to read.

My Dearest Emily,

I was so touched to read about the return of Captain Leland. Have you told him you're not his wife? Does he know the other things you've done? Let us discuss your plans. I have already arrived nearby, and will contact you soon.

S.

Emily's eyes finally blurred as she reread the threat again, and then once more. Stanwood had found her at last. She'd always known there was a chance, but as the months went by, she thought herself safe.

Matthew's return—and her crime—had finally given Stanwood new leverage against her. She impatiently pushed away her guilt, for it could only weaken her. All she could do was try harder to make Matthew love her, and think of what she'd say to persuade Stanwood to abandon any mad scheme he'd concocted. He was a murderer, and she was *someone* now, Captain Leland's wife. Stanwood had no proof otherwise.

She tossed the letter onto the open coal fire,

watched the flame light, and walked swiftly from the room.

It had been difficult to sneak away from Matthew, the entire Leland family, and the servants, but he'd managed it. Now he was hidden within an overgrowth of tropical ferns in the conservatory, watching Emily Leland through the open library doors. He could tell nothing from her expression as she read the letter. Why had she felt the need to hide from the family?

She tossed it onto the coals before leaving the room. He silently ran in and managed to pull out the charred paper. Dropping it to the marble hearth, he put out the flame with his foot, then picked it up, holding two scraps together.

Most of the letter was gone, but he did see "you're not his wife" and "will contact you soon."

He felt stunned at the treacherous implications for the family. He would have to keep a very close eye on Emily Leland—or whoever she actually was.

Chapter 7

Emily leaned her forearms against the stone balustrade of the terrace, looking out over Madingley Court's beautiful park, the one Matthew didn't remember. As she squinted up at the overcast sky, she thought again of the letter from Stanwood. Though nausea still churned in her stomach, she was determined to keep a clear head, to protect herself. This afternoon alone with Matthew, flirting and enticing, would be a good start.

Someone spoke her name, making her jump. She turned around to see Matthew's smiling face.

"My, you're jumpy," he said casually.

His gaze dipped down to her breasts, which were already rising and falling far too quickly with each breath. And his intimate look only encouraged her reaction.

She pasted a smile on her face. "I didn't even hear you cross the terrace."

"It's all my expert training in the art of sneaking up on people."

"Then you're a success."

Before she could even ask, he indicated the basket in his hand. "Treats in case we're hungry."

She smiled. "Your mother?"

"Actually, my sisters."

"They are thoughtful young ladies," she said, leaving the balustrade to walk down the broad steps to the gravel path.

Matthew walked at her side. "I spoke to Susanna. She agreed to my proposal."

Emily widened her eyes. "So easily?"

"I think she wants to please her brother who's so recently back from the dead." He grinned. "And the way marriage has changed me also persuaded her."

She deliberately brushed her shoulder against his. "We wives work magic on our husbands' stern temperaments."

He laughed. "Then we begin tonight. She'll see that she doesn't have to be alone."

"It can be a terrible thing," she said, a shade too solemnly.

He glanced at her with sympathy, then took her hand. His was warm, rough with calluses, so very different from hers.

"Much as I love my sisters," he said softly, "today I am finding you much more interesting."

She forced a laugh. "But we have all afternoon to talk."

"Don't we have the rest of our lives?"

She caught her breath. When she met his gaze, she felt the power of him, the intent focus of those changeable eyes. How could any woman resist him? She squeezed his hand.

At the main stable, grooms and stable boys were hanging on the paddock rails, staring at Matthew with open curiosity.

"I recognize no one," he said quietly.

She gave him a reassuring glance. "They're young boys. They grow like weeds in two years. Why would you recognize them? I'll tell the head groom that we'd like two horses saddled."

She went inside, and by the time she returned, Matthew was sitting on the rail between all the young stable boys.

"No, I tell you, it wasn't jolly fun to aim your musket at the enemy and fire," he was saying. "And a soldier only does so because of his duty to queen and country."

The boys watched him solemnly.

"They thought ye was dead," said an older lad, John, with several missing front teeth.

"It was a terrible strain on my family. I'm certain you all did your best to help them during the difficult times."

"Is Mrs. Leland happy now?" John asked. "She sometimes seems so sad."

Matthew's eyes found her. She *had* done her best to portray a woman in mourning.

"It is a sad thing when a wife thinks her husband is dead," Matthew said, not taking his eyes from her. "Does she come to visit the stables often, boys?"

She felt uncomfortable, uncertain of his purpose. Why did he not ask *her* how often she liked to ride?

"Usually when she goes to the village," John said candidly. "And that's a lot."

Just then, Lavenham, the head groom, emerged from the gloomy recesses of the stable leading two saddled horses. He gave her a polite nod, but was already looking past her to grin broadly at Matthew.

"Master Matthew," Lavenham said. "I saddled Spirit for you."

Matthew put out a hand and they shook. "Lavenham, good to see you're still here."

Emily relaxed when Matthew remembered his name. The two men spent several minutes talking about the breed of horses used by the army, until at last Lavenham noticed Emily watching.

He harrumphed. "Been keepin' ye from Mrs. Leland."

"I don't mind," she said.

"No, you're right, Lavenham," Matthew said. "A lady shouldn't be kept waiting. We'll speak another time."

He transferred several wrapped parcels, a corked bottle, and a blanket from the basket to a saddlebag. Before she could mount, he took the reins of both horses, leading them down the path. She knew the grooms and stable boys were gawking, wondering why they didn't ride wherever they were going. She was wondering, too.

Only when they'd passed through the more formal gardens and into a clearing out of sight of the outbuildings did Matthew turn to her.

"Since I don't know where I'm going," he said, "this would probably be easier if I could just ride with you."

Though she was surprised, she gave him the smile of a wife starved for intimacy. "That sounds wonderful."

With one powerful spring, he lifted off from the ground, swung his right leg high and settled into the saddle. Spirit tossed his head, even as Matthew leaned down and caught her hand. "Ready?"

She kept hold of her own horse's reins but swung onto his, settling into the saddle right behind Matthew, snug between the cantle and his body. He was between her thighs, his strong back against her breasts, her arms around his waist. Her skirts were stretched tightly to accommodate him—and then slid even higher up her calves. She could feel the muscles of his stomach contract as he adjusted to both of them in the saddle. Soon Spirit was walking slowly across the meadow.

Then suddenly he was urging the animal into a

gallop. She had to let go of her horse's reins, trusting the animal to follow, because all she could do was hold on to Matthew for dear life.

By the time they'd galloped across a field and had to slow down at the approach of a woodland, Matthew was finding it difficult to focus on his need to learn everything he could about Emily, with her breasts flattened against his back. All he could think about was his position between her thighs.

Where he wanted to be.

He forced himself to remember his purpose. "Where should I go?" he said over his shoulder. "It's all still a blank to me."

She spoke into his ear. "Ride up the hill. It will take us away from the park and out into the countryside."

At a slower pace, they rode through the trees and up the gradual incline of a hill blanketed in grass and autumn's purple heather. When Emily suggested she ride her own horse as they approached the cottages of tenants, he wouldn't hear of it.

They rode for several hours down country lanes as she played guide, showing him again all the places he'd haunted as a boy, which she had apparently learned from his family. He was amused by the way she recited the names of each neighbor who lived in each house, adding more details if they would be attending the dinner party that night. He let her think what she would about his lack of memory, admiring her animation and her knowledge. After all, he'd spent two years away; he should learn the local gossip. Occasionally people waved at them, and although Matthew waved back, he didn't ride close enough to talk.

At last, when the countryside spread out around them and Madingley Court sat like the gilded throne of a king in the midst of rolling hills, he drew the horse to a halt. A breeze ruffled through the long grass. It had obviously been a while since sheep had been turned loose up here.

"Shall we rest and see what my sisters sent with us?" he asked.

He closed his eyes as her warm body slid along the width of his. Her toe found his in the stirrup, and she used that and his hand to help her dismount. On the ground, she turned away from him and looked out at the view, hugging her shawl tighter about her. He didn't know how she could be cold after the heat they'd generated between their bodies.

He dismounted, removed their picnic provisions from the saddlebag, and spread the blanket on the ground. Emily's face was suffused with pleasure and contentment as she sat down beside him.

The wrapped parcels turned out to be sandwiches of beef and cheese, as well as several peaches. They took turns sipping from the bottle of apple cider. Her mouth on the same place his had been seemed

incredibly erotic—obviously he'd been without
female companionship for far too long.

They ate in silence for several minutes, and
he watched her rather than the countryside. He
stretched out on his side, propped up on his elbow,
so he could be closer to her. Emily sat so demurely,
legs folded beneath her, her yellow skirts a touch of
spring in autumn.

After a swallow of cider, she handed him back
the bottle. "I am curious why you chose the army,
surely unusual for an only son."

"Did we not have this discussion early in our
marriage?"

She didn't even hesitate. "You were an eager soldier then, ready to be away from England and see
the world."

And that was the truth, he mused, impressed by
her deduction.

"You only told me you were looking for adventure," she continued. "But as I settled in my role as
your wife and grew to understand you better, I didn't
believe that was the entire truth. A wealthy man can
find adventure traveling on the Continent."

He reminded himself that keeping to the truth
might help him—and would be easier to remember
than piling on more lies.

"Yes, I wanted to see the world, because I knew
I could do as I wished away from England, be the
man I thought I always wanted to be."

"Were you hiding yourself up to that point?"

She was far too intelligent—but then she would have to be, to have succeeded in this ruse. He rolled onto his back, hands clasped beneath his head, his elbow deliberately touching her thigh. She didn't move, and neither did he.

"I was," he said in a low voice. "I felt the need to contain myself, to set a good example for my sisters, to be a good son."

"And those were the things you hid the truth behind?"

He sighed. "They were part of the truth, of course, but I felt . . . too contained, too limited, as if I could never do what I wished, but was always doing what was expected of me. I didn't want to hurt my family, living outside the boundary of Society—even though I secretly longed for that. The military is often an answer for young men, so I decided to try it."

"You never told me any of this," she said solemnly.

"Perhaps I never had the chance, since we were only together mere months. But we're starting over, you and I, and you deserve to know the kind of husband you have."

"And what kind is that?"

She was smiling at him with amusement, and for a moment it rankled him. He wanted to unsettle her, to make her uneasy about her tenuous position here, alone with a strange man.

He came up on his elbow, and although she was still seated, her face was now close to his. "I wanted to be . . . wild."

Her smile faded.

He lowered his voice, watching her mouth. "I wanted to do whatever I wished, be reckless and live life to the fullest."

"But instead you married a simple English country girl," she countered softly.

"Perhaps it was another reckless deed on my part."

She licked her lips. "Reckless would be seducing me and leaving me behind."

"No, that would be cruel. And I'm not that. But I take what I want, do what I want."

Her smile was faint. "Oh, so threatening. Do you mean to entice me with these playful love words?"

Her fearlessness was impressive. If she was afraid he'd discover the truth, she didn't betray it.

He slid his hand along her thigh. "Are you enticed?"

"Of course. I married you, didn't I?"

"I'm a lucky man." She was surely expecting him to kiss her, even leaning toward him, a woman bent on distraction. He decided to change the subject back to her. "You didn't just sit around waiting for me to come into your life. What did you do with yourself while you sifted through the local gentlemen?"

She laughed. "I spent many hours helping our parish."

"With Mr. Tillman?" he said, feeling a heightened sense of anticipation. The man's name had been on their forged marriage license.

Her expression gradually became bittersweet as her blue eyes seemed to focus on the past. "Yes. He never married, so he did not have a wife's aid. My mother used to assist him, so it naturally fell to me after she died. I used to lead the various women's societies, the ones to provide for families with a new baby, or to help feed a family when their only source of income was cut off."

He wondered if any of this were true. She'd said Tillman was already dead, but certainly there must be others who could confirm or repudiate her story.

"I especially enjoyed working with the children," she said.

Her expression was soft and feminine, as if she longed for her own child.

"Did you wish for *my* child?" he asked.

"Of course I did."

"Then it must be difficult that I am not yet a proper husband to you."

"But you're alive. I can wait for the rest."

"And what if I don't fall in love with you again?"

She only lifted her eyebrows, her expression amused.

He laughed. "Or are you confident that we will magically find our way back to each other again?"

"We're different people now," she said slowly, looking away from him and back toward Madingley Court, gleaming even under the overcast sky. "Perhaps it won't be the same kind of love again, but I'm willing to trust in us."

He slid his hand just a bit higher up her thigh. "I find myself impatient to recapture what we had together."

She waited, her focus on him.

"Teach me, Emily," he murmured. "We need to begin to know one another again on a more intimate level. Teach me how we liked to kiss."

"I believed you proved yourself competent just this morning," she teased.

"That was just the start. I remember so little, and you promised to teach me."

Her gaze dropped to his mouth. He wanted to taste her, explore her far more than he had that morning. But he had to be patient, for he felt a wild, reckless desire for her that he'd never felt for another woman. His body was already anticipating touching her, tasting her.

He lay back on the blanket. Very deliberately, she placed her hand beside him and leaned above his body. She blocked out part of the sky, but since it was cloudy, he could see her expression, full of anticipation. She wanted the kiss, too.

And then she hesitated, her face just above his, beautiful, complex, unreadable.

"Do I initiate the kisses, or do you?" he asked. *Do you pretend to play the meek wife?*

"We both do," she whispered.

A bold answer. But then, he'd already revealed himself to be a very untypical husband who would expect an untypical wife.

Her breath on his face, a touch of autumn cider, almost made him groan. "Did I kiss you first?" he asked, hearing the huskiness in his voice.

She was lower now, a lock of her golden hair tumbling free to brush along his cheek and fall to his neck.

"Of course you did. You were courting me."

He met her half-lidded gaze. "Then it's your turn."

Her lips touched his, as gentle as a butterfly, but without hesitation. Then she slanted her head the other way to taste more of him. The rush of desire from a chaste kiss was so heady, so complete, that he barely kept himself from crushing her to him, pulling her on top of him.

Emily forgot everything but the soft moistness of Matthew's lips. He lay prone beneath her, and she had to steady herself on his shoulder or fall into him with sudden, overwhelming weakness. The sensation of the kiss was about more than their lips; she felt it in her mind, in her heart, in her loins, which so willfully desired him. She wanted to press against him, taste more of him. Her kisses grew intense, taking more of his mouth, opening to seek the true passion she'd only dreamed about.

Matthew Leland was a man back from the dead, struggling to reclaim his life—and finding her in it. Though she was taking advantage of him, she promised herself that he would be well compensated by her eagerness.

Against her will, she remembered that he had a wife, the thought dowsing her passion. She lifted her head to stare down at him. Always, this woman would be between them, until Emily could discover the truth about her. But how to do that? And what would Arthur Stanwood do with such knowledge?

"Emily? Is something wrong?"

He sat up, and as she felt both his hands on her shoulders, knew he needed some kind of explanation. She blinked as if forcing back tears, then put a hand on his chest. "You're really home," she whispered in wonder. "You'll think me a silly female if I cry in the middle of a kiss. It was bad enough that I swooned at your feet last night—"

"Into my arms. I know how to catch a woman."

She gave an unladylike snort of laughter. He pressed a handkerchief into her palm, and she dabbed at her eyes, hoping he didn't notice that the fabric remained dry.

"I don't think I've ever before reduced a woman to tears with my kisses," he mused.

He brought her hands to his chest, and she felt the strong beat of his heart. He wanted his memories back; she couldn't want the same.

But she would teach him whatever he wanted; she would make him happy. Nothing—no one—would stand in her way.

Chapter 8

Emily knew Matthew watched her too carefully. What emotions chased each other across her face, when she was trying to hide them?

"Why are you crying?" he asked.

"Because I never thought to have the chance to kiss you again," she whispered.

Then she smiled and patted his chest, turning away to gather up the remains of their picnic. When she mounted her own horse, she was surprised that he allowed it. She'd wanted him to ask her to ride with him again, but it seemed he had enough intimacy for one afternoon.

As they rode down the lane that wound between low hills, they passed a cottage that was part of the estate, remote, yet well-maintained.

"My father lived here before I was born," Matthew said suddenly.

She gave him a startled glance. "Before they were married, you mean?" She had always assumed no one was given the lease because the duke wanted his privacy.

He nodded. "My grandfather allowed the cottage to be leased, amused that a Cambridge professor wanted privacy to work, and some distance from the university. The old duke had a love of learning—if not a love of his wife."

She winced with sympathy. "Didn't your grandfather cause the first of the Cabot scandals?"

He grinned. "Not the first, but one of many. Weakness seems to run in the family."

"But not in you, of course," she said with a toss of her head.

"Of course. He gambled and womanized his way through his entire inheritance before he was twenty-five and then had to rebuild the family fortune."

"Obviously, he accomplished that feat."

"Yes, but he could never quite forgive himself for the unentailed land that had to be sold. He made no secret of the fact that he chose beauty and dowry over suitability when he married."

"How flattering to his wife," she said with sarcasm.

"Do not pity her too much. She made it obvious that she chose his title over love. But when he spent more time rebuilding his estate than paying attention to her, their shaky marriage crumbled even further. Their children—my mother, her sister and brother—were the ones to suffer. Grandfather made up for his neglect by allowing them all to marry as they wished, and not always to success."

With a smile, she said, "So here in this cottage, when a simple university professor met an unhappy daughter of a duke . . ."

"The guilty duke allowed them to marry."

"It sounds as if they fell in love."

"They did . . . I believe. But my mother came from a world where men chose business or gambling or hunting to take them away from their wives—not science. And once the scandal happened . . ."

"Your sisters explained it all to me. The female corpse, illegally purchased."

He nodded, leaning on his pommel, staring at the cottage as if he could turn back time. "I didn't tell you any of this before?"

She shrugged. "You didn't want to discuss it."

Slowly, he said, "I can believe that. When Rebecca was born, though I was young, I thought things were better between my parents. I didn't understand then how two people could . . . give in to an old passion, yet not resolve things between them." He sighed. "This is too strange, to be discussing my parents' marriage and near-divorce like this. But you've been here, you've seen them together."

"And are things not much improved in the time you've been gone?"

"They are."

"I have been . . . encouraging them to spend more time together, forcing them to talk on occasion."

"And why did you believe you could help my parents?"

She heard the doubt in his voice and couldn't understand it. Why wouldn't his *wife* want such a thing? "I simply believed it couldn't hurt. I thought they were two people who'd become used to their separate lives. If they could remember why they were first drawn together, perhaps things could be different for them. It's not yet a success, of course."

"But it is much improved. And I have you to thank for that?" He tilted his head, smiling.

She demurely waved a hand. "Oh, not entirely."

As they rode away, he leaned toward her, as if imparting a confidence. "You turned this ancient household on its ear, Emily Leland, just like you did to me."

After Matthew dressed in his evening clothes, he waited in the great hall with Peter, Reggie, and his father, until at last the women arrived. Lady Rosa and Rebecca were obviously excited, and Emily was feigning it well. Matthew almost forgot the point of the evening when he looked at Emily in the rose-colored gown that emphasized the tops of her creamy breasts and made her blond hair glow. He almost wished the evening were already over, so he could have her alone in his suite, to see where their earlier shared kisses would lead.

Susanna's demeanor brought Matthew back into the present. She looked like she was headed for the French guillotine, resigned and no longer fighting her fate.

He arched a brow at her. She heaved a great sigh and donned a smile that showed every tooth in her head.

He approached his sister and spoke softly. "I thought you only needed your spectacles for reading or painting."

"I do." Light reflected off the lenses as she gave him a stare that was almost mutinous.

"They hide your lovely brown eyes."

With another sigh, she removed them and slid them into the reticule dangling from her wrist.

"Thank you," he said, trying to be solemn.

"Oh, please." She rolled her eyes. "Do not try to make me believe you are only suffering through a brotherly duty. You are enjoying yourself."

"I *always* enjoy myself—now."

She narrowed her eyes. "That is another thing that is different about you. You didn't even protest going to this dinner, when you used to tolerate them before. You haven't even asked if there's going to be dancing—you used to hate to dance."

And he had. Every young lady he used to dance with had wanted a proper courtship and marriage—

so very boring. All he'd wanted to do was shock them with the lascivious direction of his thoughts, but he'd held himself back. Now he had his own woman to seduce, and the rest of them paled in his memory like ghosts of a forgotten past.

"If there's dancing, you will dance," Matthew said. "It's part of our bargain."

"Yes, Captain," she said grimly, giving him a salute.

An hour later, when they all stood in Lord Sydney's drawing room with another dozen guests, Matthew lost sight of Susanna in the face of an eager crowd. They gathered about him, all talking at once, the ladies dabbing their eyes and repeatedly hugging Lady Rosa, the men clapping Professor Leland on the back. Over and over Matthew explained how the mistake of his death announcement had happened. At least a half dozen times the women exclaimed over "dear" Emily's bravery until Emily blushed at last.

He noticed that Emily remained with his family and not the other women, but then again, his parents had warned him that her closest friends were his sisters.

When Reggie brought him a claret, Matthew was able to step back against the wall. He downed a healthy swallow. "It's so close in here, it might as well be summer."

Reggie glanced past him, arching a brow.

"Or perhaps there's another reason you're over-heated?"

Matthew followed his gaze and saw Emily standing with Rebecca. He smiled. "Why, yes, perhaps there is a contributing factor. But where is Susanna?" Then he caught sight of her against the far wall, amidst the elder ladies and the chaperones. He groaned. "So much for our bargain."

When Reggie expressed his curiosity, Matthew told him about wanting to help Susanna.

"She is a lovely girl," Reggie said. "I don't see the problem."

"The problem is she's not a girl, but a woman, a not-quite-so-young woman."

Reggie shrugged. "Give her time. This is only the first night of your bargain. Instead, tell me about your day with Emily."

Matthew's focus returned to his "wife," although he did look about them to make sure he could speak without being overheard. "She is wily," he began slowly.

"You still say that with admiration. The bloom is not yet off the rose?"

Matthew chuckled. "I find myself more and more intrigued. Yet I am ever practical. Do you remember a Mr. Tillman, a vicar near Southampton?"

"My mother despaired of me ever being a churchgoer," Reggie said, taking a healthy sip of his claret.

"So that is a no?"

Reggie only grinned.

"Apparently, he 'married' us. His signature is on the forged license. I sent a letter today to the duke's investigator to look into Emily's background, specifically this vicar, whom she claims she worked closely with."

"Worked closely?" Reggie said dubiously.

Matthew gave a soft snort. "Charity work with the other ladies of her village."

"Ah. And you don't believe it?"

"I don't really know what to believe. I am keeping an open mind. It will be several days before I receive an answer." His smile faded and he found himself once again studying Emily. Softly, he said, "What did she do when she found herself alone after her family's death? Assuming her childhood was as she said, why wouldn't a beautiful, well-bred woman just marry a man if she needed to support herself? Unless this marriage she'd created set her free to do as she wished."

"Yet what has she done?" Reggie asked.

"That's it, exactly. I heard today that she rides into the village often. I'll pursue that next."

"Someone approaches," Reggie said in warning.

They both focused on Peter Derby, making his way through the milling guests. Matthew watched him glance Emily's way where she stood with the rest of the Leland family.

"Is that regret in Mr. Derby's eyes?" Reggie asked.

Matthew heard his friend's smothered laughter, and though he joined it, he spoke seriously. "Am I supposed to watch a parade of men lusting after her, wondering which will be the one who isn't what he seemed, perhaps her accomplice?"

"But Peter Derby?" Reggie said doubtfully.

"He was her suitor after all."

Emily must have noticed Peter's glance, for she joined him to approach Matthew and Reggie.

Matthew greeted Peter, then let his smile deepen for Emily. She responded by taking his arm and giving it a squeeze.

"Matthew," Peter said amiably. "Quite the crowd tonight. I'm surprised you even have a moment to yourself."

"Returning from the dead makes one popular," Reggie said.

Peter grinned. "I'll have to try that."

"Oh, no, you mustn't," Emily said, her voice full of mock sincerity. When the three men stared at her, she continued, "How could you expect such a ruse to succeed twice?"

Peter laughed heartily. "Mrs. Leland, your wit is so subtle."

Matthew felt Reggie's glance but ignored it. Flirting with a woman in front of her husband was an unusual tactic. But of course, Emily wasn't his wife, he reminded himself.

Then why was he once again feeling annoyed at the thought of her with other men?

Peter's laughter faded. "But truly, Matthew, returning from the dead seems to have agreed with you."

Matthew studied his drink for a moment. "Much seems different when one returns from the other side of the world. I have seen"—*and done*, he thought—"terrible things, and it has enabled me to put my own life in perspective. I feel . . . more at peace with myself. I've chosen to stop fighting my own temperament, to accept things I once rebelled against."

Reggie and Peter were staring at him. Emily studied him thoughtfully, and he wondered if he'd revealed too much to her.

Reggie cleared his throat. "I had a very different response to being on the other side of the world. It made me want to do nothing more for a time than to enjoy good Madingley brandy, ride fine Madingley horses with no destination in mind, and even read a book in the Madingley library, with my feet upon expensive leather furniture."

They all laughed.

"What a rebel," Matthew said dryly. But he was glad Reggie had distracted their attention from him.

"I did have a pint at the inn," Reggie added. "I listened to wild stories of your death-defying return to England."

"And what were those?" Peter asked, still laughing.

"Find me another drink and I'll tell you."

The two men went off together, leaving Matthew alone with Emily. She was still watching him too closely, but her eyes suddenly sharpened as she glanced past his shoulder.

"Oh dear," she murmured, her expression full of regret.

Matthew turned to look. "Well, if it isn't Albert Evans," he drawled, relieved to see an old friend.

Albert was short and husky, with a mane of black hair and open, honest features. To Matthew's surprise, Albert hugged him fiercely. After glancing at Emily, Albert turned his determined face toward Matthew, who felt his enthusiasm suddenly wane.

"Damn, but how did this miracle happen?" Albert demanded, smiling with delight.

Matthew repeated his story, knowing this wouldn't be the last time. Albert nodded to Emily reluctantly, respectfully, his face even redder, and Matthew at last accepted the truth. Albert was another would-be suitor. Was every man after Emily?

For several minutes the two men discussed the health of Albert's family and what he'd been doing in London. Matthew would have been content to let the subject of Emily go. After all, what more needed to be said?

But at last there was a momentary silence in their

friendly conversation, and Albert glanced at Emily.

"Matthew," he said, lowering his voice, "perhaps we can speak privately?"

"I already know what you're going to say," Matthew said, sliding his arm around Emily's tense shoulders. "When my wife emerged from mourning, you showed an interest."

Albert sighed and looked away. "I feel . . . strange about it, old chap."

"Oh, please don't, Mr. Evans," Emily said softly, her face suffused with a blush.

Matthew smiled. "You aren't the only man who feels he needs to apologize to me."

Albert sighed heavily. "I saw you with Derby. So you've had this same conversation?"

"More or less," Matthew said with a shrug. He gave Emily a gentle shake. "Neither of you should feel guilty. Emily is a rare flower, and I'm a lucky man."

She stared up at him solemnly, and Matthew wondered what frantic thoughts were going on behind those clear blue eyes.

Making a decision, he continued, "Emily and I have been apart almost a year. I admit it felt strange to know that she'd decided to see other men—"

Matthew was surprised that Emily could become stiffer, but she did.

"That's not how it was," Albert quickly said, bobbing his head respectfully toward Emily. "I will speak frankly, Matthew, so that you understand the truth. I met Mrs. Leland once or twice while she was in mourning. She was polite but distant. It was only after she came to London this past summer, and your mother encouraged us all to include her as much as possible, that the rest of the male population began to see the treasure you'd won yourself."

Emily's smile was faint and strained.

"My mother wants a marriage for everyone," Matthew said, giving a crooked grin.

"All mothers do. But Mrs. Leland didn't seem to wish the same thing. I don't know a man who won more than a dance with her at a ball—and rarely two."

"Surely Peter Derby was a bit more insistent?" Matthew said lightly.

"Well, yes," Albert admitted. "But your wife— she was polite, but uninterested in any of us."

"Please, Mr. Evans," Emily murmured. "You do not need to defend me so. My husband is a most understanding man."

Albert harrumphed and rocked on his heels, looking uncomfortable. "Matthew, I just wouldn't have felt right until I'd explained everything to you."

"And you have," Matthew said. "Any duty you felt is fulfilled."

After promising to attend a dinner soon, Albert moved on, barely able to look Emily in the eyes. Matthew had no problem watching her.

She raised her chin and spoke softly. "Surely you have more questions for me than you asked Mr. Evans."

"I have met two of your suitors in one day," he said.

"And you'll probably meet other men who considered me fair game. Your mother wanted my happiness. She did not want me mourning only a brief memory in my old age. She couldn't understand that . . ." Her voice fell away.

"Understand what?" he asked gently.

Emily didn't explain, and Matthew wondered what she'd meant to say.

Without giving her a chance to protest, he took her hand and led her along the wall, toward the French doors that opened onto a terrace. He knew people gaped as they left the drawing room, but no one followed them out into the cool autumn evening. The moon hung low in the sky, providing faint light. He needed no light for guidance. He was giving in to his irrational impulse to prove something to Emily, even though he didn't know what it was.

"Matthew?"

Ignoring her query, he pulled her away from the light of the doors and along the wall of the terrace, where he crowded her until her back was against the smooth stone.

"Emily." Her name was a rumble deep in his throat. "You don't have to explain anymore. I understand everything you did while I was gone. What I don't understand is why I feel so . . . disturbed by it all. The thought of you with someone else makes me feel positively primitive with jealousy. I want to put my hands on you in public, remind them all of my claim."

She was watching him with wide eyes, but there was excitement, too, and he shared it. With her shoulders back against the wall, her breasts were thrust forward, and he looked at his leisure, where the faint moonlight dipped into the hollow between them.

He rested his hand on her shoulder, his thumb just touching the upper slope of her breast. "Were we one of those couples who cannot stop looking at each other, who cannot keep their hands off each other during any moment of privacy? Teach me the truth, Emily."

Without waiting for an answer, he kissed her, this time with all the passion he wanted to share with her. He clasped her head with his hands, used his whole body, his chest to her breasts, his hips to hers, his thighs keeping her immobile. Her mouth he plundered, tasting deeply, wanting as much of her as he could take. She put her arms about his waist, hands sliding up his back, her tongue meeting his with eager passion.

His mind went blank; they were alone in the world, cool wind tugging at their hair and clothing.

But between them rose a fire, hot with desire, little caring that it consumed their souls.

Matthew lifted his head, breathing hard.

"Did I make you forget those other men?" he asked with playful arrogance, letting his thumb slide down her cheek, then rub back and forth over her moist lower lip.

"I never forgot you," she whispered. "And I never kissed anyone while you were gone. I never wanted to."

He kissed her once again, then stepped back. "My desire for you makes me forget all my promises to help my sister."

She smiled. "It is hardly too late. Shall we return?"

He nodded, but didn't return her smile as he said, "Yes, but I'll have great difficulty in concentrating on anything but you, Emily."

She ducked her head away and led him back inside.

Emily found herself seated beside Matthew through dinner, and she took advantage of it, brushing his elbow with hers, letting their hands "accidentally" touch, leaning in to speak softly to him. She had worried that finding out about two former suitors would anger him, but miraculously, his desire only seemed to be inflamed by the challenge.

She might be winning him, she thought, trying not to be too excited and relieved.

As she ate her turkey stuffed with chestnuts, she noticed Matthew's sisters watching them. Sensible Susanna looked at refined Rebecca—and both smothered laughter. Emily tried to frown at them but couldn't quite make it believable.

"And what is wrong with my sisters?" Matthew asked, amusement in his voice.

"A fine example you set," she murmured. "They certainly saw the way you dragged me outside. Perhaps they thought it so romantic that they'll permit their suitors to do the same."

"They understand the difference between courtship and marriage," he said dryly. He arched a brow. "I assume I was a proper suitor?"

"Oh, very. My family had just died, after all. You were very respectful. Yet you made certain I knew the seriousness of your intentions."

Matthew nodded. "It is time for Susanna to know such a thing."

"You can't force it," Emily warned him. "Susanna is talking to men. She's sitting beside your friend Mr. Evans, after all. Perhaps they'll dance together."

"There will be dancing?" Matthew asked, giving a faint frown.

"I know you didn't dance much."

"That is no longer the problem." He lowered his voice. "I don't remember how."

"Oh, dear. Then perhaps you should avoid it

today. I promise to work with you before your mother's ball."

He gave her a cocky grin. "Then I have something to look forward to."

After dinner, the guests returned to the drawing room to find all the rugs rolled up and the furniture moved against the walls. A quartet of musicians had begun to play from a corner of the room.

Emily followed Matthew as he retrieved Susanna, who'd already lined up with the chaperones and spinsters against one wall. Susanna followed them willingly, with only a touch of resignation.

When the three were far enough away from the musicians to speak, Matthew put his hands on his hips and loomed over his sister. "And what do you think you're doing burying your loveliness against a wall?"

"That is very sweet of you, Matthew, but—"

"I do not remember such shyness from you, Susanna. Tell me what happened."

Flustered, she spread both hands. "I don't know what you mean."

Matthew softened his voice. "Do you think you cannot trust me?"

"I—" She gave Emily a look that appealed for help. "It isn't that," she said. "It's all so silly, really. You'll think me a fool. It's just . . . easier to remain unnoticed, to do what I want with my life."

"Easier?" Emily repeated, wondering what Susanna was keeping hidden. Then she had an inspiration. "Tell us, Susanna. Let us help. Is it something about Mr. Derby?"

Thankfully, Matthew remained silent as his sister folded her arms over her chest.

Finally, Susanna responded in a low voice. "I knew I could not hide my reaction to him this afternoon. And now Mama has invited him to stay!"

"Is it because he courted me?" Emily asked.

She shook her head. "This problem happened years ago. I—I thought he was interested in me, and then I began to hear that he was spending much time with another girl as well. I understood that; there was no commitment between us. But then . . ." She trailed off, then abruptly turned a furious gaze on Matthew. "If you do anything about what I tell you, I will never forgive you!"

"I'm supposed to give my word so blindly?" Matthew said, spreading his hands wide.

"Yes!" Emily and Susanna said together.

"Very well, you have my promise, so you may proceed," he said, his voice cool.

"I overheard this certain young lady and her friends discussing me and laughing. I know there is much for proper girls to laugh at, believe me," she added, with only a faint trace of bitterness. "I don't mind being different. But Mr. Derby—he only laughed *with* them. He didn't defend me."

Matthew's head swiveled, looking for Mr. Derby. "Self-centered bastard—"

"You promised," Emily said, touching his arm.

"I promised not to do anything, but I can have my thoughts."

Susanna sighed. "We were younger, Matthew, all of us. He probably just didn't want to look badly to—this particular young lady."

"And you won't tell us who?" Matthew demanded.

She shook her head. "I understand that Mr. Derby, being a younger son, has not the freedom to do as he wishes, like you do."

"A freedom I seldom exercised," he said with bitterness.

Emily tried not to look too curious. Matthew had said, several times, how he'd "changed" in India. What had happened to him? And did it have something to do with the unseen wife she was determined to find?

"I have forgiven him, truly," Susanna continued. "And isn't it foolish of me to remember such a minor slight?"

"Not foolish, no," Matthew said. "But little sister, people *can* change, including you and Peter."

Emily found herself stiffening in defense of Susanna. "Are you telling her to forget?"

"No, but perhaps to forgive. You yourself see Peter's lot in life, Susanna. I think if he asks you to dance, you should do so, for your own sake. Why let something that happened in the past alter your future? I've changed, as you've been quick to point out. I don't know yet if Emily has changed, but I'm learning."

Emily blinked at him. She *had* changed, she thought, and not for the better. Long ago she would never have been able to imagine how easy it was to lie to good people.

Susanna looked between them thoughtfully, and Emily wondered what she saw.

"Very well," Susanna said at last. "I will try to do as you wish."

"Good." Matthew slid his arm around her. "Now tell me what you did this afternoon."

"You mean since our bargain?"

He laughed.

"I did not go to the laboratory—though I wanted to. I cut flowers for the tables."

Emily winced. That was not her favorite activity, either.

"I arranged them quite . . . artistically," Susanna added. "And then I read a book."

"And was it so very difficult?" Matthew asked.

Her hesitation said it all.

"I am giving this a chance, Matthew," Susanna said softly. "But only for you."

Albert Evans soon came by to ask Susanna to dance, and Emily saw the approval in Matthew's eyes. Mr. Evans certainly saw how to improve his standing with Matthew, she thought.

And later Mr. Derby came forward to claim Susanna for a dance. Susanna only smiled and then graciously accompanied him. Emily met Matthew's gaze.

"I won't say you're right about everything," she whispered. "I'm not certain you are. But somehow Susanna needs to overcome her sensitivity. As for giving up painting—I'll believe it when I see it."

Matthew took her hand in his. "I can work miracles." Then he bent lower and whispered provocatively in her ear, "Just wait until tonight."

Chapter 9

Late that evening, Emily was surprised when she opened her own door and saw Matthew sitting at her desk—*his* desk—writing.

She didn't think he heard her at first, since he sat with his back to her, head bent over what he was doing. He wasn't wearing his coat, and the width of his broad back beneath the fine linen shirt enticed her.

Matthew turned his head. "Emily?"

She came farther into the room, walking softly. "I am sorry to disturb you."

He only nodded, then bent his head to finish whatever he was writing. He had moved all of her books out of the way, and she wondered what he thought of her reading choices: biology, history, and mathematics. But he didn't question her. When he kept his head down, she went past him to the dressing room and found both her maid and a valet talking softly as they waited. When they saw her, they stood up, and the valet bowed as he retreated to Matthew's room.

"Your bath is drawn, Mrs. Leland."

"Thank you, Maria. After you unhook my gown, you can retire for the evening."

Maria, short and dark, looked past her as if she wanted to see into the bedroom. She winked at Emily, wearing a smile.

When Maria had gone, Emily stepped into the bathroom and closed the door. After removing the rest of her clothing, she took the several stairs up into the tub, then sank down into the heat, letting the soap bubbles pop all around her. She sighed, content that Maria knew just what she liked.

But she couldn't relax. She washed as quickly as possible, and had just emerged from rinsing her hair beneath the surface when she heard a soft knock on the door. Wiping streaming water from her face, she opened her eyes to see Matthew standing there. Her instinct was to sink deeper into the water, but she resisted. As it was, soapy bubbles covered most of her, leaving her knees showing like little islands.

Though a lamp and several candles lit the room, Matthew's face was still in shadows. "This is strange," he finally said, chuckling. "I'm your husband, yet I don't remember. Surely we were familiar enough for this . . ." He waved his hand at the tub.

She laughed, leaning her head back against the

tub. "Of course we were this familiar. We spent six months traveling everywhere together."

He perched on the edge of a table near the door. "I imagine life aboard a steamship would be cramped with two people sharing a cabin."

"Oh, it was. So you seeing me in my bath is nothing."

His gaze moved down over the water, and she wondered what he could see between the soap bubbles.

"We were intimate on more than one level," he continued, speaking deeply, softly, "sharing the same bedroom."

"Yes, we were." The answer came so easily. She wanted intimacy, she needed it. How else could she make him see that their future could be good?

He rose and came to stand above her. To her surprise, she felt the faint weakness of needing to cover herself, but didn't give in.

"Did I bathe with you?" he asked, his voice suddenly hoarse.

Matthew saw the changing emotions pass over Emily's face: passion and need. The desire he felt for her was beginning to override everything else.

"Bathe with me? No, we were not able to, although you expressed a wish to do so." Her blush was as pretty as a bride's. "We were constantly traveling, and we were lucky if we had access to a small hip bath, let alone a tub big enough to . . ."

Her voice faded away, and though she smiled meaningfully, the blush became scarlet, spreading down her neck and chest to where it disappeared under water. Was she actually embarrassed? The bubbles were gradually subsiding. He could see the line of her cleavage and the curve of one hip. His head felt light, his groin felt heavy.

Softly, he said, "My wish to bathe with you is surely as strong as ever."

She wore a faint smile, her eyes half closed as she watched him. He reached out and touched the only curl that had come to rest in front of her shoulder. Using his finger, he tucked its sleek wetness back behind her ear. She shivered, closing her eyes.

He leaned down over her, bracing his hands on the tub. "We have been away from each other for so long."

He cupped his hand at the back of her wet head and kissed her. He was greedy for the response that had haunted him all day. And she must have been, too, for her tongue met his. They explored each other's mouths deeply, leisurely. Before he knew it, his hands were touching her, feeling the wet softness of her shoulders, caressing the long delicate arch of her neck.

At last he slid his hand beneath the water and cupped one of her breasts. She moaned low into his mouth. Her flesh was warm from the water. She fit well into his palm, and the brush of her hardened nipple made him at last concentrate his efforts there. She shuddered as he played with her, teased her.

"It has been so long," she whispered against his lips.

Whose touch was she remembering, since it wasn't his?

He straightened and stepped back, angry with himself for this unaccountable jealousy. His hands trembled from touching her, as if he were still a green youth. Why did any of this matter? She was *offering* herself to him. He only had to take her.

Her wide eyes stared at him with bewilderment. "Matthew, what is wrong?"

How could he tell her? And what would he even confess? He shrugged and gave her a deliberately awkward smile. "I'm sorry if I'm confusing you, making you think one thing, and then I do another."

"We could talk—"

"No, you go ahead and finish your bath. I'll bathe afterward."

"I'll hurry."

"Don't. We have all the time in the world."

When Emily was done with her bath, she removed the stopper to empty the tub, still amazed at the convenience of such a thing. When one was a duke, one could install permanent tubs.

Her hands still trembled as she toweled herself dry, her breasts too sensitive. Matthew had touched her with such gentleness, yet such knowledge, as if he would know just how to pleasure her.

Then she'd somehow said the wrong thing, because he'd left her alone. Was it some vague memory that she wasn't his real wife?

She couldn't go on wondering about this woman. It was time to learn the truth. After she donned her nightgown and wrapped her dressing gown over it, she knocked on Matthew's door to tell him that the bathroom was free. And then she waited in her own room. She heard a door shut, and she cautiously peeked in, only to see that it was the bathroom door. She waited another few minutes, hearing the water run. Tiptoeing closer to the bathroom, she heard him settle in the water, even heard his sigh of pleasure. It sent a welcome little shiver down her neck.

For a moment she thought of joining him in there. Surely he wouldn't refuse her.

Yet, she couldn't ignore this opportunity. She ran to the bedroom he'd been using. There was only one desk, and on top was a leather folio. She went through that as quickly as she could, but found only papers related to his military service. A battered trunk rested against one wall. Although it was unlocked, she could tell when she opened it that no one had been given permission to go through it yet, for the smell was overpowering with musty dampness and unclean clothing.

She ran back into the dressing room and listened at the bathroom door again. At first she only heard silence, and she froze. But then she heard the gentle slosh of water, and realized that he must be enjoying soaking in the tub.

On her toes, she ran back into his room and began to lift things out of his trunk: clothing, a pistol, and books. Wedged against the bottom she found another leather folio whose papers had been stained with water. Some were stuck together, others damaged beyond repair.

And then she made out a smudged letter that began with: "We send our condolences on the death of your wife." Relief flooded through her. Matthew was a widower. There would be no woman come to claim her rights. He was all hers.

She didn't even read any more of the letter, only checked the rest of the papers to make certain that nothing mentioned his wife. She put everything else back the way she'd found it and closed the trunk. She couldn't leave the paper buried in there, in case it was discovered. And then what would Matthew think? That he had two wives he couldn't remember?

No, he'd realize the truth.

As she was moving through the dressing room,

the letter clutched in one hand, she was staring at the bathroom door more than watching her path. She bumped the washstand and barely caught the pitcher and basin before they crashed to the floor. The rattling seemed as loud as a gunshot.

"Emily?" Matthew's voice was muffled.

"Yes?" She stared wildly around her, wondering where to hide the letter.

"I forgot towels. Could you bring them to me?"

She rolled her eyes even as she stuffed the letter in her own wardrobe, back beneath the dresses. After picking up the small stack of towels, she knocked softly on the bathroom door.

His voice was amused as he said, "Emily, shall I assume it's you?"

She winced, then forced her expression to ease. As she opened the door, she caught a glimpse of him, rising head and shoulders out of the tub, which suddenly looked too small for an average bath. Or too small for an above-average man.

As his wife, she would have seen all of this before. So she bustled like a maid, setting down the towels, smiling at him as he sat in the tub. She saw his dark hair slicked back with water, the red glints hid by wetness.

And then she saw his scars.

His left arm was a web of unnaturally white skin, flattened, pulled, and rippled, distorted by scars that spread across three-quarters of his arm. They continued to his side and beneath the waterline, as if the flames had leapt the chasm between arm and torso, to continue their cruel destruction, fading and growing sparse as they approached his left shoulder. The right side of his body seemed unmarred.

She gasped—she couldn't help it. Never had she seen such suffering, nor imagined it. She raised her eyes to his—and found his gaze calm, without any hint of emotion beneath.

"Oh, Matthew," she whispered. She touched his wet arm, her fingers trembling, as if she might feel his pain and was afraid of it. "Do they still hurt?"

He shook his head. "Not really. Ugly, aren't they?"

He hadn't quite said they didn't hurt, and with the way they seemed stretched over bone and muscle . . . "No, oh no, they aren't ugly. They're a mark of your bravery."

He cocked his head and smiled with chagrin. "It's not exactly brave to be unable to get out of the way of a mortar exploding," he said as if he were discussing the weather. "And don't forget about the bayonet I didn't see coming."

That scar must be below the waterline—or hidden by all the others.

"But it was brave of you to travel halfway around the world," she said, "to put yourself in danger for your country. And you suffered terribly for it. It must have taken a long time for you to be well

again. You said you recovered at a mission? Were
the missionaries English?" She was trying to discover something, anything, about his late wife.

He nodded. "The mission was there to convert
the 'pagans'—not that they wanted to be converted.
And some were even grateful for the help, for the
food and clothing and rare medicine."

"Some?" she echoed.

He leaned back against the rim of the tub, much
as she'd recently done, looking up at her from beneath lowered eyelids. There was suddenly a lazy
stillness to him—lazy, yet with a hint of danger beneath. He was looking down her body, his glance
casual, as if he thought about sampling her wares.

And then she had the strangest feeling that he
was deliberately distracting her with his interest. She
frowned down into those always smiling eyes.

"You said only some people were grateful for the
aid of the missionaries," she said. "Were the rest . . .
angry with England? Perhaps, because you were so
ill, you didn't really understand if—"

"I may have been recovering, but I was never a
fool," he said mildly.

"So what did the other people want from the missionaries?" she asked softly, sinking down onto a
stool beside the tub. *Or want from you?*

"They wanted what crafty people can always get
from ignorant fools—everything they could, and
then more."

"I don't understand," she said.

He reached out and took her hand from where it rested on her knee. His skin was wet and warm.

"You are an innocent, my dear. Here in this corner of Cambridgeshire, you don't need to know what the rest of the world is capable of."

He was watching her, studying her. Again she had the feeling that he was deliberately trying to intimidate her, which was totally unlike the man he'd been showing her.

It was time to let him think he succeeded—for now. She would not have been able to carry off her masquerade during the last year without realizing she possessed a knack for reading people.

"You are surprisingly cynical," she said at last.

He arched a dark brow. "I wasn't always?"

Back to dangerous waters. "No, I do not think so. At least you did not show it so readily."

A faint smile curved one corner of his wide, elegant mouth. Perhaps losing his wife had made him cynical.

"I've been telling you that India changed me," he said.

She clasped her hands in her lap. "I am not *that* different, and neither are you."

He reached for a facecloth and the ball of soap. With lazy movements he began to lather his chest, his hands forming slow circles that seemed to hypnotize her. She remembered them on her body, cupping her breasts, giving her such intense pleasure that she hadn't been able to imagine to what heights he could take her. Her brain seemed to freeze, all higher function shutting down. He washed himself almost too slowly, hands moving down his torso, disappearing beneath the water.

And then some part of her brain remembered the night's incomplete mission. "Good night, Matthew."

He chuckled. "Good night, Emily."

She came to a stop in the middle of the shadowy dressing room, confused and uncertain. She'd wanted him to call her back, to take her as a husband took a wife. Why hadn't he? Short of throwing herself at him, how much more obvious could she be?

But the condolence letter still had to be dealt with. Quickly, she pulled it from her wardrobe and hurried into her bedroom, wishing she could lock the door. Perched on the edge of her bed, she read it quickly. It was a formal letter from the wife of his commanding officer, expressing her sorrow that Matthew's wife had finally succumbed to a lingering illness.

Lingering illness?

Had Matthew nursed her in her last days, watching the woman he loved wasting away with her suffering? She didn't want to think about that poor woman, not when she was replacing her. She couldn't afford to feel sympathy or guilt. Life had taught her that.

At the hearth, she set the letter afire, dropped it fluttering onto the coal grate and watched it burn, forcing herself to feel nothing but determination. She no longer had to worry about Matthew's first wife—but there was yet Stanwood to confront.

Chapter 10

Matthew prowled his new bedchamber, unable to sleep. He ached with sexual frustration, and even found himself in the dressing room, standing at her door—*his* door—ready to claim his "marital rights." He froze with his hand on the doorknob, swayed by overpowering desire that he'd been unable to satisfy.

And then he heard the muffled sound of Emily crying out. He opened the door and strode inside.

The draperies were open to the moonlight, il-luminating Emily, who tossed upon her bed—*his* bed—her head rolling back and forth on the pillow, the sheets and her nightgown tangled about her bare legs.

He moved cautiously to the bed and saw that her eyes were shut, great tears streaming from beneath her lashes.

"Papa," she whispered, her head lolling away as if she were searching for him in her dreams. "Papa!"

He didn't know if he should wake her. He thought

about what it must have been like to watch her entire family die, to think she was about to die with them, only to be rescued. But rescued into what situation? Where did a young woman go when everyone had died?

He'd always had his family to return to, even when he wanted to be on the other side of the world from them. But what would he be like without them, if tragedy had struck? He'd said those words to Susanna, but now he applied them to himself.

Still Emily cried in her sleep. He touched her shoulder and said her name.

She gasped and arched back. He looked at the nightgown tightened across her breasts, glanced at her long pale legs glistening in the moonlight.

"Papa!"

Her voice was almost a scream now, and he didn't want to draw any attention to their bedroom. He put his hand across her mouth. "Emily!" he said more urgently.

Her tossing turned to thrashing and she grew even more upset. He leaned down to put his arms around her, anything to quiet her. She suddenly clung to him, arms around his waist, face pressed into his chest.

"Emily?" he said, quieter now.

When she didn't release him, didn't answer, he found himself climbing on top of the counterpane next to her. She wrapped her arms even tighter, pillowing her head against his shoulder. His skin dampened with her tears, but at least she was shedding no more of them. Her expression had eased, her body seemed to wilt into exhaustion.

Matthew was left staring up at the dark canopy, thinking of her willowy body pressed along his side, legs bare, breasts unbound beneath her nightgown. There was only her sheer garment between their upper bodies, for he was wearing trousers. It was almost too much for a too-long celibate man. He told himself he would only lie here for a few minutes, until she was calm.

And somehow he fell asleep.

Emily slowly awoke as if from the depths of a deep, summer pool. She felt . . . content, refreshed, and so deliciously warm. Something intruded at the edge of her happiness—and she realized that the warmth surrounding her was a man's body.

She opened her eyes and found herself staring across the bare, sculpted chest of Matthew Leland. Somehow, without even trying, she'd lured him to her bed. She raised her gaze and saw his profile, calm and peaceful in sleep, dark eyelashes fanned across his cheeks.

When had he come to her? And why hadn't he woken her?

She took stock of their position and realized that her knee rode over his clothed thighs. She was pressed along the left side of his body, her cheek against his smoothly fleshed shoulder, just above the scars across his ribs. His left arm was about her shoulders.

She slowly raised herself up on her elbow and found him watching her. She froze as his gaze drifted almost lazily down her face. Only then did she realize that her nightgown had slid off her right shoulder, leaving it, along with the top curve of her breast, bare.

Heat centered hotly between her thighs, right where she was pressed against his leg. She wanted to rub against him shamelessly. Instead, she reached to touch the side of his face.

"Matthew?"

His gaze had dropped to her breasts, even more exposed as she leaned over him.

He closed his eyes for a moment, before asking in a voice husky with sleep, "Is this how we awoke every morning?"

She nodded. "I don't remember you coming to be with me last night."

She felt his hand cup her shoulder.

"I was in the dressing room and heard you cry out."

The nightmares, she thought, sitting up and drawing the nightgown back over her shoulder. His hand came to rest on her lower back.

"You were very upset," he continued from behind her. "Your pillow must be wet with your tears."

Oh God, she thought, rigid with dismay. What had she done, what had she said?

As if in answer to her unspoken questions, he said, "You called for your father, and would not be comforted until your arms were about me."

If she'd betrayed her lies, he would not be here with her, treating her with such compassion. She forced herself to breathe normally. She hadn't given anything away.

"I wish I could remember if you had these nightmares when we were together," he said.

"Only at first," she said, choosing her lie carefully. "But you made me feel so safe, that at last my fears faded."

"Fears of what?"

She couldn't look at him. "Fears of being alone, of being helpless."

He sat up and his arm came around her back again, his hand riding low on her hip. "And then you thought I'd died. Did the nightmares resurface?"

She nodded. "But your family banished them again."

"Then why have them now that I've returned?"

She'd made a mistake—his return should have been joyous for a grateful wife.

"It's my amnesia, isn't it?" he said softly, leaning

down until his face brushed the side of her head. "I have made you feel lost again. Your husband, but not your husband."

"Oh, no, don't think that!" she said, turning her head toward him.

Their faces were too close. She felt his hand tighten on her hip.

"So what did I do when you had nightmares at the beginning of our marriage?" he asked.

She looked down, only to find herself staring at his nude chest. She had never imagined being unable to think when he was near. "You held me, just like you did last night. How did you know to do that? Did you remember something about our marriage?"

He slid his legs over the edge of the bed, then rose. As he turned away from the sunny windows, she saw his back starkly, the burn scars that faded away before reaching the center of his back—and a white line low on his right side, where the bayonet must have pierced his flesh. He was lucky to have survived.

She deliberately avoided her dressing gown, not wanting to cover herself from him.

"No, I haven't remembered anything new about our marriage," he said at last, smiling. "Surely it is natural to hold someone in comfort." Walking toward the dressing room door, he called back, "What are your plans for the day?"

"I am not sure yet. If you have need of me, of course I will be available." That was a very open invitation.

"I am going to be busy with correspondence and some business matters today," he said.

She nodded with disappointment.

Matthew spent the early morning writing letters to his cousins, after asking a stable boy to alert him if Emily requested a horse. When he'd last looked in on her, she was in the drawing room with Susanna and Rebecca, each of them sewing.

Unobserved, he'd watched Susanna yank out stitches, saw the patient way Emily worked with her. But he didn't disturb them. He was waiting to see what Emily would do with her day.

After several hours spent with his father, going over new investments, he'd gone looking for Emily, only to see Susanna walking aimlessly through the conservatory, ripping the occasional leaf into shreds. She looked so glum, so sad.

And then he knew that Emily was right. He could not take away all of Susanna's favorite pastimes, even if only temporarily.

He approached her, and her demeanor brightened.

"Good morning, little sister."

"Almost time for luncheon," she said. "I thought it would never get here."

"The day is slow for you?"

Her hesitation was a good answer.

Smiling, he said, "I thought of a way for you to combine something you love into your busy new social schedule."

"And what is that?" she asked warily.

"We'll have a picnic tomorrow and invite a mix of young ladies and gentlemen."

"Well, I love a good picnic but—"

"We'll set up easels at the castle ruins, so you can give them all art lessons."

Her mouth opened, and for a moment nothing came out. "Give lessons?"

"They'll all see how talented you are, how generous with your time, how patient—"

"Mathew!" she said, rolling her eyes.

"And you'll be able to paint," he finished softly.

Her eyes glistened as she took his arm. "You are sweet to me. How glad I am to have you home with us."

"Then let's discuss who to invite, so we can send the invitations this afternoon. I want to take advantage of the beautiful weather."

As they strolled back into the library to begin making their lists, Matthew casually asked, "Have you seen Emily lately?"

Susanna looked at him over her spectacles. "I have not seen her in several hours. Last I knew, she was heading into Comberton. She didn't tell you?"

He gave a tight smile. "No, she didn't." And the stable boy hadn't, either.

"I would have thought she wanted to show you..." Her words faded away.

"Show me what?"

"It's her place to tell you, not mine," Susanna said, smiling even as she raised both hands.

He hesitated, caught between two compulsions: one to help his sister, the other to see what Emily was up to in the village.

"You should go," Susanna said, laughing at him. "I can see how curious you are."

"But the invitations . . . "

"I will write them and have them delivered. Our lawn will be filled with people tomorrow. And I'll find Mama, who will be so happy to help me plan the picnic."

Matthew grinned and kissed her cheek. "Then I'll go find my wife." He walked away, saying over his shoulder, "Tell Mother I won't make luncheon today."

Chapter 11

When Matthew reached the stable, he questioned the boy, only to discover that Emily hadn't requested a horse or a carriage.

She'd walked into the village? What secret was she keeping, one that his entire family wanted her to reveal to him? It must be innocent enough if everyone knew—but then, it could mask something else.

He reached the village swiftly on horseback. Comberton had grown where two streams met, in the midst of gentle hills. There were thatched cottages along the lane and several small shops on the main street near the village green.

As he passed the grocer's, there was a flurry of movement from behind the window, and the door opened as he passed.

"Captain Leland! Captain Leland!"

He sighed at the delay, but smiled as he turned around. "Yes?"

A woman wearing a too small bonnet, and an

immense shawl over her girth, waved even as she grinned. "Captain Leland, I had heard of your return, and hardly thought to believe it—but here you are!"

The name suddenly came to him. "Mrs. Winston, how good to see you."

She twittered with laughter like a pleasant bird. "And of course it is marvelous to see you! To think, your poor family was rewarded with your happy return."

"It was good fortune for all of us. I only regret that they had to suffer thinking me dead." Matthew thought he might have danced several times with Mrs. Winston's daughter, but for the life of him—

She touched his arm and tilted her chin with pride. "My Matilda is happily married now."

"I am glad to hear it, and not surprised, of course." The woman's talkativeness might be of help. "Mrs. Winston, do you know my wife?"

She blinked at him in bewilderment, then chuckled as if she thought him silly. "Why, of course I do, Captain. Who doesn't? Such a sweet-natured young woman. I must confess, when I heard you'd married so unexpectedly I didn't know what to think. But once I met the poor dear, even in the midst of her mourning, I could see why you fell in love with her."

Emily had easily fooled so many people, an impressive feat.

"I imagine your reunion with your family—and your wife!—has been wonderful," she continued.

"It has, Mrs. Winston. I have so missed my Emily that I feel I just cannot be apart from her. I know she came into the village today. Have you seen her?"

"Well, no, but she's usually at the inn, of course."

He grinned with satisfaction and curiosity. "Of course." He touched the brim of his hat. "Thank you, Mrs. Winston."

"Do take us up on the dinner invitation we sent, Captain," she called as he walked away. "My family would enjoy seeing you."

He passed the village green, where farmers and craftsmen had set up stalls for Market Day. The inn was nearby, situated at the crossroads, a small, two-story building in classic Tudor black trim on white plastered walls. A sign above the door advertised the inn, as well as the popular taproom within.

Could Emily be regularly meeting with someone? But surely she wouldn't do so in a public place.

He ducked under the low doorway into the entry hall, where the innkeeper was helping several people at the counter. He looked in the first open door and saw the taproom, where several tables were full of villagers eating the midday meal. His own stomach growled, but he ignored it.

A door across the hall suddenly burst open and at

least a dozen children of varying ages ran past him, laughing and talking loudly.

To his surprise, Emily then appeared in the doorway, smiling and waving. He stepped back into the taproom before she noticed him, then peeked into the hall again as she withdrew back into the private room, leaving the door open. Her expression stayed in his mind, the softness in her gaze, the simple pleasure curving her mouth.

Curious, not knowing what to think, Matthew crossed the hall, leaned near the doorway as if he belonged there, and peered inside. There were several tables and chairs scattered about, and he realized he was looking at a private dining parlor, usually reserved for upper class guests.

And then he saw Emily sitting across the table from a strange man.

He stepped back before they could see him. He leaned against the wall, crossing his arms over his chest in a bored pose, as if waiting for someone.

To his relief, they spoke loud enough for him to hear.

Emily said, "But Mr. Smythe, I have had no word when the man will arrive from London. It was good of you to take my place these past days, but I assure you I can continue as before."

"But Mrs. Leland, what about your husband?"

Matthew had clenched his jaw in jealousy when

he was distracted by a shout from across the entry hall.

"Captain Leland!"

Matthew turned and saw the innkeeper and his guests staring at him, and several people from the taproom were following the man who'd called his name.

"It really is you!" the young man said, practically bounding across the hall to shake his hand.

Matthew recognized him as one of the younger brothers of Albert Evans, who had recently been courting Emily.

And then Emily appeared at his shoulder. "Hello, Mr. Evans!" she said quickly, loudly.

Matthew realized she thought he couldn't remember the man's name. For the next several minutes, he accepted the well wishes of half a dozen men and women, all of whom Emily casually spoke with before Matthew had to. As she deliberately repeated each of their names, he found himself amused by her concern for his memory.

At last the crowd dispersed and Emily took his arm to lead him back into the dining parlor.

"Captain, why didn't you tell me you were coming into the village today?"

She spoke brightly, glancing at the other man, who'd risen to his feet. He was several inches taller and much thinner than Matthew, and he bobbed his head repeatedly, wearing a rather silly grin.

Matthew looked down at Emily and said softly, "Why didn't *you* tell me you were coming into the village today?"

"I thought you didn't want to be disturbed." She smiled, then turned toward the other man. "Captain Leland, may I present Mr. Smythe?"

Mr. Smythe bobbed his head even as he bowed, looking rather like a bird.

"It is a pleasure to meet you at last, Captain. You're a rather famous war hero in these parts."

"Mr. Smythe is new to Cambridgeshire," Emily confided.

"And what do you do here, Mr. Smythe, besides meet with my wife?"

Though Matthew spoke pleasantly, he saw Emily's smile fade a bit as she blinked at him.

Mr. Smythe never stopped grinning. "I'm the local parish curate, sir, assistant to Mr. Wesley, the vicar."

Matthew nodded. "I remember Mr. Wesley, a favorite guest at Madingley Court."

Emily squeezed his arm, grinning up at him as if his sudden recollection was such a *good* thing. He blinked down at her, distracted from his curiosity by her loveliness.

"Mr. Wesley is in London this autumn," Emily said, "preparing for his upcoming wedding. So Mr. Smythe came up from London to assist the parish. We've been so grateful for his help."

"And how do *you* help?" Matthew asked Emily.

Emily grew pink, and Matthew could not miss the way Mr. Smythe regarded her with fondness.

"You had so much to deal with when you first arrived home," she said softly. "I didn't want to overwhelm you with things that weren't immediately important."

Mr. Smythe cleared his throat. "She is being far too modest, Captain Leland. Her work is very important to the village. And to think, these children had to go clear to Cambridge for any sort of education. Most didn't, you know," he confided solemnly. "How would their families have taken them there? It was all Mrs. Leland's idea to make things easier for the children."

"The children who just went running past?" Matthew said, beginning to understand.

"Those are some of our students," Emily said with pride in her voice.

"You're their teacher?" Matthew asked in disbelief.

"Only until I can convince the village justices that there is enough interest to have our own national school here in Comberton. More children than ever are attending. Few came today because they thought I would be too busy at Madingley Court with your homecoming. But I had enlisted Mr. Smythe's help to teach when I couldn't."

"This is an interesting school," Matthew said, glancing again at the dining parlor.

"She rents the space herself," Mr. Smythe said, grinning at Emily.

Emily gestured about the parlor. "It costs little, and it is so important for boys—and girls—to have access to schooling. Everyone needs to better themselves."

"I saw the books on your desk," Matthew said.

She nodded happily. "You didn't ask about them, so I wondered what you thought."

"I wish you would have told me. I've been curious what you did while I was gone."

She slid her hand into the crook of his elbow. "It is not so important a thing as defending your country," she said, smiling. "I thought it could wait."

Mr. Smythe cleared his throat. "I'll be off, Mrs. Leland. When I hear word about the new schoolmaster, I'll let you know."

When he was gone, Emily told Matthew, "The village is close to hiring a schoolmaster. They'll decide after they interview him. And next I shall convince them to find space for a permanent schoolroom."

So she and Mr. Smythe had been discussing a schoolmaster while he'd eavesdropped like a jealous fool.

Now that the curate had gone, Emily gathered a

stack of books, glancing over her shoulder at him, saying nothing.

He took the heavy books from her—she'd *carried* these on her walk?—and set them back down. "Do you have somewhere you need to be?"

"No, of course not," she said slowly.

"The innkeeper can watch over your books. Today is Market Day. Many villagers are here. As you saw earlier, I can't remember everyone's names. Would you walk with me and reintroduce me to them?"

She brightened with pleasure. "I would love to!"

Why was she so happy in this little village, teaching children, escorting her amnesiac husband? It just didn't make sense.

"Perhaps you have friends here you'd like me to meet," he continued, still open-minded about a fellow conspirator, but beginning to think that Emily's plans and motives were all her own.

But she didn't respond to his interest in her friends.

As they walked back toward the market stalls, she gestured toward the year's appointed constable, and once she said the name, Matthew recognized him.

"The constable, eh? I remember Blake as being a rather angry young man."

He noticed that Emily seemed nonchalant about the man's profession and its implicit threat to her activities—but then, he knew she was very good at hiding any guilt she might be feeling.

"How wonderful that you remember such things!" she said, squeezing his arm. "Surely the more you're home, the more your memories will return. That might be sad for me, because then I won't feel as useful. I like helping you." She wore an almost wistful expression. "Blake has been a good constable. He's the local miller now, and he's married, with a second child about to be born."

As they walked down the street, many people stopped to welcome him home. All of them seemed to know Emily. She continued to tell him people's names, and several times it honestly helped him. As a young man he'd always enjoyed London more than Cambridgeshire, and once he joined the army four years ago, he'd seldom been able to come home. Now, he was flattered by how many people were glad to see him and happy for his recovery.

At the mercer's shop, he impulsively bought ribbons to decorate Emily's hair. Next, he purchased paper and pencils for her students. By the soft expression in her green eyes, he might have been buying her jewels.

After they wandered through the market stalls, he purchased them each a meat pie, and they sat on a bench near the covered well to eat them. Soon, her students began approaching to meet the man returned from the dead. Emily gently corrected their impertinent questions, listened intently to each child's plans for Market Day, and behaved like the kind schoolmistress everyone would wish to have. A person who didn't love children would never have chosen teaching to pass the time, he reflected. She was working hard at something that people were only beginning to realize was important.

What did Emily really want?

When they at last had a moment to themselves, he quietly asked, "Did we discuss children before our marriage?"

She gave him a shy smile. "You mean in that whirlwind two weeks?"

"The two weeks when you were in mourning for your family," he added, then regretted his words, not wanting to bring her attention to his suspicions.

Her smile turned rueful. "I imagine that to a man who isn't involved in the immediacy of our courtship, it can seem—unbelievable."

But as he looked at her, her champagne hair glinting from beneath her bonnet, the sun bringing a lovely blush to her cheeks, he knew that desiring her was very believable. He felt it now, the simmering tension, the way he thought too much about the coming night, when he could be alone with her and take their intimacy another step further.

"My heightened emotions surely played a part," she continued quietly, watching the villagers mill randomly through the stalls. "But you were also preparing to depart, and the fear of never seeing each other again was . . . pervasive. But to answer your first question, no, we did not discuss children. We didn't need to. We were so . . . in tune with each other, wanted the same things out of marriage, that . . ."

Her voice faded, and to his surprise, she turned her face away and dabbed at the corner of her eye. Was that a tear? He waited for her to explain, but she said nothing, and he sensed her uneasiness.

"You do not need to be uncomfortable," he said at last. "I know that my mother had hoped you were with child when you arrived. Did you want a baby so much?"

Emily could not believe that they were having this discussion on the village green, her students running nearby, their parents wandering through the Market Day stalls.

"Yes, I wanted your baby," she whispered, lying, yet not, for she did want children. But now she could not stop thinking of the threat to this idyllic marriage she planned to give him.

He put his hand on hers, where it rested in her lap. "Now you have another chance for a child, a lifetime's worth of chances."

Oh God, her eyes were stinging again. What was wrong with her? This was what she wanted!

"Matthew, I guess I didn't tell you about my work with children because I was worried you might disapprove." She held up a hand as he began to speak. "Most men do not look kindly on their wives working, and even though I was not earning wages, I was doing something Society would frown upon for a lady. After all, we have the standards of a dukedom to uphold. You and I never discussed such things early in our marriage. Yet today you accepted my work, and even offered your help. Thank you."

"It was only the purchasing of supplies."

"You have me as your wife, yet you're willing to share me, to allow me to do something I feel strongly about. It is a very open-minded way of thinking."

And even though they were surely being watched, he hugged her briefly to his side. But as they rode back home together on his horse, and she was nestled sideways across his lap, a more demure way of riding through the village, she could not help dreading what he would think if he knew that the woman he thought of as his schoolmistress wife had done something worthy of blackmail.

A day had passed since she'd received Stanwood's threatening letter. Worried about what he'd do, she almost hadn't come to the village today. But Stanwood wasn't the sort to openly confront her and risk jail rather than a reward. And she could not cower within Madingley Court. She needed to meet this threat head on, see what he wanted, and deal with it.

The life she wanted was within her grasp; more and more, Matthew was believing in their marriage, willing to accept it. She was determined to make it happen.

Chapter 12

When Emily set her school books on her desk, she saw a sealed letter tucked beneath the ink bottle. She frowned, remembering that Matthew had been writing letters just that morning. But there was no address, and the wax was a blob without a proper seal—just like the one that had arrived for her yesterday.

She frantically tore it open, her heart beginning to pound.

My Dearest Emily,

Have you been looking for me? I have been watching you, waiting for the perfect time for our little talk. First the schoolchildren were in the way today, and then Captain Leland. They can't protect you from me for long.

S.

Oh God, Stanwood had written again, but this time he hadn't used the post. Someone had set it here on her desk, not that long ago. If it had been hand delivered to the front door, at least her name would be listed, but there was nothing.

How could a stranger have possibly gotten into the house, with hundreds of servants everywhere?

Or . . . could Stanwood have persuaded one of the servants to his side? She shuddered, remembering his talent for coercion.

Was she supposed to be afraid now, in this house where she'd always felt safe? No, she wouldn't live like that. Harming her would gain Stanwood nothing. He wanted her fearful so that she would succumb to whatever he demanded.

She would wait, as he wanted her to, but she would not do so idly. Someone within this house had put the letter on her desk.

Emily went to look for her maid, Maria, who could not remember seeing anyone near Matthew's suite. Emily knew she even had to suspect Maria, so she casually questioned the other maids who looked after the women of the family. No one had seen anyone unusual. Dozens of servants had permission to be in the family wing.

This kind of questioning would get her nowhere, she realized with frustration.

* * *

Before dinner, Emily waited for Matthew to return to change his clothing. He'd gone shooting with his father for several hours. She listened at the closed door to the dressing room, and when she heard him enter at last, pressed her ear to the wood, waiting what she thought was a suitable amount of time for him to change. She did not hear the voice of his valet, which no longer seemed so strange for Matthew. He was a man used to caring for himself.

At last she knocked, and when he called for her to enter, she hurried in, smiling at him. He was partially dressed in his evening clothes, wearing his trousers and shirtsleeves, feet still intimately bare.

He looked up at her, cravat in his hand. A slow smile lit his eyes, distracting her from her troubles, making her feel warm all the way to her toes.

"I saw you riding with Professor Leland," she said, surprised at her breathlessness. "Did you enjoy yourself?"

"Shooting defenseless birds is always a pleasant time." He grinned.

She waved a hand. "You are teasing me. I am sure Cook appreciated whatever you brought back. But did you and your father have a chance to really talk?"

"About what? About you?"

She gave him a wry smile. "I don't know—do men talk about their wives with their fathers? Oh, don't answer that. I was with your mother this afternoon, and she, too, was glad that the two of you spent time together."

"We spoke of Lady Rosa."

He blinked at her, as if he were surprised by what he'd revealed.

"He has long ago forgiven her for her disbelief in him," Matthew said. "Even now he feels very guilty that they came so close to divorce. But the improvement in their relationship has been a great comfort to him. He said a scientist does not make a very proper husband for the daughter of a duke."

He walked slowly toward her, and just his impending nearness seemed to take the air away that she needed to breathe.

"Just like you're not a proper wife—"

She tried not to stiffen.

"—or so you've told me."

Her knees went weak with relief. He was standing so close that if she took a deep enough breath, her breasts would touch his chest. It made her feel . . . languid, sensual.

"Would a proper wife know how to tie a cravat?" Matthew continued with a sudden grin.

He was so very large, so intimidating, so . . . male. Different than her in every way. She liked the feeling.

And then she realized that he'd asked for her help. "Where is your valet?"

"I have not used one in several years. I can draw my own bath, and dress myself . . . or at least I could." He looked at the starched cloth in his hand. "And I used to be able to tie one of these. But the ability is gone."

Before he could be bothered by his memory lapse, she touched his chest, palms flat against the heat of him, even as she looked deeply into his eyes. "Allow me to help."

When he only handed her the cravat, she tried not to show her disappointment. But then his large, firm hands settled on her waist. She slid the cravat about the high starched points of his collar and gathered it together to form a loose bow.

"And where did you learn to tie a cravat?" he asked.

His breath on her face was soft and warm, and her reaction felt so very . . . intimate, deep within her body. She straightened the white bow, then slid her hands down his chest, smoothing the creases—feeling the curve of hard muscle.

"I had three brothers and few servants. There was not money for personal valets."

"But was there money for tutors?" he asked.

Surprised, she raised her face to his. "Yes. They were gentlemen, after all."

"But you were not tutored with them."

"No, I wasn't." She smiled. "I was taught the

things a lady needed, like reading and arithmetic, and of course needlework, drawing, and—"

"Not skills that would have enabled you to work as, say, a governess when your entire family died."

A frisson of unease went down her spine. "No, I didn't have to worry about such things. I had cousins I could have lived with. I would have been safe."

"But you fell in love with me."

His hands slid up over hers, where they rested against his chest.

"And I took care of you," he continued.

Somehow that annoyed her, and she spoke without thinking. "And I took care of you."

"Did you?"

Her palms were growing unnaturally hot against his chest, and she could feel the beat of his heart, so solid, so normal, unlike hers, which raced with nervousness and excitement.

"I know you're caring for me now," he continued, before she could speak. "I am a rather helpless man, my memory full of holes. But how did you care for me when we were first married?"

"You didn't marry me only because you thought I needed to be rescued." She tossed her head.

He laughed. "You will no doubt say that I loved you, that I needed you."

She found herself shuffled backward until she was up against the wall. He leaned his hips into her.

"Were you always so spirited?" he asked.

"Always. It's one of the reasons you fell in love with me."

Abruptly, she pulled his head down and kissed him with all the passion he aroused in her. She invaded his mouth, tasted the essence of him, and wanted more. She wanted to show him the kind of woman she was, wanted him to see that he could not do without her. He needed to see her as his wife.

He pushed his thigh between hers, spreading her legs within her skirts. The feeling was shocking and too pleasurable. He didn't stop there, but kept moving against her with his thigh, almost rhythmically, his hips thrusting into hers. His hand slid down over her right hip, down the back of her thigh, only to lift it so he could fit better against her body.

If there were no clothes between them, how much better this would feel . . .

She gasped as his mouth left hers to trail down her neck. She wore her evening clothes already, and his lips were able to find a path down to the valley between her breasts. She unabashedly held his head against her, her hips arched forward wantonly, taking deep pleasure in his movements against her. Her rising need grew into hot, sharp urgency. He suckled the upper curve of her breast, taking her skin into his mouth. It should have hurt—but it felt provocative and wild. She wanted to pull the gown down her body, bare herself, have his mouth where his hands had been just last night, when she'd been in her bath.

He pulled her knee higher, pushing himself hard between her thighs. She groaned and clutched him.

He lifted his head, his mouth wet. "We seem to share an intense passion for one another. Did I bed you before we wed?"

"No!" She laughed, her shock too obviously fake. "You didn't have to marry me for honor's sake. Only for your own."

He smiled down at her, even as his eyes fiercely swept over her. His hand, which held her knee high, now slid beneath her skirt, along the bare, sensitive skin behind the knee. Their gazes were meshed together, sparking with heat, and she could only pant when his hand moved higher, sliding over the fine linen of her drawers. His palm traced the underside of her thigh, and his fingers touched and trailed the inside. Her breath came faster and faster, his hazel eyes smoldered on her, and all she could think was that he could touch her . . . anywhere, and she would revel in it.

His fingertips touched the edge of the slit that parted her undergarment. A moan of need escaped her. She wanted him to touch her. When the tips of his fingers brushed the bare place at the highest point of her thigh, she trembled so hard that he was forced to hold her up. Her head fell back against the wall. He leaned over her, and she watched through half-closed eyes as his tongue traced her cleavage— while his fingers traced the warm, wet cleft of her body.

She whimpered helplessly, her body shuddering as it was buffeted to and fro by the pleasure invoked by his mouth and fingers. His lips traced over her garments to the peak of her breast, and then he gently bit her through her bodice, even as his touch probed the private depths of her, stroking, stroking, sliding deeper. Every feeling, every emotion, surged higher within her, his teeth nibbling, his fingers exploring, circling, making her gasp and cry out and shudder and—

Explode. That's the only word that did justice to the shocking release of pleasure that soared outward through her body, as if to press against her very skin. She shook helplessly in his embrace, even as he continued to caress her, pushing deeper, his breath harsh against her breasts. She slumped against him, spent.

Chapter 13

Matthew wanted to unbutton his trousers and take her now, against the wall. His fingers were hot and wet inside her, and it felt so good. He pressed a little deeper, heard her whimper in pleasure—

And then he lifted his head so he could see her face. In that moment when she met his gaze, looking so vulnerable, he saw the wonder before she could mask it by closing her eyes.

Wonder. He realized that she'd never experienced her woman's climax before. In his feelings of confusion, he found himself wishing that he'd looked into the beautiful face of such innocence and pleasure on his wedding night.

Shocked by the strange feeling, he took his hands from the depths of her body and released her leg. He had to remember their real relationship, the game he was playing.

"My hands have not forgotten how to pleasure you," he said in a low voice, putting them on her shoulders now. "How did you used to pleasure me? Teach me, Emily."

He thought she would hesitate, but she was bold as she raised trembling hands to run them down his chest. To his surprise, she lingered at his nipples, rubbing them gently through the cloth. He sucked in a breath. And then she leaned into him, pressing her mouth to his neck in gentle kisses, before licking a path up behind his ear. Now she had him shuddering, this woman who'd never experienced pleasure.

He wanted her with a desperation that overwhelmed him. When she pulled his shirt out of his trousers and touched his bare stomach, he groaned against her hair. He wanted to rip off his own clothes, to be inside her—

But he leaned back against the wall and took a shuddering breath. What was he trying to prove by pleasuring her? He was only showing her that they would end up in bed—which was exactly what she wanted.

Much as he wanted it, too, should he give her what she so obviously craved? Strangely, he felt trapped between the repressed man he'd once been and the devil-may-care soldier. A few years ago he never would have risked his family's safety, risked scandal, for a night in such a woman's bed—much as he might have wanted to.

In India he'd taken such chances without a second thought, and suffered the consequences.

But now he wasn't the only one who would suffer if he made the wrong choice with Emily Grey.

"I can't, Emily," he said slowly, moving away from her at last.

She caught his arm. "But why? I'm your wife, and I want you."

Her words actually made it easier for him. "I desire you, you know that. But . . ." He let himself trail off as if he were confused.

She sighed and leaned her cheek against his shoulder. "I didn't mean to push you into something you were not ready for."

He wanted to laugh—it was almost as if she played the man's part in a seduction. "You weren't. I just . . . don't feel like myself yet. And I want to do what's right for you." He could have snorted at that. What was "right" had nothing to do with Emily and him.

He donned his evening jacket, his fingers still trembling.

While they had dinner that night with his family, he found himself staring at the red mark just visible on Emily's breast, the one he'd caused with his mouth, and the way she kept trying to pull her bodice higher to cover it.

After dinner, when the gentlemen joined the ladies in the drawing room, Emily watched Matthew laughing over something with his friend,

Lieutenant Lawton. She felt . . . not herself, frustrated, aching, and it wasn't just with desire.

For he'd satisfied *her*, but not himself, and it made her uneasy. Why would he deny himself pleasure with his willing *wife*? Was she mistaken in thinking he had no suspicions about her?

She knew she could go mad with these fearful thoughts. He'd given her not one reason to suspect him. Surely she was just overly suspicious because of Stanwood's threats and the tension of wondering what he would do next. She needed Matthew's loyalty and protection, and she was using him to get it, but at least she would return the favor with pleasure to the best of her abilities.

If he let her.

She sat still for a moment, looking at everyone in the drawing room, these people who were so important to her. Lady Rosa and Professor Leland sat together, talking softly, even sharing the occasional smile. Rebecca and Mr. Derby were having an animated conversation, and Rebecca pulled Susanna over to join them. Rebecca could have monopolized the eligible gentleman, but she hadn't.

Emily's gaze returned to Matthew and his friend, and for just a moment, Lieutenant Lawton glanced at her. It was so swift she almost didn't see it, but something in his eyes gave her pause.

And then things began to rearrange themselves in her mind. She had never even received a word from

Stanwood until Matthew returned home—and his friends moved in for a visit. She had questioned the servants this afternoon, but perhaps she was limiting herself and should consider others as well. Stanwood might not be using a servant at all. What if Lieutenant Lawton, or Mr. Derby, were more than they seemed?

Immediately she told herself she was being ridiculous. Matthew had served with Lieutenant Lawton and had grown up with Mr. Derby. They couldn't be criminals like Stanwood.

As Matthew and Lieutenant Lawton approached her, she willed herself to be calm. For the last year, she'd overcome one complicated situation after another. She told herself she would succeed here as well. She had to.

Then she looked at Matthew, and for a moment the sense of danger receded to the back of her mind. The way his gaze held hers betrayed an intimacy that warmed her, stunned her.

But Lieutenant Lawton was looking at her, too, and he was smiling that easy, cocky smile, as if everything amused him.

She linked her arm to Matthew's, as if staking her claim. "I am so sorry I've monopolized the captain these past few days, Lieutenant."

He shook his head. "There is no need for an apology, Mrs. Leland. You have not seen your husband in well over a year—and you thought him dead.

You have every right to his attention. After all, he wasn't dead to me. Sometimes I was downright tired of him."

She laughed along with Matthew.

"So what have you been doing with yourself while we were in the village today?" she asked. "We didn't see you there."

"I followed Matthew's good example and wrote letters to my family, Mrs. Leland. Matthew so urgently needed to return here that I never had a chance to notify them."

"And where are you from?"

"Southampton, ma'am. Matthew wonders how we never met."

But had Lieutenant Lawton met Arthur Stanwood there? she wondered with a sinking feeling.

Though the lieutenant was smiling, Emily noticed that Matthew had no reaction at all to what could have been taken as a very pointed observation.

"I was seldom in the port town itself," she said calmly. "I am from Millbrook. Have you visited the village?"

"No, ma'am."

Yet while she was supposed to be married to Matthew, she'd been living in Southampton itself. Where had the lieutenant been then? Obviously not with Matthew, because he didn't seem to know anything about Matthew's brief first marriage. And she knew she couldn't risk inquiring too closely.

As Matthew and Lieutenant Lawton's conversation turned to the extensive Madingley stables, Emily considered the fact that the lieutenant was seldom visible except at meals. And he'd been taking many long rides. Could he have somehow become reacquainted with Stanwood? Could he now consider her a criminal?

She glanced across the room at the Leland sisters and Mr. Derby. He was another newcomer to the household, and had a completely different reason to be easily swayed about her past. It wasn't a secret that he'd been courting her and was rejected.

Mr. Derby saw her watching him and gave a brief bow from the waist. Then Rebecca gestured for her, and Emily excused herself from the two men and crossed the room.

"Did Matthew tell you about the picnic we're hosting tomorrow?" Rebecca asked with excitement.

"No, he didn't." Emily prayed she wasn't blushing as she remembered what she'd been doing with Matthew.

"They only spent the whole afternoon together," Susanna said, rolling her eyes.

The two women laughed, but Emily felt uneasy as she glanced at Mr. Derby. It was not very nice to remind him that he no longer had a chance to woo a widow. Maybe it even made him angrier.

But he was smiling at Susanna as he said, "Surely

the picnic was your idea, to reintroduce the young people to your brother. You're very thoughtful."

Susanna shook her head, and though her smile seemed the slightest bit strained to Emily, at least it was cordial.

"It was all Matthew's idea," Rebecca gushed.

Emily started in surprise.

"He wants everyone to see what an incredible artist Susanna is," Rebecca continued, elbowing her sister. "She'll be giving art lessons so we can all paint the ruins."

Emily smiled warmly at Susanna, who smiled back. How thoughtful of Matthew! Though he'd been resistant to Susanna's "inappropriate" use of her hobbies, he'd finally realized how important painting was to her.

Emily turned and caught Matthew's eye. She gave him a wide smile, not caring if Lieutenant Lawton or Mr. Derby or any of the servants watched and disapproved of her—or secretly plotted against her.

When Matthew heard the dressing room doorknob turn, he lifted his book and pretended to read once again. Still wearing his shirtsleeves and trousers, he was lying on the bed in Emily's room, pillows supporting him.

When Emily saw him, she paused on the threshold. She was clothed in a dressing gown, her hair wrapped in a towel, her skin glistening in the candlelight. He'd just come from the dressing room, where he'd listened at the bathroom door and imagined what made each splash.

He was a fool—a panting, lust-filled fool who was allowing his overwhelming desire for Emily Grey to make him forget that he needed to discover her secrets.

She smiled at him and moved toward the hearth. He gave up trying to read and simply watched her, the way she drew a chair before the hot coals in the grate, removed the towel from her hair, and began to comb through the blond curls. His mouth went dry as she spread her hair wide, combing over and over again, her face in profile, her eyes focused far away. It was a dreamy moment, filled with her slow, fluid movements. His eyes ached from the strain of staring at her; his breathing sounded harsh in his ears. How could she not hear it? It reminded him of the way she panted in his arms when he'd given her the fulfillment she'd never experienced before. He wished he could show her everything about the intimacy between a man and a woman.

Perhaps then she'd trust him.

That's what it came down to, he realized at last, stunned. He wanted her trust. He wanted the truth from her lips, uncoerced.

But she hadn't trusted his family, whom she'd known for a year. And she'd only known him for a few days.

At last she braided her hair in one long plait and moved away from the hearth. He found himself able to breathe easier when she sat down at the desk, retrieving a notebook. She consulted one of her books—mathematics, he thought—then wrote something down. Was she studying for her own benefit? Or preparing to teach?

He thought about her admission that she had no training as a governess. Had she desperately needed such skills after her family died? This elaborate charade, using his family and her new position, could not simply be a way to educate herself. It just didn't make sense.

Emily felt as if her back was on fire. Matthew was staring at her—he always stared, which pleased her. Surely he was remembering what they'd shared earlier, when she'd surrendered to his caresses, allowed him to do as he willed with her.

She couldn't concentrate on mathematics equations. Matthew was in her bed, clothed, but here nonetheless.

An unusual scent suddenly drifted past her, and she lifted her head, inhaling. It was sweet and fragrant, but not the roses Maria often brought her from the greenhouse.

She turned—and saw him watching her openly, the book set aside. In his hand, he held a flower she didn't recognize at first, twirling it in his fingers.

"Come here, Emily," he said in a low, soft voice.

Full of rising gladness, she rose from the desk and moved slowly toward him. She focused on the flower, white with a yellow center, and faint pink at the tips of the petals. "I recognize that," she said. "It's a lotus. They're grown in the pond in the conservatory."

"Do you recognize where else it is from?"

"India." She was proud of the studying she'd done on the country she was supposed to have lived in for six months.

"Sit down, Emily."

She sat on the edge of the bed beside him, and to her surprise he leaned forward and tucked the flower behind her ear. Its sweet, fruity scent enveloped her, and she knew he must have just picked it.

"Did I give you flowers in India?" he asked.

She nodded, finding it difficult to speak. Her mouth was too dry.

"The flowers in India were like no others I'd ever seen," he murmured.

He continued to stroke along her ear, then lower still, through her hair. Her braid had fallen forward across her shoulder, and he removed the ribbon, then threaded his fingers through the long waves of her hair. It was far too pleasurable; his hands were so near her breasts. She wickedly wanted them there, already craved again the sensations he'd made her feel only hours before.

"Do you tell your students about India?"

She nodded, struggling to focus on his words, not the play of his hands. It was like he was weaving a spell about her. "I tell them about the torrents of rain in monsoon season, how I missed it by leaving the country too soon."

"You wanted to see the rain?" he asked, a brow arched in surprise. "It was so hot and humid my clothes were damp constantly."

"A wool uniform must have been unbearable."

"I became accustomed to it. What is your favorite memory to tell your students?"

"Being on the river," she said immediately. From her studies, and the sketches in books, she could practically see it in her mind, almost as if she'd been there. "The white egrets flying low over paddy fields, the surprise of an occasional temple peeking through groves of mangoes. I tell them about the crushed seashells lining garden paths to keep out the snakes. It was all so very foreign to me—so beautiful."

Though she was glad she was well-prepared for her masquerade, she felt almost ugly saying such lies. Why did it seem harder to lie to him? She had to ignore that.

"Tell me about our bed," he murmured.

She inhaled swiftly, giving him a teasing smile. "Surely even if you've forgotten me, you remember sleeping in the bungalow on your string-cot."

He cocked his head as he studied her, eyes narrowed but still glinting with amusement. Was he trying to picture her in his bed each night? Or sorting through his suspicions? No, she had no proof of that.

"I imagine I will begin to remember such things soon," he said softly, "for I plan to spend my nights in this bed from now on."

Hope surged through her, then confusion. After calling a halt to their lovemaking that afternoon, now he wanted to sleep with her?

He added, "Perhaps you won't have such terrible nightmares if you know you're not alone."

That didn't seem like enough of a reason.

He grinned. "And this bed is much more comfortable."

An outright exaggeration on his part.

His expression sobered. "But I don't want you to think I'm teasing you, Emily. This afternoon . . . I lost myself in pleasuring you. Yet I've also lost every memory we shared, and it bothers me."

"You aren't teasing me, Matthew. You're my husband, and your presence in this bed is your right."

"My mind strains to put you in my memories of India. I imagine you sailing upriver with me—"

"But not very far," she interrupted. "You were concerned about the danger I would be in. When you were transferred up the country, that's when you sent me home."

She went to the desk and put out the lamp. She'd stood for a moment at the windows, where the draperies were still open, and looked out on the dark night. A cold autumn rain fell against the glass, rattling it. Then she lowered the draperies, checked the coal grate one last time, and came to the bed, where the last lit candle illuminated him in a gentle golden glow.

Matthew slid to the far side, still fully clothed, and watched as she removed her dressing gown, to lay it across the chest at the end of the bed. She wondered what he could see beneath the sheer fabric of her gown, hoped it enticed him. She slid beneath the covers, pulling them up to her waist.

She glanced at him. "Are you not coming to bed yet?"

He nodded to her and stood up, shrugging out of his shirt and trousers, leaving his drawers in place as he slid beneath the covers on his side of the bed.

She leaned to the side and blew out the candle, enveloping them in darkness. The pleasurable tension between them was a physical thing. She slid up against him.

"You're warm," she murmured.

To her disappointment, he started to talk.

"This is so strange," he murmured, pillowing his head on his bent arm.

She snuggled against him, her hand on his chest. "Strange for you, but not for me."

"There's still some part of the proper gentleman in me, who feels that sharing a bed with you, even innocently, is like seducing a virgin."

"I am not innocent." She winced, thinking she spoke too firmly.

He only chuckled. "But you're my wife. I would certainly assume you're not innocent."

Chapter 14

After breakfast the next morning Matthew sat alone on a bench in the conservatory, looking at the rain that drizzled down the glass windows.

"You can't believe how difficult it was to find you."

Matthew turned at the sound of Reggie's voice and smiled. "I didn't mean to hide."

"I saw Emily drive off in the cabriolet," Reggie said, sitting down on the bench.

Matthew heard the question in his voice. "I told her to take it because of the rain. She's teaching again today."

"Teaching," Reggie mused. "You mentioned something about that last night, but we didn't have a chance to talk. *Teaching*?"

Matthew laughed softly. "That's what she's been doing in the village. And here I followed her like an army spy, thinking she might be meeting someone in secret."

"She still might be."

"I haven't been able to tell," he said with a shrug.

"You'll know more soon, when the report from the investigator arrives."

Matthew only nodded.

"You seem . . . contemplative this morning."

"Contemplative. What an interesting choice of words." He gave a half smile. "I am thinking of Emily, of course."

"Of course." Reggie grinned. "You retire to a private suite each night with her. How could she not be on your mind?"

Matthew recognized the hint for what it was, but ignored it for the moment. "She has this uncanny ability to have an answer—a fabricated answer—to everything I say. There's not even a hesitation."

"She's very intelligent."

"I don't know if she made herself that way with all the studying she does for her students. She even talks about India like someone who's been there."

Reggie laughed. "Maybe she has."

"Unless her father took her there, I don't think so." He lowered his voice. "I keep wondering why she's doing this. The more I know her, the more I see how my family loves her, all that makes sense is that she was desperate to survive. Her family died, and she had nothing."

"Other women who have nothing—and look like her—marry quite easily. Or perhaps she knew she could not prove herself a virgin on a wedding night."

For an insane moment that made Matthew bristle. He was getting too close to Emily, entwined with her, sympathizing with her. She was swaying him, and he seemed helpless to stop it.

"I don't know if she's a virgin," he said at last.

Reggie only arched a brow.

"She says she's not innocent. Yet, without going into details—"

"Oh, please do."

Matthew smiled. "I don't think she's ever known a woman's pleasure before. And I know all that could mean is that no man took his time with her." He paused, looking back outside at the wet park, feeling awkward but needing to talk. "I think I'm getting caught up in her, Reg. I thought pursuing and taking her to bed would be fun. After all, didn't she ask for that by being here, by lying? But . . ."

"But?" Reggie finally urged.

"But that's what she wants."

"And that is a bad thing?" he asked with disbelief.

"I'd be falling right into her little plot. And what if she became pregnant? That would change everything."

Reggie sighed. "Not an easy decision, I'll admit. Not ready to confront her?"

"No. Not until I hear from the investigator. There's some part of me—" He ran a hand through his hair, feeling like a fool. "God help me, there's a part of me that almost wishes it were real."

"Her passion? Or the marriage itself?"

With a groan, Matthew pushed to his feet. "Forget I said anything. I'm just confused."

"I think you're thinking too much."

"I used to be very good at that, overthinking everything. I put it behind me in India—and then I came home to this." He donned a perfunctory smile. "So what are your plans today? Are you coming to our picnic?"

"Of course! More eligible ladies. This visit is proving so entertaining."

"What are you doing before the picnic?"

Reggie shrugged and glanced outside. "I don't know. I might ride."

"In this weather?"

"We've seen worse."

As they left the conservatory together, Matthew had the distinct feeling that Reggie was holding something back. But everyone had secrets, so his friend was welcome to keep his.

Emily drove the two-wheeled cabriolet, keeping the carriage hood up over her as a defense against the fine mist of rain. She was uneasy all the way into Comberton, and knew she couldn't blame the gloom of the countryside.

Was Stanwood—or one of his minions—watching her even now?

In the taproom of the inn there were more strangers than usual, and she felt watched as she hurried through the entrance hall and into the private dining chamber. She tried to relax through the morning of teaching, but her nervousness never quite left her. When only one man threatened her, it had seemed easier to handle, to plan for. Now she didn't know from which way a confrontation might come.

Yet—why didn't Stanwood just get it over with?

As she drove out of the village, the itchy feeling between her shoulder blades returned, as if someone was staring at her. She urged the horse into a canter.

Behind her, she suddenly heard the sound of a horse galloping quickly, as if to overtake her. Calm, sensible Emily was replaced by a vulnerable woman whose mind raced with plans of escape that made no sense at all. She flicked the reins, urging the horse faster.

"Emily!"

She gasped at the sound of her name, then saw Matthew's bobbing head as he peered beneath the carriage hood from the back of his racing horse.

She sagged against the bench in relief, pulling up on the reins.

"I must have missed you in town," he said, slowing down to ride beside her cabriolet.

She gave him a bright smile. "I am sorry, too."

Why had he been following her?

But he was smiling down at her with such happiness.

"The picnic," she said suddenly. "Did the plans change?"

His smile broadened into a grin. "No. But I was worried you might think so because of the earlier weather and delay your return. But it stopped raining several hours ago, so the picnic will continue. I had the servants raise several pavilions, just in case."

He was only being a good brother, she told herself.

The old castle seemed to stretch to the sky, replicated in the nearby pond. As a child, Matthew had spent hours exploring the ruins, pretending he was a knight in armor, fearless and reckless in battle. As an adult, he'd become a soldier. Had he made those childhood dreams come true?

Nearby were two colorful pavilions, with tables and chairs haphazardly spread about, the remains of their picnic feast still evident. The elders of the party still lingered there, talking with his parents, and to Matthew's surprise, he saw Reggie among them.

A half-dozen easels were spread across the lawn, and young ladies sat before them, contemplating how to capture the view. Susanna moved among them, talking, teaching, looking so at ease with her skills. Several young gentlemen milled among them all, and Matthew was pleased that she easily answered their questions, smiling.

Peter Derby said to Susanna, "Haven't you drawn or painted this view a hundred times?"

She raised her nose primly. "Every day is different, every sky different, and even my talent is different year to year. And I never tire of such beauty and history."

Matthew knew he didn't have to worry about her. He spread a piece of canvas for protection against the damp earth, then a blanket over that. He threw several plump cushions on top, ready to relax against them.

"You aren't going to paint?" Rebecca said as she approached.

"Of course not. My hands are far too clumsy." He smiled, but it faded as he studied his sister.

To his surprise, she sat down on the blanket, legs folded demurely beneath her.

"Rebecca, are you feeling well?"

"I'm just tired," she said, waving a hand. "We

stayed up late with Mama, discussing who was coming, how we should behave."

"As if you don't know that by now," he said dryly.

She giggled, then plumped several cushions behind her and leaned back. She fell asleep too quickly. Her pale face reminded him of the terrible illnesses of her childhood.

He hadn't realized that Emily was also watching Rebecca soberly. He rose, inclined his head toward the ruins, and held out his hand. She took it without hesitation, and they walked around the pond toward the old castle.

They were silent as they entered. He wondered if she knew it as well as he did. "I remember a room where the roof had collapsed . . ."

"This way," she said, moving before him down a dank passage, before heading up a flight of stone steps and out beneath the sky.

The sun shone down on her, broken walls towering around them. But one was only a half wall, and they could see the entire countryside spread around them, the autumn trees shining with the many colors of Susanna's palette.

He glanced at Emily, whose face was serene as she took in the view. Strands of pale blond hair had come loose and now fluttered gently about her face. God, she was truly beautiful. Long ago he would have courted her, he realized with a start. If he had simply met her in Society, he would have wanted to know her better.

"How was Rebecca while I was gone?" he asked.

Emily looked at him then, her blue eyes full of understanding. She read him too well.

"Don't let her taking a nap make you think the worst," she said.

"But there are over a dozen people here. And she fell *asleep*?"

"Susanna told me of Rebecca's fragile health in childhood. But I've been here a year, and she's only had a cold or two, nothing worse."

"She almost died," he said softly, looking away from her. "More than once my family feared the worst."

"But she's so strong, she was able to recover," Emily said in a gentle voice.

Perhaps the whole family would recover when at last they knew the truth about Emily. But would they forgive her?

"Your concern for your sister is touching," Emily continued. "There are not many men who would show such emotion."

"I once thought it very easy to lock emotion away," he found himself saying ruefully. "Sometimes I didn't think I'd ever let myself feel truly alive again."

"But you were doing a soldier's duty. You had to protect yourself."

He let her think he was talking about his service in the army. She was such a sympathetic listener, facing him now, her eyes blue mirrors of understanding and solemnity. To his surprise, she reached up and cupped his face. Her touch brought to life the latent desire for her that never went away.

"Don't think of what you had to do," she said quietly, her face close to his. "Circumstances can change us, but it doesn't have to be forever."

She was warm and sweet, and he leaned down to kiss her, enjoying the twin heat of her hands on his face. He pulled her into his arms so he could feel all of her, the softness of her breasts and belly against his body, the lushness of her hips as he ran his hands over them to hold her against him. Their kiss grew more and more urgent, deeper, greedy, and he let himself sink into the raw desire he felt for her.

"You know I'm going to make love to you soon," he said against her lips, breathing hard.

"I know. But do you love me, Matthew?" she whispered between the gentle kisses she pressed to his lips.

Words froze in his throat; he couldn't lie about this, not as easily as she could. But she hadn't said she loved him.

At his continued silence, her gaze was sad but understanding, like that of a real wife. He found himself wishing he could take what was offered.

They walked back to his sisters arm and arm, and he saw the way Susanna and Rebecca exchanged a knowing, happy look upon seeing them together. Then Susanna took Emily away to discuss her plan to sketch the ruins from inside, her students and their male admirers following behind. He remained with Rebecca.

Smiling, she poured him a glass of cider, and he drank deeply. "You know," she began thoughtfully, watching the others disappear inside the castle, "you left marks on her chin from your whiskers."

He coughed into his glass, barely able to keep from spilling it.

Rebecca laughed merrily, bringing a pretty blush of pink to her cheeks. He was glad that his foolishness could make her look so.

"I know the signs of a man's kisses," she continued, eyes sparkling.

"I hope not from experience."

"Of course not!" she said too quickly, then laughed. "What is it like to court a woman you're already married to?"

He stretched out, leaning back on one elbow as he regarded his sister with amusement. "It is a challenge, but a pleasant one."

"I am glad you think so. Many men would be angry and frustrated by everything they couldn't remember."

"Again, you know that from experience with the opposite sex?"

She lifted her chin haughtily. "I'm well read." Then she laughed and regarded him thoughtfully. "For the first day or so, I thought you would be one of those other men."

"My feeling angry at this insane situation would have disappointed you?"

She shook her head. "No, of course not. If important parts of *my* memory were just—gone, I think I would handle it far worse. I value every precious memory, perhaps because I don't have as many as people who've lived ordinary lives."

He studied her thoughtfully, thinking of the weeks of her childhood she'd spent ill and weak in bed, while life went on for everyone else. "You've grown too wise, little sister."

She laughed merrily. "I'm not so wise. If I were, I would be able to settle on a husband."

"Perhaps you have not met the right man," he said, trying to be gentle.

"Is that how you felt when you met Emily?"

He couldn't help it—he laughed.

Rebecca playfully pushed him. "You did marry her very quickly."

"And you blame me, too, as Mother must, for not being at the wedding?"

She shook her head and raised both hands. "Oh, no, I thought it all quite romantic."

Romantic, he thought, lying back again, closing his eyes against the sun. He wouldn't even need romance to take Emily to bed now.

Leaning against a stone wall, Emily enjoyed the warmth of the sun, watching Susanna sketch out her ideas for a more elaborate painting from the high point of the castle. Her students had spread out among the ruins, but Mr. Derby still lingered nearby. At last Susanna seemed to notice his interest, and her expression became polite, but unreadable. She closed up her notebook and started back toward the picnic pavilions.

Emily took her arm. "Oh, don't return yet," she said impulsively. "We all enjoy watching you work."

Susanna sighed, her eyes glancing toward Mr. Derby. "Emily, you've spent a year watching me work, so that can't be all of the truth." She lowered her voice. "I just feel . . . uncomfortable around Mr. Derby. I know he wasn't the one who said cruel things about me, but—"

"Haven't you ever been in a situation where you didn't know how to speak up? Or know the right thing to say? Perhaps those were his problems. I am not making excuses for his benefit, only for yours, so that you can forgive and forget."

"I know," Susanna said. "And I remind myself of that. I promise that I'm trying."

Emily let her go, and Susanna, with a brief smile for her, and even a pleasant nod toward Mr. Derby, went back through into the ruins.

When Mr. Derby moved to follow Susanna, Emily called his name.

Smiling, his blond hair gleaming in the sun, he nodded to her. "Yes, Mrs. Leland?"

She looked about, making sure they could not be overheard. "Would you mind a very small piece of advice?"

His smile grew stiff, and he said nothing.

She had probably made a mistake by interfering, but it was done now. "Give Miss Leland time, Mr. Derby. She is . . . the sort of young woman who needs to take things slowly."

"There is no need to couch your words, Mrs. Leland. I know you don't want me connected to this family."

She gaped at him. "I never—"

"You made it abundantly clear before Captain Leland returned."

"My reluctance to become involved with another man had nothing to do with you, Mr. Derby."

"But I was the man you wouldn't become involved with," he said with sarcasm.

"You were not the only man—you could not be blind to that. There were several men expressing subtle interest, but there was something inside me that just knew . . ." She paused, hand to her heart, then continued softly, "I just knew I wasn't ready."

But he must not have believed her, for he continued coldly, "I know I do not have the sort of wealth the granddaughter of a duke might wish for, but your beginnings are not any better than mine. Yet you think yourself a suitable wife for Captain Leland?"

How to answer that? "I do," she said in a calm voice. "And you might be just what Miss Leland wants and needs. But if you push her right now, it will all be for naught."

He opened his mouth, but then seemed to think better of speaking, for he turned on his heel and marched away. Emily closed her eyes for a moment. Part of her wanted to read deeper into everything Mr. Derby said, but what was the point? If he was helping Stanwood, she could hardly confront him about it.

She faced the very real possibility that the safe world she'd constructed for herself could come crashing down around her. Though Matthew's return had complicated everything, she was growing more certain that they could be happy together. She'd practically melted when he confessed his concern about Rebecca's health, his deep fears about how the army had changed him. And then she'd foolishly asked him if he loved her. What had she been thinking? What a perfect method to push a man away, just when she was so close to having all she wanted.

He was telling her more and more about himself—and she was falling for the honorable man he was. That wasn't part of the plan.

But she could adapt. And she wouldn't let Mr. Derby—or Stanwood—get in the way.

Chapter 15

Late in the afternoon, as Emily was approaching her suite to change for dinner, she came around the corner and stumbled to a halt as she saw Lieutenant Lawton outside her bedroom door. Without conscious decision, she backed around the corner and then peered out at him.

He was just standing there, looking down as if he were debating something. Opening the door perhaps?

Or did he have something he wanted to leave for her?

That infuriated her so much that she marched around the corner. The lieutenant's head came up and he smiled at her with natural ease, but she wasn't misled. She, too, was very good at behaving as if nothing was wrong.

"Lieutenant, are you looking for me?" she asked directly. "If I am not mistaken, we just came from the same picnic."

"No, Mrs. Leland, I was actually looking for Matthew."

"Then why not knock?" she asked. "I saw you just . . . standing here, doing nothing."

He grinned and shuffled his feet like a boy. "You'll think me foolish, but I couldn't remember which bedroom he was using."

A very good excuse, she thought. "That is my room," she informed him.

"Forgive me."

"Of course," she answered, forcing a smile. "I was simply surprised to see you here. You have not been often at Madingley Court, and even at the picnic I saw you talking to others rather than Matthew."

"I did not want to intrude on your time with him," he said smoothly.

He was watching her deliberately, his eyes full of open amusement—and it bothered her.

"Where do you go when you leave us?" she asked.

"Riding, ma'am. It is so refreshing to be among the cool English countryside after the heat of India."

"Then you've been riding for many days."

"And letter-writing," he reminded her. His manner suddenly became less cocky and more serious. "Mrs. Leland, might I offer a word of advice?"

Hadn't she just said those same words to Mr.

Derby? she thought with exasperation. "Of course, Lieutenant."

"You seem . . . uneasy. If there is something wrong, I suggest you discuss it with Matthew. He is of an understanding nature."

She arched a brow and coolly said, "And I would not know that about my own husband?"

He spread his hands wide even as he bowed. "Forgive me. I will not presume to bother you again."

Then he walked around her and was gone.

When Matthew returned from the picnic and saw that a thick envelope was waiting for him on the silver tray holding the post, he took it to the library and started to close himself inside. Someone pushed on the door from out in the hall.

"Matthew?" Reggie said, peering in the crack.

Laughing, Matthew opened the door wide.

"When I couldn't find you upstairs," Reggie said, "Hamilton told me I could find you here."

"And I thought I had hidden myself as well as one could in a palace with hundreds of servants. Count on Hamilton to know everything that is going on. Come in."

Matthew sat down in a leather chair near a window, and Reggie did the same nearby.

"And why hide yourself in here?" Reggie asked.

Matthew held up the envelope. "The investigator's report. We can't have prying ears hear about this."

"Ah." Reggie eyed it with interest. "Would you like to read it alone?"

"You and I have no secrets," Matthew said, smiling as he shrugged. He unsealed the envelope.

"Will you be glad to know the truth?" Reggie asked, leaning back in his chair as he clasped his hands behind his head. "Or has it been great fun figuring it out on your own?"

Matthew continued to grin. "The latter, I think. But this was a necessary step. The next one will be up to me."

The investigator had filled several sheets of paper with details about Emily Grey's childhood in a village outside Southampton, how she was the beloved little girl of the family, and how they'd died tragically. None of what he read was different from her own story up to that point. As he finished each page, he handed it to Reggie to read.

Emily had told him she'd had cousins to go to, but the investigator reported that the cousin who inherited Squire Grey's entailed land had not wanted Emily, and even claimed he didn't have a place for her.

"What a cold man," Reggie said thoughtfully.

"It's hard for a woman to marry well in that situation," Matthew said pointedly.

"And her meager inheritance would barely keep her in food and clothing, let alone under the safety of a roof. Useless as a dowry."

"I wonder what purpose it served to lie to me by saying her cousin wanted her?" Matthew wondered aloud.

"Perhaps she didn't want to appear too pitiable."

"Well, she did have Mr. Tillman, the vicar who'd sent a letter to my parents informing them of the marriage before Emily's arrival."

Reggie looked up at Matthew dubiously. "I rather thought Tillman would be a shady character."

Matthew nodded. "I'd been prepared to hear of a man well versed in persuading his parishioners to donate their money, a man who bent God's rules as he saw fit. But the investigator says that Tillman was elderly, and already living on a meager retirement sum in a single rented room at the time of the Grey family tragedy."

"He could hardly take Emily in."

Matthew held up the paper that Reggie hadn't read yet. "She rented a room from a hard-faced spinster, who was glad to tell the investigator that Emily often had trouble paying the rent, that her sewing seldom earned her even a meager living."

He lowered the pages to his lap for a moment, unable to erase the image of Emily sewing by candlelight, trying to support herself in a world that showed little compassion for penniless women. He didn't like the emotions racing back and forth inside him, from anger to pity. Emily wouldn't want that from him.

"So what did she do to survive?" Reggie asked.

"The landlady suspected that Emily had found another way to earn a small amount of money, but didn't know what it was." Matthew rolled his eyes. "Since Emily had no visitors, proper or improper, the landlady insisted she made it a point not to pry."

"How charitable of her." When Matthew remained silent, Reggie cautiously said, "If Emily hadn't been able to keep up with the rent, what was she forced to do before news of your death gave her a way out?"

"All the investigator could find out was that on the night Tillman died, Emily simply vanished with her small amount of belongings. No one had cared why, or tried to discover what happened to her. Her only friend was dead, and she'd had no one else."

"Sounds like a desperate situation."

"Then why not tell the truth once she arrived here?" Matthew said, elbows on his knees as he spoke earnestly to his friend. "My family would have helped her in any way they could. Instead, she simply claimed to be my wife."

"Tillman claimed it first."

"It doesn't make any difference how she announced the plot. It was a bold move. Something more must have happened to force her into it. She'd done her best to support herself, and she's proud enough that she would have continued to do so if she'd had any chance of success."

"How can you know her well enough to know that? This life is certainly easier."

"Only in some ways," Matthew reminded him. "And now that I'm home, it's even more difficult for her."

"But now she's stuck with the part, isn't she?" Reggie seemed to hesitate, then at last said, "She seems . . . nervous to me."

Matthew tilted his head, intrigued. "Really? How?"

"Just a little while ago I was looking for you in the family wing. You'd have thought I was about to burglarize your suite by the suspicious way she confronted me. Nothing happened beyond that, and her manner became cordial once again."

"I guess we can't blame her for being cautious," Matthew said, but he was already turning over in his mind again the question of how Emily might have been earning extra money in Southampton. The investigator was unable to confirm another employer. What had she done that forced her to flee?

After a dinner filled with discussion about the imminent arrival of the rest of the family, Matthew was surprised when Emily drew him aside in the corridor outside the dining room and spoke in a soft voice.

"Matthew, with the Madingley ball in two days' time, would you like to practice your dancing? You said that you didn't remember the steps." She looked up at him sweetly, her eyes full of concern.

He grinned at her. "Excellent idea. Susanna?"

His sister looked over her shoulder at them.

Emily slid her arm into his and pulled him close, whispering, "What are you doing?"

"She can play for us."

"Unnecessary. Let her talk about her triumph at the picnic today with Lady Rosa. You'll remember how the music sounds. Or we can hum."

So, it would be another attempt at seduction, Matthew thought, anticipating it even though he knew he should resist.

"We aren't going to join you in the drawing room," Emily called to his sister. "We have something to discuss."

Susanna arched a brow devilishly, but Emily ignored it.

Matthew wasn't going to take the risk of being interrupted. "We're going to practice dancing," he told Susanna. "Alone," he added meaningfully.

His sister covered her mouth, but her eyes shone with merriment.

"Do wish good-night to your parents for us,"

Emily said, then steered Matthew down another corridor.

Side by side they walked upstairs to the ballroom on the next floor. At that time of night the room was dark, a cavern of blackness, but Emily brought in a lamp from the corridor and set it on a small table. It only illuminated a glow about her, leaving everything else dark.

Matthew enjoyed looking at her. She was wearing a pale blue gown that just hid the tops of her breasts, yet displayed her slender waist and the swell of her hips. She looked ethereal in the near darkness, a glow of beauty that lured him to fly too near and risk incinerating himself.

Soon he'd have his hands on those delectable curves, and she'd be touching him—

She put her fists on her hips and spoke briskly. "We'll begin with the quadrille, which will open the dancing at the ball."

"Ah yes. I was taught at a young age to have a store of small talk on the tip of my tongue, ever ready to amuse my partner."

A faint frown furrowed her forehead. "But I thought you said you didn't remember."

He kept smiling as he shook his head. "I don't remember the steps, it is true. But how can one forget the endless admonishments of dance masters?"

Though she probably hadn't been taught by dance masters, she nodded and tried to smile again.

Clearly, she was troubled by his misspoken words. She began to instruct him about the four couples participating in the dance and the necessary steps, from the *chasse* to the *glissade*. She stood at his side and demonstrated each, and he gained secret amusement at teasing her with his inability to follow. When she finally bent to pull his thigh forward, she froze, looked up at him, and they both began to laugh.

The merriment lit her face into an angelic glow, even as she stumbled back, holding her hand to her side. Her laugh was hearty, not missish, and he enjoyed the sound. It made him think of earthy pleasures and ticklish kisses. He thought it was a good thing she wasn't still bent over his thighs, or she'd see the tight fit of his trousers.

"I think I'm remembering now," he said at last. "Let's begin the dance again."

After several false starts—and without other couples to dance with—they were able to complete a quadrille without mistakes.

He liked touching her hand and waist so much, he betrayed his eagerness by saying, "Now on to the waltz."

She was obviously trying to use her professional schoolmistress voice, but it was difficult to be serious when she was manipulating his hands to place them on her body.

He tried to pull her close, enjoying the brush of

her feminine skirts, and then the impression of her thighs. When she pushed him back, again demonstrating the proper form, he murmured, "But surely it is different between a husband and wife."

She managed to breathlessly say, "When a married couple is dancing in public, they must behave as properly as everyone else."

As she began to demonstrate the turns involved, he deliberately stumbled as he followed her, pulling her tight against him so she didn't trip. She eyed him boldly, he answered with an innocent smile, and they tried again. He let himself look surprised, as if by a memory, then confident, and soon they were truly dancing. The sweep of the dance took them away from the faint glow of the lamp, into darkness, but that did not deter him. He was too caught up in how well they moved together, how they anticipated each other's every step as if they'd practiced forever.

Her face grew flushed, her smile faded, and soon she was just staring up at him and he was staring down at her. He was consumed with the promise of the night, their own bedroom, and the battle within his thoughts about taking her to bed.

The circle of the dance took them back into the lamplight—and the sound of applause. Matthew and Emily broke apart, only to see his parents standing in the doorway, still applauding, their expressions full of delight. Did Lady Rosa actually wipe away a tear?

He smiled perfunctorily, irritated by the interruption. "So you found us."

Lady Rosa bustled forward. "And it was necessary. Tonight we were going to discuss all of the guests we've invited to the ball, so that you will be armed with enough knowledge."

Emily touched his mother's arm. "That is so thoughtful of you, Lady Rosa. Matthew will do best if he feels at ease. That's what we were doing here tonight."

Matthew saw Professor Leland give an abbreviated snort as he looked away.

"Rosa," the professor said, "perhaps the young people wish to be alone."

"But the family arrives tomorrow, Randolph. There won't be time for this discussion. And Matthew certainly doesn't wish it to be in front of his cousins." She turned to Matthew. "Are you planning to tell them about your memory loss, dear?"

He glanced at Emily, who watched him with interest.

"I haven't decided," he answered truthfully.

He knew that his mother loved him, and she obviously wanted his homecoming reunion with the rest of the family to be as normal as possible. To make certain of it, she led them back to the drawing room and went on in detail for several hours, explaining every family in the shire and their relationships. Matthew tried to protest that more and more of his memories were returning, but she didn't believe him.

And during it all, Emily fell asleep at his side, head resting at an awkward angle against her shoulder. When their conversation hit a momentary lull, they all seemed to notice her at once.

Lady Rosa sighed and whispered, "I do believe we might have gotten carried away."

Matthew and the professor exchanged a glance.

"It is time for us to retire," Matthew said quietly, getting to his feet.

His mother wrung her hands. "Have I told you about the family dinner party tomorrow night?"

"You have," he said, striving for solemnity, "and I appreciate all the trouble you're going to."

She looked shocked. "Trouble? You think that the return of my son from the dead would cause me trouble?"

He grinned and leaned down to kiss her cheek. "Of course not. I just wanted you to know that I appreciate you—and that I missed you."

Mollified, she playfully pushed him away. He gathered Emily into his arms, half expecting her to awaken, but she only snuggled against him, her head coming to rest on his shoulder. When he turned around, his parents watched him holding

Emily with twin expressions of hope that made him uneasy.

Wishing them good-night, he strode away.

Emily was light and pliable in his arms. He traversed corridors and staircases, moving in and out of faint circles of lamplight stationed at intervals. More than one servant passed him silently, some wearing the same hopeful expression as his parents.

Thankfully, their bedroom door was ajar, and he shouldered it open. The blankets and counterpane had already been turned back, and he was able to gently lower her to the cool sheets. She still didn't awaken. He closed the door, then began to loosen his cravat as he returned to the bed to stare down at her. After tossing the cravat on a nearby chair, he removed his coat and waistcoat.

With a heavy sigh, Emily rolled onto her side, away from him, her cheek pillowed on her folded hands. Matthew waited, but her breathing continued slowly, evenly.

He took the opportunity presented to him and began to unhook the back of her gown.

Chapter 16

As Matthew unhooked Emily's gown, he felt certain that she would awaken any moment. She would never give up an opportunity to have him in bed, to seal this marriage she wanted so desperately. He found himself breathing unevenly, wanting to fulfill every promise of pleasure they'd been creating these last few days, even as another part of him knew it might be a mistake.

Every hook he tugged on sent an answering tug deep inside him. When he found her corset as her gown separated, he untied the laces, letting his fingers brush her back through her chemise. As he loosened the corset he thought she would surely notice that she could breathe easier. Yet her breathing had the same, even cadence.

He rolled her onto her back, and her head fell to the side, facing away from him. He removed her shoes, then drew her gown forward off her shoulders, pulling her arms out of the sleeves. As they fell back like the limbs of a stuffed doll, he knew she was not going to awaken. She was losing her chance at the perfect seduction, he thought, smiling, and knew she would regret it greatly in the morning.

Gently, he slid her dress down beneath her hips, drawing it past her legs. His smile faded as his mouth dried. He was making this even more difficult on himself, but he couldn't stop. He was able to pull the corset off her as well, although it took some tugging.

Her face scrunched up and she made a sound. Matthew froze, his hope—and other things—surging. But she only sighed and seemed to slip into a deeper slumber.

It was his turn to sigh. She was lying before him in her chemise, cut low in the bodice to allow for a more revealing evening gown. For a wicked moment he debated removing that as well. But it would be so much more enjoyable if he could watch her expression as he did so.

Had he given up and decided to take her after all?

He slid his hands up her legs to remove her garters and roll her stockings down. At each brush of her flesh his fingertips seemed to burn.

He wanted her to open her eyes and reach for him, to bring him down to her. Why did he care if he was giving her what she wanted—when he wanted it, too? He was the one in control after all, the one who with just a word could end this whole masquerade.

But still she didn't awaken, her face was so innocent in sleep. Leaning over her, he brushed her hair from her eyes, then at last pulled the covers up over her and left.

The next afternoon, with Emily at his side, Matthew stood at the front portico of Madingley Court and watched the caravan of carriages and wagons coming slowly down the long drive. All of his relatives were arriving at last. It had been two years since he'd seen the two men who'd been more than cousins to him—they were like brothers, with only a few years' difference in ages between all of them. They'd been raised together and went to school together until separating before Cambridge. Daniel and Matthew went to university, but Christopher's father had died, making him the duke at eighteen, and burdening him with too many responsibilities and duties for Cambridge.

It would still be several minutes before the carriages came to a stop. Matthew was curious when Emily spoke his name in a hesitant voice.

"Yes?" he said.

"I have debated if I should speak to you all day," she said slowly, "and then I decided I had to say something."

He arched a brow. "About what?"

"Lieutenant Lawton. Yesterday, I found him outside our bedroom."

"Yes, he mentioned it when he finally found me."

She smiled with chagrin. "Oh—never mind."

"No, go on," he said, glancing at the slowing carriages. "You obviously feel it's important."

"It's simply that . . . I almost felt like he was . . . following me."

Matthew kept his smile in place. Reggie's concerns that she was suspicious of him were correct. How interesting that she would mention it. "Following you? Why would he do that?"

"I know I sound foolish, but I felt I had to mention it, especially after my maid, Maria, told me that Reggie was seen by the servants sneaking back into the house before dawn this morning."

Arms folded over his chest, Matthew leaned against a column and grinned at her. "He is a man long away from England. Surely you can understand that he would want to search out amusements that an old married man like myself could not participate in."

Her cheeks blushed red. "Of course you're right. I hadn't thought of that."

"You're my innocent wife," he said softly, cupping her cheek with his palm. "Why would you feel you had to be suspicious of him?"

She looked away, breaking their contact as she spread her hands wide. "I don't know."

And then there was no more time to talk. The

first carriage, with two bewigged footmen perched on the rear and the ducal crest as an announcement on the door, came to a stop before the front door. Daniel Throckmorten emerged first, and then Christopher Cabot, the duke himself. Both men had inherited the dark Cabot looks and the impressive height. But Christopher, being half Spanish, had an olive cast to his skin that marked him as decidedly different.

Matthew started down the stone stairs, grinning, but they both turned to help out two ladies, obviously their wives. Just that morning, Emily had supplied him with all the information he needed. Christopher, his once very proper cousin, had done the scandalous thing and married a female journalist, a woman with brown hair and a lush figure. Of course, Daniel, the biggest rake of the three of them, was not to be outdone where scandal was concerned. He'd won the hand of his petite wife, Grace, in a card game with her mother.

Emily descended the stairs at Matthew's side. He saw her happy wave, and the answering waves of his cousins' wives. Though the two women hugged Emily, they stared at him with curiosity and amazement. Even Daniel's and Christopher's expressions were solemn.

"Have I changed so much?" Matthew asked, smiling.

He reached out a hand to the duke, and to his

surprise, Christopher hugged him hard, then passed him to Daniel, who did the same.

Matthew stepped back and grinned, feeling almost too choked up to speak.

"It is good to see you," Christopher said softly.

Daniel added, "Always had to make an entrance, didn't you?"

Before Matthew could respond except with a laugh, a footman opened the door to the next carriage. His aunt Isabella, the dowager duchess of Madingley, descended first, still regal, with only a touch of silver in her black hair. Behind her came his second aunt, Lady Flora, Daniel's mother, dressed in dark blue rather than black. Matthew remembered her wearing the color of mourning since her husband's death, when he was a little boy. He was glad her mood had at last improved. Both women were widows. Not for the first time, he realized how lucky he was that his father was still alive and still had the ability to find a second chance at happiness in marriage.

"Matthew!"

The shriek came from his youngest cousin, Elizabeth, Christopher's sister, who jumped from the carriage without waiting for assistance. She'd still been in the schoolroom when he left, but had blossomed into a lovely young woman. She flung herself at him, and he swung her around.

"Help, she's choking me!" he called, gasping.

She pounded his shoulders as he let her down. "I am allowed my happiness, after all the mourning you put us through."

He sobered and saw his aunts dabbing at their eyes, and that even spirited Elizabeth blinked hard against tears. Though there had been years of squabbling with so many families living in the same household, it wasn't until he was away from England that he'd realized how rare it was that his family all loved each other.

He'd unknowingly put them all through hell. "I . . . I can only say how sorry I am that I did not realize the terrible news you'd been told."

Christopher rolled his eyes. "We would go through it all again as long as we were guaranteed the same outcome. You're home, restored to your family—and to your wife."

Everyone laughed and applauded. Emily blushed, but didn't meet Matthew's eyes. He thought Daniel looked between them with too much curiosity, but there would be time to answer that later. More carriages filled with servants and wagons piled with trunks were waiting to rumble past them, heading both to the servants' entrance and the luggage entrance.

Matthew gestured up the portico stairs, where the butler and many downstairs servants were already lined up to greet the duke. "Let's go inside, shall we? You all need to rest and prepare yourselves for dinner." He looked at Christopher. "If His Grace doesn't mind me speaking for him."

Daniel laughed. "His Grace is becoming far too used to having others speak for him." He lightly tapped Abigail, the duchess, on the arm. She elbowed him back.

After dinner, as the ladies were leaving the gentlemen, Emily paused in the doorway and watched Matthew for a moment. His face was alive with animation as he spoke with his cousins. She knew they'd practically been raised as brothers, and it was obvious they had all missed each other during the two years he was in India.

Right now he was distracted from her concerns about Lieutenant Lawton. She had planted a seed, and hoped it would be enough to make Matthew see his friend in a different light, but she was uncertain that she'd made the right decision. Perhaps he would become so curious about what the lieutenant was doing all day—and night—that he would confront his friend. If Lieutenant Lawton knew the truth about her, would he reveal it? He hadn't so far, and to be fair, she didn't even know if he was her enemy or not. But something had to change within this household, allowing her to discover Stanwood's accomplice, even if it placed her at greater risk.

Mr. Derby was polite, but distant, as far as she was concerned. He was still affronted by the sug-

gestion she'd made to him about Susanna, and she
had not forgotten his hints that she wasn't worthy
of Matthew.

Feeling frustrated and impatient, she turned to
leave the men alone in the dining room and found
Grace Throckmorten and Abigail Madingley watching her thoughtfully. They were alone in the hall, as
if they'd been waiting for her.

Emily smiled. The women each took her arm
and led her into a cozy parlor. They were not the
closest of friends—she couldn't afford to allow
herself friends—but had socialized often with her
when she'd spent the past Season in London. She
liked them, and knew that they were very intelligent
women. Abigail might be the trained journalist, but
they were both regarding her thoughtfully and with
too much interest.

"Emily, we were so stunned at the news!"
Grace said. "I have never seen my husband so
emotional."

Abigail glanced at Grace in surprise, then turned
back to Emily. "And Chris was the same. We were
glad for our husbands, of course, but neither of us
could stop thinking about you!"

Emily smiled. "Thank you. We have all truly
been blessed."

"All?" Abigail said deliberately. "Of course Matthew's sisters and parents are thrilled, but . . . what
about you?"

"I feel the same," she said simply, serenely.

"Yet, after not seeing one's husband for a year," Grace said quietly, "was it almost like beginning anew?"

"It has been more . . . challenging than I expected. Fighting for England has changed him in some ways."

"We have only heard stories about him, of course," Abigail said, "but he seems like a very nice man. Much more open and carefree than I'd assumed from the stories I heard. Of course, the fact that our husbands love him like a brother says much about him."

"He is more than a nice man," Emily said in a low, fervent voice. "He is a *good* man, who's seen too much unhappiness. It has been difficult for him, but we are doing fine."

Abigail exchanged a look with Grace, as if they would say more, but in the end she only said, "Then we are happy for you. If you don't mind a little advice, be patient with him. Our husbands come from stubborn stock."

Emily nodded. "That, I already know."

When everyone gathered in the drawing room after dinner, Matthew enjoyed the lively hum of conversation and laughter. He stood a moment in the doorway, looking at his family, feeling full of happiness and satisfaction. Daniel, Christopher, and their wives were talking to Emily. Earlier in the day he'd decided to tell his cousins everything, but now, seeing how friendly their wives were with Emily, he changed his mind. She'd been a part of his family while he was gone. How could he tell his cousins the truth, when they would mostly likely confide in their wives?

While the ladies decided to begin a lively game of charades, Christopher, Daniel, and Matthew shared a knowing glance and tactfully retired to the other end of the drawing room to play cards. Matthew invited Professor Leland, Peter, and Reggie to join them.

To Matthew's surprise, Emily trailed along behind, and it didn't take long to see why. She hovered near his shoulder as the cards were dealt, and before he could even make a move, she whispered the correct play in his ear.

He realized her need to aid his memory, and smiled up at her. "Join the ladies, Emily. I am fine."

Smiling, she touched his shoulder softly and then walked away.

When Matthew turned his attention back to the game, Daniel and Christopher were watching him closely.

Clearing his throat, the professor said a little too loudly, "She always likes to help, our Emily."

Matthew could have groaned. His father trying to cover up Emily's actions was only making it worse. Then someone childishly kicked him under the table, and he frowned at his two cousins, who wore matching innocent expressions.

For a while they played with little focus, mostly discussing Matthew's time in India, his injuries, and how the miscommunication about his death had happened.

During the evening, by ones or twos, the ladies gradually retired, and the men began to drink a bit more. The professor at last said good-night, helping Reggie escort an inebriated Peter to the bachelor wing.

Only Daniel and Christopher remained with Matthew—and they were both pointedly staring at him.

"Explain," Christopher said abruptly. Though his expression was amused, there was an underlying order in those words. The master of the house—the duke—had spoken.

Throwing down his cards, Matthew spread his hands wide and leaned back in his chair. "Explain what?"

Daniel rolled his eyes. "Why did your wife feel like she had to help you play cards?"

Matthew hesitated, but there was only one way to answer that short of lying. "Emily and my family believe I'm having memory problems since recovering from my injuries."

" 'Believe'?"

Christopher had unerringly focused on the important word. Matthew sighed. He'd told himself that he wasn't going to ask his cousins' advice, that involving more people would only increase the chance of a disaster happening.

But . . . they'd always confided everything in each other. And maybe they could help.

"What kind of memory problems?" Daniel asked before Matthew could speak.

"I told them I . . . forgot being married to Emily."

Christopher actually gaped. "Why would you do that if it wasn't true?"

Matthew took a sip of brandy, then glanced to the empty doorway and lowered his voice. "Because . . . it was either that or tell the truth: that I'd met Emily only once, never married her before I left, and that she'd been lying to them about being my wife all along."

The silence was abnormally long. Christopher's expression went from stunned to furious, and Matthew knew it was because he took her behavior as a threat to the family.

But Daniel just started to laugh, and he continued until he was wiping his eyes. Christopher gave him an annoyed look, but Matthew couldn't help smiling as he shook his head in exasperation.

"Why wouldn't you just tell the truth the moment you returned?" Christopher demanded.

"I understand why," Daniel said, saluting Matthew with his glass. "It goes back to scandal, dear cousin, and your avoidance of it at all cost."

Matthew lifted his glass in return.

"Truthfully?" Christopher said, mouth agape. "You let a criminal have the triumph of her lies, you *pretended* to be married, all to avoid a scandal?"

"Well, that's not the *only* reason," Matthew said with amusement.

Daniel grinned. "Upon meeting Emily, I would have gone along with the pretense as well. Does she share your bed?"

"That's not the point!" Christopher cried, then swore, flinging his chair back and crossing the room to close the drawing room doors.

"She's not a criminal," Matthew said.

Daniel's grin deepened.

Christopher groaned as he sat back down. "You're falling for her."

"I haven't slept with her," he insisted.

"But you want to," Daniel said with a knowing smirk.

"I've had her investigated." He explained how he'd rescued her from drowning, and his belief in her desperation to survive. "I *told* her to come here for help. I just don't yet know why she posed as my wife."

"And you haven't discussed it with her," Christopher said heavily. "You've let this farce go on for days trying to figure her out."

"But don't you already have a wife?" Daniel asked slowly, his smile fading. "Your mother told us so last year."

"How did she—oh, now I remember," Matthew said. "I sent a letter home about it. Good Lord, I set my family up for Emily's charade."

"And the other wife?" Christopher prodded.

"She's dead." Matthew was surprised that he sounded weary rather than angry. Perhaps if he'd questioned Rahema more, she wouldn't have been so desperate, either. Had she been too frightened to confide in him—just like Emily?

Christopher put a hand on his shoulder. "I am sorry to hear about your wife."

"Which one?" Daniel asked softly.

Matthew gave a quiet laugh.

"So what is your plan?" Christopher asked. "What do you intend to do with her?"

"I—" And then Matthew stopped. "I don't really know."

"You're going to reveal her, of course," the duke continued.

"And turn the whole family upside down? Open up another new Cabot scandal?"

"You weren't here for either of ours," Daniel said dryly. "It's your turn."

Ignoring Daniel, Christopher spoke in a measured voice. "But you don't want to lose her."

Matthew shrugged.

"You can't just pretend to be married forever," Christopher said sternly. "Lies always surface."

"I know. I want the truth from her, willingly. I think she might almost be there. She loves my parents and sisters."

Daniel narrowed his eyes. "How do you know?"

"I just do."

"Be very careful, Matthew," Daniel continued. "She fooled our entire family; she fooled your parents, who were with her all the time. She is a very good actress." But the moment must have been too sober for him, for he added, "But then Chris might give you some direction on that. His wife did a very good job fooling him. She pretended to be a house party guest, all while investigating him for her father's newspaper."

Matthew smirked, glad for the change of subject. "Tell me about that, Chris. I'm glad to know I'm in good company where women are concerned."

Several hours later Matthew's cousins were almost too drunk to make their way to their rooms. They shushed each other and tried not to laugh as they staggered down empty corridors. Daniel and Matthew had to practically hold Christopher until they saw him to the master chamber.

Matthew wasn't quite as inebriated. When he was alone, he remembered Emily's concerns about Reggie. He went to find his friend, and to his surprise, Reggie was donning his overcoat, about to leave his room.

Matthew stood in the door, holding the jamb so he wouldn't sway. "Going somewhere?"

Reggie grinned. "I bet you wish you could go with me, like the old days."

Strangely, he didn't, but wouldn't say so. He shut the door behind him. "I thought you should know that Emily came to me about finding you outside our bedroom door."

"Really?" Reggie said, pausing in the center of the room. "I would have thought our encounter worthy of secrecy."

"Me, too. But she's suspicious, and obviously wants *me* to be suspicious—even if it makes her place here more perilous."

"Bold of her."

"Yes, we've known that from the beginning," Matthew said dryly. "But . . . let me deal with her. You don't need to bother yourself." And in that moment he realized he was feeling protective toward Emily, which was truly strange. He had sworn to himself that he would never feel that way about another woman—especially one who was lying to him.

Reggie's lips quirked with amusement. "Trust me, I don't wish to interfere."

"Busy, are you?" Matthew responded idly.

"Very. Important meeting tonight."

"At midnight?"

"Those are the most important kind." Reggie touched the brim of his hat, moved around him and left the bedroom. Matthew followed, shutting the door, watching his friend walk briskly away. What was Reggie doing with himself late into the night? Surely a woman had to be involved.

In his suite, Matthew swayed and caught the bedpost as he looked down at his own woman, his slumbering "wife."

"You've escaped me tonight, sweetheart," he murmured, sober enough to know he wanted to remember the first time he bedded Emily. "But I won't wait *another* night, I vow. And then you'll tell me everything."

Chapter 17

In the morning, Emily left a slumbering Matthew undisturbed. She wrinkled her nose at the smell of alcohol, but shook her head in amusement. She was glad he had his cousins.

Tonight was the Madingley ball, where all the local gentry and nobility would gather to officially welcome Matthew home. But first she would teach her students. She was not going to imprison herself in the house, waiting for something else to happen. Stanwood had shown her that he could get to her anywhere—and she wanted the confrontation over with. She decided to drive the carriage into Comberton. Ever since she felt she was followed—even though it was only Matthew—she'd realized that she was too vulnerable on foot.

The children gave her great joy. For the first time in years she had a purpose, building and guiding the little village school community. Even after a new schoolmaster was hired, she planned to remain involved.

In the early afternoon she gathered her books together after the children had been dismissed. Walking across the entrance hall, she nodded absently at the innkeeper, and out of habit glanced into the taproom—

And froze in place, the books clutched to her chest. Arthur Stanwood was sitting alone at a table, smiling at her, his teeth so white, his hair so black about his thin face.

Her brain seemed unable to process anything but *Run!* Yet she knew she couldn't. He wanted her to be afraid, to cower, to give in to him. He thrived on it. But she wasn't that same vulnerable girl he'd used.

He lifted a hand and calmly gestured for her.

Keeping her expression cold, her back stiff, she walked toward him until only the table remained between them. He stood up, all politeness.

"Hello, Emily."

The sound of his voice made her shudder. She took a deep breath and met his eyes, pale gray as ice.

"Well, now aren't you brave," he said softly. "Do sit down, Emily."

She pulled out a chair and perched on the edge of it, the books still clutched to her chest. When she realized how frightened that made her seem, she deliberately set the books on the table, proud that her hands weren't shaking.

He sat back down opposite her. "I read about your *husband*," he said, emphasizing the word.

"So you said."

Lowering his voice, as if politely confidential, he continued, "What a happy coincidence that he is alive, for I seem to remember you only claimed to be his wife once he was dead."

"I *am* his wife," she said through gritted teeth.

He tsked softly. "I did my research on you, my girl. I know when he rescued you from drowning—and I know when his ship left. He didn't marry you. And if he had—wouldn't you have gone to the bosom of his family?"

"I did."

"No, you tried desperately to support yourself. And I gave you decent employment, didn't I?"

She said nothing.

"Didn't I?" His voice took on a touch of menace.

She nodded.

"And all I wanted was a little kindness," he said sadly.

"But you want something else now."

"You have a secret, and you don't want anyone to know."

"I do not have a secret. I'm married—otherwise my husband would have denied me on his return."

He regarded her intently, and his gaze almost

felt like a violation when it settled on her mouth.

"An excellent try, Emily, but I don't believe you. I don't know how you convinced him to let you stay—or perhaps it was what you *did* for him."

He grinned without restraint, and she knew that if anyone had been looking at him, they would have seen the kind of man he was, evil, conscienceless. But there was only one other couple in the taproom, and they were eating at a table behind him. She could hear the innkeeper talking with a customer in the entrance hall. They were all innocent people, and she would not involve them.

"Or perhaps," Stanwood continued with exaggerated thoughtfulness, "Captain Leland didn't want to embarrass his family. Whatever the reason, I'm afraid you've made him vulnerable, my girl. And what a nice family he has."

"Leave his family alone—leave his friends and servants alone. I don't know who you coerced into helping you invade the house, but I want it stopped."

"Coerced? Whatever are you talking about, Emily?"

"Do not think you can make me believe you're acting alone. You don't have that kind of power."

He grinned. "I have enough power to stop you."

"Who's helping you!"

His smile vanished, and though he didn't move a

muscle, he suddenly seemed even more threatening.
"Lower your voice. I will only tell you what you
need to know."

Inhaling swiftly, she said, "Then stop trying to
scare me and just tell me what you want."

He cocked his head. "I'm not certain what I want
yet. I'll make a decision soon. Perhaps I should
attend the ball tonight, to make a more *informed*
decision."

"They will not admit you without an invitation."

He gave her a withering stare, as if saddened that
she underestimated him. He leaned toward her. "I'll
want money. Plenty of it."

"But I don't—"

"Then start thinking of where you'll find it."
He got to his feet. "What a lovely village you have
here—and such sweet children you teach."

She blanched as if he'd told her which child he
meant to target.

"I shall see you soon, Emily."

And then he left the taproom. She didn't bother
to watch him go, only sat for a moment, trying to
remember how to breathe evenly.

It was obvious he did not mean to reveal her as an
imposter, she thought, staring blankly at the hearth,
where the coal grate gave off meager warmth. He
only wanted money.

But how much, and how was she supposed to get
it? Steal it from Matthew and his family, who'd only

been good to her? The thought made her sick. She could only wait for Stanwood to contact her again, and find some way to talk him out of it, to convince him that she was incapable of stealing without giving herself—and him—away.

Hugging herself, she wanted to laugh at how foolish she'd once been to think she could outrun her past, to feel that she was safe with the Lelands.

When Matthew entered the dressing room to prepare for the ball, Emily gave a cry, then put a hand against her wardrobe as she breathed rapidly.

"I am sorry if I startled you," he said in amusement.

Her face seemed a bit too pale as she nodded.

"Emily, is something wrong?"

She smiled. "Nothing is wrong," she said lightly. "We are only holding our first Society ball since I've been married to you. Why should I be nervous?"

He grinned and walked toward her, staring at the assortment of gowns hung in her wardrobe. "Choosing what you'll wear?"

"It is not a difficult choice," she answered. "I did not purchase that many ball gowns since coming out of mourning."

Her breathing gradually eased, but her color didn't return. There were marks of strain visible by wrinkles between her eyes. He had not thought a ball would make fearless Emily nervous. Or perhaps she was worried about Reggie revealing her secrets. *No,* Matthew thought. He would never allow them to be revealed to others—he wanted her secrets all to himself.

"What will you wear?" she asked.

He blinked at her. "My evening clothes, of course."

She tilted her head. "Not your uniform?"

He met her eyes then, understanding. "No. I won't be going back to the army."

As a pretend wife, she should look happy, but instead she studied him too closely.

"I didn't realize you had made your decision," she said.

"My father is not getting any younger. I would like him to be able to concentrate on his research, while I handle our investments. Even Chris asked for my assistance with his vast holdings. And besides, why would I want to leave you?"

For just a moment there was a bleakness in her gaze, but her smile wiped it away. Why was she revealing what she was usually so good at hiding?

"Is your maid here?" he asked, glancing toward the open bathroom.

Emily shook her head. "She'll be here soon. She's so good with styling hair that I lent her to Grace and Abigail."

He moved close, until her back was against the wardrobe, her head tilted toward him. He couldn't resist cupping the slim length of her neck, rubbing his thumb along her jaw and cheek.

She inhaled, her lashes fluttered. He loved how responsive she was to his slightest touch, the way she trembled as he continued to stroke her.

He leaned down and kissed her temple, speaking against the soft tendrils of hair. "Tonight will be a special night, Emily."

She put a hand on his chest, and he didn't know if she was steadying herself—or wanting to touch him. Just the thought of the latter made him hard.

With his mouth lightly against her ear, he whispered, "Tonight I will be reintroduced to Society—and reintroduced to the intimacy of your bed."

He heard her faint moan, saw that her hand clutched the lapel of his coat. He nuzzled his face against hers, then kissed the shell of her ear, and behind it on her neck. She arched, letting him have his way.

"Yes," she suddenly whispered, her hand pulling him closer. "Yes."

Desire almost overpowered him. It was all he could do not to throw her onto their bed and tear her clothes off. But no, he didn't want to be rushed, knowing he would be interrupted by family members or servants eager to see them at the ball. He wanted to enjoy every moment of his seduction of Emily, anticipating it, drawing it out, until both of them were mad with passion.

He kissed her then, showing her with his lips and tongue how much he desired her. She answered him without hesitation, with a touch of desperation that aroused him even more. She entered his mouth with urgency, put her arms around his neck to clasp him hard against her. He pushed her back against the wardrobe, his hips seeking hers. They groaned into each other's mouths—

And didn't hear the knock on the door.

"Oh!" cried a feminine voice. "I will return later."

Matthew lifted his head, not looking at the little maid, Maria. "No, my wife needs you." He stepped back, meeting Emily's stunned gaze.

Emily blushed, and he turned and went to the other bedroom, where the valet he seldom used had already laid out his evening clothes. Smart man, giving the women the dressing room on such an important evening.

It would be important in so many ways.

Chapter 18

When Matthew entered the ballroom with Emily on his arm, he saw every pair of eyes turn toward them. Thousands of candles glowed above them in their globe lamps, artificial roses festooned every column, but none of it was as beautiful as Emily, so poised, so serene as she stood at his side.

Her gown was a demure navy blue velvet. He imagined her intention on purchasing it had been to remain unnoticed. But she didn't seem to realize that the dark color set off her pale skin, and made her champagne blond hair shine like a precious metal. The bodice was cut straight across, showing the fine bones of her shoulders and just the beginning swells of her breasts, making a man only think of seeing the rest. Her chin was lifted and a faint smile curved her sweet lips. But her face was still pale. Surely she knew all these people, so why should she be nervous?

From the moment of their arrival they were surrounded by eager guests, who—briefly—deserted the receiving line in front of the duke. Emily never left his side, helping him by greeting people by name if he didn't do so immediately. For at least an hour it was a blur of becoming reacquainted, of hugs and curtsies and bows, and over it all, well wishes for his renewed marriage to their "dear Emily."

He only wanted to call her "lover." He met her gaze often and smiled knowingly, until he made her blush each time.

They led the quadrille at the upper end of the ballroom, the place of honor. When he performed the steps perfectly, Emily beamed at him. Instead of pale, she now seemed quite animated, almost too excited. Was she anticipating the end of the evening as much as he was?

But it was during the waltz where he tried to make her see that the two of them were all that mattered. Though they began the dance at the prescribed distance apart, he felt like he was falling into her eyes as they began to whirl around the ballroom. He liked the strength in her back as she moved, and the confidence of her hand in his. She was a true partner, not a decorative doll to be led about. Without realizing it, he pulled her closer through the turns, then allowed their thighs to brush. Though Emily blushed, she never stopped looking at him. When his thigh dipped between hers, her eyes became dreamy and her pink lips parted. He almost kissed her right in front of everyone.

Only when the music ended did he realize that they'd become the center of attention. Most of the dancers had retreated to the edge of the floor. Now everyone applauded, and he bowed as Emily swept into a deep curtsy. His family was clustered together, and he saw many of them wiping their eyes. Then he looked down at Emily, so beautiful, so willing, and only let himself think of the coming night in her arms. He kissed her gloved hand and led her to the refreshment room that opened off the ballroom.

After handing her a glass of champagne, he clinked his own to hers. "Be glad you're not one of the unmarried girls being put on display; otherwise you'd have to fortify yourself as best as you were able with lemonade."

"There's nothing wrong with lemonade," she murmured, looking out over the crowd as they energetically danced a daring polka.

They were near a bank of exotic flowers from the Madingley greenhouses, and he used their edge of concealment to put a hand on Emily's waist. She gave a little start but did not cease studying the crowd.

"Looking for someone?" he asked, letting his fingers drift down over her hip.

She took a deep sip of her champagne. "No."

He loved how with just a touch he could affect her.

"There is Lady Rosa," she said abruptly.

He sighed. He did not want to be thinking of his mother when he was seducing his wife.

"She is like a butterfly among them," Emily continued softly, a fond smile on her lips.

"A butterfly?" he echoed with amusement.

But he found himself watching Lady Rosa as she floated from couple to group, her hands moving animatedly as she spoke, her smile glowing. Professor Leland remained with the other members of the family, but Matthew saw him watching his wife, his expression one of fond contentment.

"Your father seldom accompanies your mother as she speaks to people," Emily said, her head tilted as she studied them.

Matthew glanced at her. "What?"

"Haven't you noticed their deliberate separation? He watches her, but they remain apart when they socialize at dances. Being a widow"—she laughed up at him—"and a stranger in Society, I didn't have the opportunity to dance as much, so I had time to observe them."

"What about all your suitors?" he asked, admitting to himself how jealous he was that other men had spent more time with her than he had.

She smiled and batted her lashes coquettishly. "There were only a few of them. They could not take up a whole evening of dancing." She looked back across the ballroom floor at Lady Rosa and spoke softly. "Twenty years have passed since the scandal that shook the trust in their marriage. Your father might not admit it, but he deliberately hangs back and lets her socialize as she wishes. I think he believes he's trying to help, but he's wrong. They're both worried too much about how others feel about the scandal in their past."

Hadn't that been his own problem? Matthew mused. He'd always cared too much what others thought. But he'd gotten over it. Perhaps his parents would do the same.

And then he exchanged a surprised glance with Emily, for the professor was leading Lady Rosa onto the dance floor.

"They don't usually dance together," Emily said, eyes wide.

"I know."

Then Emily and Matthew were separated by the duke and duchess, who each claimed the next dance. When it was over, Matthew returned Abigail to her husband, who was speaking to Emily.

Already he was tired of sharing her, although the night was young and the orchestra hadn't even halted for a supper announcement yet. He smiled at Christopher, and without a word took Emily's hand and led her away.

While Christopher laughed, Emily restrained

herself, her eyes alight. "But I was talking to your cousin," she said to Matthew.

"And I'm finding myself overheated from all this dancing. Let's go out on the terrace."

On an autumn night, the glass doors were thrown wide open to allow air to bathe the dancers. Many other couples strolled in the torchlit darkness. The music faded a bit, no longer assaulting their ears. Matthew led her to the balustrade, where they could look out over the gardens. They were lit with globe lamps hung from the trees along the paths, but he did not see many people taking advantage of the privacy, which fit in well with his plans.

When he tried to pull Emily toward the stairs, she resisted. "Why can't we stay here?"

"It's too public," he said. He leaned closer. "And I'm going to put my hands on you in a very inappropriate manner for public display."

Her mouth sagged open and her eyes glazed over as the torches reflected in them. Then she seemed to shake herself.

"I'll be too cold," she protested.

"I'll keep you warm." He tugged again, and she took several hesitant steps until they reached the top of the great stone staircase that flowed wider and wider until it reached the ground.

"So you'd like me to carry you?" he asked.

She gave him a strained smile, and Matthew realized that she was only humoring him.

He took both her hands. "You don't wish to be alone with me?"

She squeezed his hands. "It's just . . . this night is about you, and if we go out there in the dark, we'll come back disheveled. I don't wish to embarrass your family."

"I think they'll believe it's about time."

But he relented, instead drawing her farther down the terrace, where the torches ended and the shadows deepened. She gladly came into his arms, raising herself on her toes to kiss him. Her willing warmth was a seduction itself, and he lost himself in the sweet way her tongue explored his mouth, then met his. She'd learned quickly what pleased him, and he thought of how much more he wanted to share with her.

"Soon," he whispered against her mouth.

Waiting proved the hardest, for at last he had to take her back inside. Emily stopped before him so suddenly that he ran into her back.

"Is something wrong?"

She looked over her shoulder and smiled. "Do you see Susanna?"

It was difficult for him to think of anyone but Emily, but at last his mind refocused and he remembered his sister and his efforts to help her find happiness. Feeling guilty, he followed Emily's gaze and saw Susanna, several gentlemen in attendance.

"Besides Peter, I recognize those men," Matthew said. "They attended our picnic yesterday."

"You should feel eminently successful."

Although they could not hear the conversation, they could see Susanna looking between the men, speaking politely but with little animation. Gradually, Matthew realized that she wasn't enjoying herself.

"Damn," he murmured softly.

Emily reached behind her to touch his arm. "Give her time. This is all overwhelming."

"How overwhelming can it be for a twenty-six-year-old who was born into the household of a duke?"

Emily said nothing, and they continued to watch. Two of the gentlemen left, leaving Peter Derby, who spoke to Susanna, his face composed and serious. Another man approached, and Peter displayed a look of brief impatience before smiling politely. Susanna continued to cast glances at Peter even as she spoke with the newcomer.

Then it was just Peter and Susanna, and they left the ballroom together.

"Are we supposed to be happy with this result?" Emily asked dubiously.

"I don't know. If it were me in my more repressed days, and I was able to be alone with a woman, I would always behave like a gentleman."

Her voice sounded subtly amused as she said, "But now?"

"We should go to Susanna."

Though she was obviously holding back laughter, it soon faded from her face as they made their way through the crowd and away from the ballroom. The trouble was, Susanna could have gone with Peter—anywhere.

Emily seemed to read his mind. "Besides sketching in the laboratory—where she would hardly take a man—she enjoys painting in the conservatory."

"Let's go."

As they entered the library, the conservatory doors on the far side of the room slammed open and Peter walked out, looking furious.

Matthew felt his gut tighten, his hands ball into fists. What had happened with Susanna?

Emily again touched his arm, quickly whispering, "They weren't alone together for long."

A brief look of anger and frustration twisted Peter's expression when he saw Emily. It faded to impassivity as he nodded to Matthew.

Though Matthew wanted to confront Peter, he let him go. He'd seen how pinched and white Emily's face had become just before she increased her step to enter the conservatory. Good God, could the man hold a grudge against Emily just because he had returned from the dead to squash his courtship?

They found Susanna standing near the central fountain, wiping away tears.

"What happened?" Matthew demanded.

She groaned and looked away. "Nothing happened," she snapped. "And that's the problem."

Matthew sent a bewildered stare at Emily, who took hold of his sister's shoulders.

"Susanna, tell me," Emily said quietly.

"I'm trying to do what you both want!" she said to Emily, then repeated it as she faced Matthew. "What else do you want me to do? But I feel— nothing! These men now gather around me—I'm not different, you know. I only stopped wearing my spectacles and moved away from the wall. It was enough to make them remember I'm related to a duke," she said bitterly.

"That's not true," Matthew said.

"And don't forget how blind men can be," Emily said, her voice soothing.

"Excuse me?" Matthew was hoping to lighten the mood.

The women ignored him.

"Sometimes they only see what's obviously in front of them," Emily continued. "And now they see you."

Susanna found a handkerchief in her sleeve and blew her nose. "What's wrong with me? Other girls go on and on about the excitement of a man looking at them, but I never feel that way, not even with Mr. Derby, who I once thought I cared for a great deal."

"Then he's not the right man," Emily insisted. "You can't find him in a week's time, Susanna."

Susanna hugged herself, looking miserable. "I just want my old life."

"It was safe, wasn't it?" Emily spoke matter-of-factly.

Matthew glanced at her in surprise.

"No risk involved," Emily continued.

And then she looked at Matthew, and he couldn't look away. He and Emily were both drawn to risks, powerfully attracted to them. It crackled between them so much he could almost let himself be consumed—if he weren't so aware of his sister's pain.

"That's not fair," Susanna murmured.

Emily nodded. "Perhaps not. But it's the truth. How will you know if you can find happiness unless you risk everything?"

Susanna looked between them, and whatever she saw made her take a deep breath, even as her shoulders sagged. "Very well, I'll keep trying to find someone who intrigues me."

"Good," Matthew said firmly. "The right man is out there."

She gave a faint smile. "If *you* could find the right woman, then there's hope for me."

Emily chuckled while Matthew pretended to sputter a protest.

He was leading the two women into the ballroom

just as supper was announced. He steered them to the dining room and adjoining drawing rooms, where tables overflowed with food, gold plate glistened in sumptuous displays, and people stood about as they ate and talked. Susanna, composed once again, left them to join several of the young women she'd painted with at the picnic.

When Matthew went to fill Emily a plate, he returned to find her talking to someone he recognized well. Miss Sanborn was a woman he'd once flirted with, coming close to a courtship but not quite, because he'd considered himself far too young to settle on one woman.

She was beautiful, with her dark hair and flawless skin, he thought, as he paused before approaching them. He remembered her as being rather free with her affection, a little too loud, a little too in love with Society's entertainments. He realized that he would much rather be married to Emily, quietly intelligent, hardworking, yet strong-willed enough to do what she had to in order to survive.

And in that moment, he'd had his fill of sharing her with everyone else. He couldn't wait any longer to have her, needed to get her alone—regardless of the risks he had to take.

Emily's face lit when he approached. "Captain, surely you remember Miss Sanborn."

It took every bit of control he had to make small talk, hear about her fiancé, all the while watching

Emily eat, watching her mouth. When enough time had passed for the sake of politeness, he led her out of the dining room, avoiding family, avoiding people he knew too well.

"Matthew?" she called from behind him. "Surely you're hungry—"

He just looked at her over his shoulder, and her eyes went wide and she grew silent.

Emily hurried through the house with Matthew, leaving guests behind, all because his eyes had looked at her with such dark hunger that she'd lost any will of her own. His black evening clothes should have made him seem stiff and formal, but instead made her think of the sensual man beneath and the intimacies he was about to share with her. Dancing in his arms had been like a cherished dream. He'd watched her so intently, even while conversing with friends and family, that she'd been breathlessly aware of him all evening.

Yet always, there had been moments when she watched the crowd or scanned the dark gardens, looking for black hair and an evil, knowing smile. But she never saw Stanwood, and hoped he would not risk attending the ball.

But she would not think of that now, she told herself. She was safe with Matthew as they went up the broad staircase to the family wing. She had to hurry to keep up with him, her skirts flying out behind her, her hand hot in his.

And then he pushed her past him into their bedroom, shutting the door behind him and leaning
against it to just stare at her. A lamp glowed on the
bedside table, softly lighting his white cravat and
shirt. Her mouth was dry and her body trembled
with excitement and anticipation and desire so
heady she hadn't imagined a woman could feel this
way without being feverish.

The dressing room door suddenly opened, making
her jump.

Maria looked in. "Mrs. Leland—" Then she saw
Matthew and gasped.

"She won't need you," Matthew said in a low
voice. "And I won't need a valet."

"Yes, Captain."

And the door shut.

Emily gave a low laugh.

Without saying another word, he loosened his
cravat and stripped it off, then started on the buttons of his waistcoat. She said nothing, did nothing, just watched him, as if disturbing the moment
would end everything between them. He slid his
tailcoat and waistcoat off, then pulled his shirt over
his head. She'd seen his chest before, but that didn't
stop her from inhaling sharply and staring at his
muscular body, so very different from hers. His
scars were too white, and she couldn't miss them,
but they didn't matter to her—they never had.

He kicked off his evening shoes, then sat on the

edge of the bed to remove his stockings, never breaking eye contact with her. When he stood back up, his hands were already at the buttons on the front flap of his trousers.

She fisted her hands, so tense with expectation that she wanted to cry out for him to hurry.

He finished unbuttoning, then bent as he pulled off the trousers and drawers. When he stood up and walked toward her, some distant sense of self-preservation reminded her that as his wife she would have seen all this before, that she shouldn't stare too much. Then again, surely he would think his wife would look for more scars. But the scars on his left side faded away as they crossed his hip bone.

His sex was erect with his desire for her—she'd caused that, had made him want her so much that he'd left a party in his honor, deserted his family, all to be alone with her.

Matthew stopped in front of her, and she could barely control her breathing. He lifted a finger and very slowly ran it along where her neckline met her skin, shoulder-to-shoulder. She shuddered, eyelids fluttering—even though he could have practically touched her the same innocent way in public.

But when a naked man touches one's skin, it takes on another level of meaning.

"A demure bodice," he murmured, eyes on her body. "But the little I could see . . ." He slowed to rub his finger over and over the very top of her breast. ". . . made it more enticing than any other woman's overly displayed cleavage."

Breathlessly, she said, "I—I chose it hoping to dissuade suitors."

"It didn't work."

Suddenly, he turned her around and began to press his lips along the column of her neck. Bending her head away from him, she let him do as he willed, even as his hands unhooked the ball gown and slid it down her torso. The sleeves were tight, and she pulled her arms out so impatiently she could have torn the delicate fabric.

He chuckled against her neck, then gently bit her. She gasped.

Again his hands moved behind her, and she was torn between the tugging on her corset strings and the sensations of his mouth trailing down her shoulder. As the corset came loose, she took a deep, shuddering breath. He was watching over her shoulder, knew her breasts rose with each inhalation. She wanted him to touch them as he had before, but instead he pulled the corset down her body and she stepped out of it. She wanted him to see the low-cut front of her delicate lace chemise, but he wasn't leering over her shoulder anymore.

She felt his hands on her lower legs, and her lips parted in shock.

"Lift one foot," he murmured.

She did so, and he pulled it back to remove her slipper and stockings. She was so unsteady she put a hand on his shoulder before falling over from the sheer dizziness of overwhelming passion. How would she feel when he touched her more intimately?

Oh, she already knew—she remembered. The hot feeling of rising, uncontrolled passion she felt when he'd touched her between her thighs, when he'd nipped her breasts through her clothing—it had lived in her dreams—and daydreams—ever since.

And she wanted to experience it again so badly that when her second shoe was gone, she started to turn around.

"No." The word was a hoarse command.

But she wanted to see his face when he saw the sheer fabric of her chemise, so daring that she was almost embarrassed to look at herself in the mirror.

Then she felt his hands lift the hemline of her chemise. A hot, shaky feeling swept over her. His fingers caressed one ankle, yet . . . something was wrong. It felt wet and—

It was his mouth. He was kissing her ankle, then lifting her chemise and following the path up the back of her leg with his lips and tongue. She gave a low moan, catching herself in a hug about the waist, as if she could keep in all the excitement. She shuddered when he licked the back of each knee.

Surely he was going to stop, to finish taking off her chemise, to . . . and then she felt him lick a line between her closed thighs.

"Spread your legs," he whispered.

His breath on the wetness of her skin set off a ripple through her body. *Oh God* . . . But she did as he asked.

She closed her eyes, torn between shock and disbelief and arousal. As he continued kissing his way up the back of her thighs, she felt the cool draft across her backside, and knew he was looking—there. She wanted to squirm; she wanted to collapse.

"Turn around."

She gasped, and without volition, regardless of her shocked sensibilities, her body obeyed him. He was kneeling naked before her, holding her chemise bunched just at the top of her thighs. If the fabric moved at all he would be at eye level with . . .

Her thoughts simply faded away as she looked into his hazel eyes, half-lidded, dangerous. His gaze swept up her body, and his nostrils flared when he saw the sheer lace across her breasts. But he didn't stand up.

"Lift your chemise over your head."

With trembling fingers she took it and slowly raised it high, knowing he saw everything now. When she pulled it over her head, it dangled from her now lifeless fingers before falling to the floor.

She was naked, and so was he, and there was so much dark satisfaction on his face.

"Beautiful," he murmured.

She was trembling so violently, on fire with the need to be touched. But he had her in his control, obviously wanted to do things his own way, in his own time, so she said nothing.

And then he leaned forward and kissed her where before only his fingers had touched. She cried out with shock and searing pleasure, not knowing whether to push him away or clutch him closer. She hadn't imagined that anything like this existed between a man and a woman.

It was his turn to moan, and he licked her, pushing her thighs apart. She covered her mouth to stop her cries, but her moans were uncontained, and she shuddered with the sudden rising sensation of pleasure rippling through her, sensitizing every inch of her skin, seeming to burn her. She would have fallen if he hadn't held her up with one arm. And then he lifted his other hand and his fingers found her left breast, where he gently tugged and caressed her nipple.

The climax swept over her with more power than she'd remembered. She was shuddering over him, her body uncontrolled, responsive only to him.

As she fell, he caught her in his arms and swept her up to carry her to the bed. He laid her down, and then he was partially on top of her, the length of his body hot as he took her mouth in a demanding kiss. She clung to him, feeling his erection large and hot against her thigh, and she arched to press her naked breasts harder against his chest. His dark, fine hairs rubbed against her nipples. She wouldn't have thought it possible for her passion, so explosive, to begin to rise again, but it did, even as he kissed his way down her neck and for the first time took her bare breast into his mouth.

"Matthew!" she cried out, holding him to her, writhing beneath him.

She felt his hips settle between her thighs, felt him probing, even as his mouth moved to torment her other breast.

Then he came up on his arms above her, looked into her eyes, and thrust deep inside her.

And then he started moving, and she arched her back, crying out, "*Yes!*"

With a groan, he came down on top of her, where their mouths mated roughly, even as their bodies moved. She understood the rhythm almost immediately, meeting him, lifting herself with her heels so she could experience even more. Everything he did to her made her shudder and cry out, as she flung her head back and forth. She couldn't get enough of the feel of his skin over the hard muscle of his body, rippling so sinuously with his every movement. She loved his shoulders and chest, the very width of which made her feel so delicate and feminine. When she brushed his nipples, he inhaled sharply, and she gladly caressed him as he had done to her.

He drove into her deeper, even more out of control, his face contorted as he shuddered.

And then he collapsed upon her.

In that moment, she held him, felt the damp hair on the back of his neck as he pressed his face against her shoulder. She had succeeded in making him want her; she would have this intimate connection to him forever. And then she knew that it went beyond her need for protection—it was love that she wanted to offer him. Lifting her knees, she hugged his hips hard, wishing he never had to leave her body.

At last, Matthew lifted himself up on to his elbows. She smiled at him, framing his face in his hands. He was damp with perspiration, the hair on his forehead darkened with it. He looked as tired and sated as she felt, and it was a wonderful feeling.

His smile was faint. He studied her with such seriousness that she grew afraid that she'd done something wrong.

He slowly pulled out of her, and the shock of emptiness made her gasp. He sat back on his heels, looking down between her thighs. Embarrassed, confused, she started to close her legs, but he put his hands on her knees to stop her.

"Sit up," he said softly, reaching for her hands.

She told herself to remain calm. She didn't know what he was feeling, what he could be thinking.

When she was upright, he said, "Look down."

Her confusion vanished, to be replaced by understanding and regret. She'd had a plan all along for how to hide her innocence, but with her passion, she'd forgotten everything. Across the bedsheet, flecks of blood were scattered—the evidence of her virginity.

Chapter 19

Matthew stared at the bloodstain on the sheets, and his last fear that Emily might be under another man's control faded away. Relief and gladness swept through him. He'd been right about her. He'd trusted his intuition, and it hadn't failed him. She was simply a desperate, traumatized woman, and he wanted to help her.

He looked up into her face and almost winced. She'd gone chalk white, lips bloodless in fear. He didn't want her to feel that way about him.

But before he could speak, she spoke with regret. "I knew I was close to my monthly. I am so sorry it had to spoil such a wonderful evening."

He could only admire her composure in the face of such overwhelming evidence of her lies. When she folded her legs together and tried to leave the bed, he gripped her shoulders. At last he found a weakness, for she was trembling, but trying valiantly not to show it.

"Matthew, please, I need to clean myself." She spoke in a low voice.

"Emily, you cannot hide this from me. I knew the moment I took you that I was taking a virgin."

At last she met his eyes, hers full of incomprehension. He had to give her credit: she was an accomplished actress. But, of course, she'd had to fool so many people.

"Matthew, what are you talking about? It's been over a year since we were together. I just wasn't used to—"

"Emily!" He gave her a little shake. "Stop lying to me. It's over."

How could he make her trust him enough to tell him the truth? With a feeling of desperation, he wanted her trust, though he had no idea what it meant for their future.

At last he realized that the only way to get her to admit the truth was to tell her *his* truth.

"Over?" she whispered. "Matthew, I don't know what you mean. How can our marriage be over, after everything we shared this night?"

"There was no marriage," he said softly, gentling his hold, stroking her upper arms with his thumbs. "I came home with a perfectly sound mind to find you claiming to be my wife. To give myself time to discover the truth, I lied to everyone by saying I had amnesia."

Emily sat frozen, distantly surprised to feel that his hands were still gentle on her arms. She was naked in front of him—in more ways than one. The fear was creeping up on her, but she was so shocked, it didn't seem quite real . . . yet.

"Your memory—" She broke off.

Nausea threatened to overtake her, but she held it back, tried to pull away from him, but he wouldn't let her go.

"It's fine," he said softly. "My memories are fully intact. When I first arrived home, all I wanted was to make my family glad with the news that I lived. And then I found you claiming to be my wife. You can imagine what I thought."

He was actually smiling at her? she thought in stunned amazement. Smiling, as if this web of lies she'd begun and he'd embellished was . . . not important to him?

"Say something, Emily," he urged, searching her face. "You look too pale."

She suddenly felt so naked, and regardless of what he might think, she crossed her arms over her chest. She said in a low, even voice, "Was this your way of discovering if I was a virgin?"

His expression grew pained. "No! By this point I'd already assumed you were innocent, and yes, it confirmed it, but it wasn't why I—"

She pulled away from him to back up against the

pillows and headboard, tugging on the sheet until he lifted his hips to release it so she could cover herself.

He'd known she was a criminal. She'd been under suspicion from the moment he returned home. He'd known about her lies, manipulated her just as she'd been trying to manipulate him. With wonder, she studied him; she'd never guessed the truth.

But as always, she was alone; she could only rely on herself to solve her problems—and that included Stanwood.

She wanted Matthew to put clothes on. She didn't want to see his body, to know how she'd fallen in love with him—and was still going to keep lying to him. She couldn't deny part of the truth anymore, nor could she remain silent.

Trying to sound matter-of-fact, but letting some hurt through, she said, "So while I was trying to seduce you for protection, you were trying to seduce me for sport."

He rubbed his hand down his face. "Yes, at first. I couldn't believe the incredible masquerade you'd pulled off. I wanted to know everything about you."

"It sounds like you went along with me for jolly fun," she said bitterly.

"Well, yes. It was either that or throw you in jail."

She flinched, shocked by how close she'd come to that without even knowing it.

"But I never wanted to do that. My family loved you, and I reasoned that you could not be so terrible if you inspired that."

She gasped. "Then Lieutenant Lawton—"

Matthew nodded. "He knows the truth about you."

"You must have thought me a fool when I complained that he was following me."

"For what it's worth, I haven't had him follow you. I wanted to keep you all to myself."

That didn't make her feel any better. And didn't assuage her worries where the lieutenant's loyalty was concerned.

"I don't know how I feel now," Matthew continued, "except that we both wanted this." He reached for her. "Emily—"

She flinched away, tucking the sheet under her arms. The soft feelings she'd had for him seemed pointless now, foolish. What was wrong with her? She should be rejoicing. After all, he didn't seem at all angry with her betrayal.

She hadn't even made a mistake until she'd slept with him—and fallen in love with him. Of course, she'd never tell him of such ridiculous, useless emotions. How could there be love between two people who guarded their real selves? Even though she told herself she could make this work, why did she feel so badly?

"Why don't you hate me?" she whispered, hugging herself with both arms.

At last he took a blanket, wrapped it about his hips, then sat back down, facing her. She didn't know if the fact that he covered himself made her feel better or worse, but at least they were armored with clothing against one another.

"The more I came to know you," he said, his expression gentle, "the more I knew you could only do something like this out of desperation. At first I thought you might have tried to pass off a bastard as mine."

She winced.

"But there was no child," he said. "You took only a little of my wealth and used it for a school. You didn't want clothes or jewelry, or a Season meeting rich, eligible noblemen."

He took her hand.

Wearing a faint smile, he said, "I remembered you after you reminded me of the boating accident."

"I wasn't even in your company long. You don't truly remember anything about me."

"No, but I've listened to everything you've told me, and you can tell me the truth right now." He squeezed her hand a bit tighter. "Tell me, Emily."

She had to be careful what she confessed, and

hide what she still needed to. He would not let her stay if he knew about Stanwood's threat against his family. Her plans had certainly not changed, not with Stanwood out there, lurking like a spider, holding her with a web of threats.

"You owe me," Matthew said, wearing a faint smile.

Owe him? she thought, feeling a bit hysterical. Yes, she owed him, but hadn't she paid for it by offering up her innocence?

But she did owe him some of the truth. After all, he'd at last confessed his.

Leaving her hand in his, she met his gaze. "After the accident, although you were leaving for India, you seemed so concerned about me. I told you I had a cousin who would take me in. That wasn't quite true. I didn't feel right confiding my troubles to you, since it wasn't your place to worry about me. You were a stranger."

"So you had nowhere to go," he said.

The sympathy in his eyes made her feel like the lowest worm. If he only knew the evil she'd brought close to his family—no, he could never know.

"I have skills," she said defensively. "I am an expert seamstress. And that is how I made my living."

"And you tried for six months, but it wasn't enough, was it, Emily?"

Biting her lip, she shook her head.

"Then you remembered me, and my offer of help."

She gave a reluctant nod. "I talked to my vicar, Mr. Tillman. From the beginning he thought I should go to your family, but I was a stranger to them. I was determined to support myself."

"They would have helped you without all these lies," he said softly.

"I know." Her voice came out as a croak, and she had to clear her throat. She would not cry. "Mr. Tillman thought I needed more protection from unscrupulous men. When your name appeared on the casualty list, he insisted it was a sign from God that—that I should use the tragedy of your death to help myself."

In a voice filled with disbelief, he said, "Your *vicar* told you to pretend to be my wife?"

She nodded solemnly. "I swear I refused. I know you won't believe me, but I intended to ask for a bit of help, just a bit, and I would have been on my way."

"But Tillman sent a letter to my parents telling them you were my wife."

Wincing, she hung her head. "I didn't know! By the time I had recovered from my dreadful fever—it rained the whole time I traveled here—your mother had quite . . . fallen in love with the idea of having your wife with her." He opened his mouth, but before he could speak, she quickly said, "I am not using her as an excuse. You asked what happened, and I'm telling you. I was so . . . sick, so weary of being alone. Lady Rosa found the marriage license in my portmanteau—I had no idea it was there! Then I realized that Mr. Tillman had copied your signature from the letter you left for me. He was dead and I had no one. And your family was so kind. You were . . . dead, too, and I kept telling myself that I would leave soon, that I just needed to get strong again."

"Emily."

When she would have spoken, he covered her mouth with his fingers.

"And they fell in love with *you*, not just a woman they thought was my wife," he said softly.

Her eyes widened and she felt tears rise close to the surface. She ducked her head away from his touch. "And I fell in love with them. Growing up, I had never imagined I would ever be alone, not with three strong, healthy brothers. Then they were all just—gone, and my home was gone, entailed to a distant cousin. All of my possessions, my mementos of my parents, he took them all." Her voice shook.

Although her words were only partially the truth, and she was convincing him of her sincerity, she was surprised to feel guilty. But his acceptance was what she needed.

When he said nothing, she took a deep breath. "What are you going to do with me?" She had to know, so she could make new plans to counter his.

Matthew crawled up to sit beside her against the headboard, his arm touching hers. Did he think her cold? Did he think he was giving comfort? Instead all she could think of was the way he'd held her when they made love, when she'd been blissfully playing out their marriage as if it were real.

"I don't know what I'm going to do," he said at last. "If I pretend to divorce you, it will hurt my family."

She knew he'd been thinking all this through ever since he arrived home. And he still hadn't decided? At least she'd succeeded in distracting him, she thought with relief.

Lifting her chin, she played a hunch. "Don't think that you can seduce me again. We both know the truth now."

He flashed her an amused smile. "We also know how much we desire each other."

His gaze seemed so very heated, so possessive as it moved down her barely clad body.

"How can you want me, when you can't trust me?" she whispered. She was playing her wounded part, but it was far more difficult now. Lies upon lies upon lies.

He leaned over her, and she pretended to shrink back against the pillows, the sheet held tight to her chest. His nearness, the heat of him, made her melt inside with just a touch.

But he only bent his head and pressed a soft, brief kiss to her lips. "Trust has nothing to do with it."

Then he unwrapped the blanket from his hips and slid beneath the bedcovers. He didn't hide his arousal from her, nor did it seem he was going to act upon it, which disappointed her. But she could show patience, too.

Deliberately remaining unclothed, she sank beneath the blankets on her side of the bed. Coming up on her elbow, she blew out the candle, telling herself she wasn't hiding.

She chose her next words carefully. "So you'll continue to lie to your family?"

"Yes. And you will, too."

He had no problem with this—he truly *had* decided to do whatever he wanted with his life.

"Trust me, lying will wear on you," she said softly.

After a few minutes of silence, when she knew by his breathing that he wasn't asleep, she said, "While you were in India, you wrote your family that you were married." She heard his inhalation, but went ahead quickly. "I was worried that you had forgotten her, and that I was wrongfully taking another woman's place. If she needed you, then it would be my fault. I couldn't have lived with that. So I searched your trunk."

He sighed, but when he spoke, his voice was lightly amused. "You're very thorough, aren't you?"

She relaxed a bit. "All I found was one letter of condolence. I burned it. I had nowhere to hide it where it wouldn't be discovered. I'm sorry, Matthew. I didn't mean to treat lightly the memory of your wife. And now because of me you cannot even share your grief with your family."

"I would not be sharing my grief, regardless of you," he said impassively. "She's dead, she's in my past, and I don't need to talk about it. Good night, Emily."

She heard him roll over, and before she could even compose another question, he was softly snoring. It was that easy just to forget every revelation they'd exchanged? Of course, it hadn't been a revelation to him; he'd known about her lies from the beginning. Her mind returned to everything they'd done in the last few days so she could examine it all in a new light.

Matthew awoke to the now familiar morning ritual of Emily sleeping against his side. They were tangled pleasantly together, her knee between his, her arm flung across his chest.

But this morning she was naked, and that made everything so much better. Her smooth breasts were pressed against his side, and he could feel the warm moistness between her thighs against his hip.

He looked down at her face, so sweet in repose.

Much as she'd brought him infinite trouble, he really was back from the dead. All the lies had been revealed. Why couldn't they just start fresh, enjoy each other, and see what happened?

He came up on his elbow, letting his fingers smooth the blond hair back from her cheek. She wrinkled her nose, then began to move, stretching her body sleekly against his side. He could have groaned with the pleasure of it.

Blinking once or twice, she opened slumberous blue eyes and looked up at him. He smiled, and before she could overthink the situation, he leaned down and kissed her. Her lips were so soft, so sweetly plump. When he deepened the kiss hungrily, she pushed a hand against his chest.

"Matthew, don't!" she said firmly. "You know this can't continue."

"I don't see any harm in continuing as we are for now," he said, pressing kisses along her cheek and down her neck. He felt her stiffening but he didn't stop.

"I don't want to be just your mistress," she whispered.

He slid farther down her body, kissing the wings of her collarbones, the hollow in the center, then farther down to the warm valley between her breasts. "I've already paid for you with comfort and security. You accepted it. How can you be squeamish now?"

She said nothing for a moment, but how else did she expect to be treated after everything she'd set in motion?

He tugged the sheet a little farther, not quite uncovering the luscious peaks of her breasts. He ran his tongue along the edge. He could hear her breathing quicken. To stop any more protests, he tugged the sheet to her waist, baring the beautiful bounty of her bosom.

As he bent to them, she put her hand in his way. He arched a brow as he looked up at her across her naked body.

She was blushing, her lips parted with her ragged breathing, but she whispered urgently, "Matthew, I don't want a baby to become entangled in this mess!"

"There won't be a baby," he said, easily dismissing her concerns. "I was mindless last night, but I won't make that mistake again."

And then he began to slowly taste her nipples, licking and suckling until she writhed under him, her protests forgotten. The scent of her captivated him; the smooth, silky texture of her skin drew his fingers.

He rolled onto his back until she was above him, straddling him, her breasts bouncing until he thought he'd go mad if he couldn't have them again.

"Take me, Emily," he said hoarsely, arching his hips, letting her feel his erection between her thighs. He ran his hands over her thighs and hips, urging her to lift herself.

Her expression was full of innocence and passion and dawning understanding. He taught her to guide him into her, and when at last she sank onto him, surrounding him with her moist heat, they both gasped together.

"Am I hurting you?" he said.

"No." As she adjusted to the feel of him, she leaned forward on her hands and murmured hesitantly, "But then . . . I assumed it would hurt just the first time."

He held her hips still so he could focus on her. "And you hid your pain from me?"

She lowered her eyes. "I can't talk—like this."

The heat and tightness of her seduced away his senses, but he had a last moment of clarity. "Don't hide your feelings from me, not ever again."

She met his gaze, searching his, he knew. She didn't trust him. But they didn't need trust to enjoy each other, now that the truth had been revealed. He lifted her hips and pulled her down on him again to prove that to her. She moaned and arched back, taking him even deeper.

"Now you," he said, lifting himself up on his elbows until his lips just brushed her nipple.

She cried out his name and pushed her breast against him, but he dropped his head back.

"Move on me, use me to find what pleasures you, Emily."

And then she was moving, awkwardly at first, but when she found her rhythm, when she took the control away from him, he thought he'd die from the bliss. He molded her breasts with his hands, used his mouth to seduce delighted cries from her, all the while feeling his own pleasure rush over him. He held back, aching with the need to succumb as she increased the pace.

When he felt her release shudder through her body, he rolled until she was beneath him again, gave a couple thrusts that were too close to the edge, and then withdrew, climaxing against her thigh.

To his surprise, Emily held her arms about his shoulders, running her fingers through his hair.

He met her gaze at last. "No baby," he said, wearing a wry grin.

She nodded, her expression more solemn than his, but he understood. She was the one who would bear the burden, not him. But although she probably wouldn't believe it, he would never let her bear it alone.

"Now we need to face the day," he continued, wiping away his seed with a sheet, then rolling off her and bounding out of bed. It was amazing how good revelations—and sex—could make a man feel.

"Get up, sweetheart, so I can pull this sheet off the bed."

She frowned in confusion, so he picked her up and deposited her feet first on the floor.

"We don't want your maid to see the evidence of your virginity," he said.

Her blush swept right down her body, and he enjoyed the sight as he threw back the counterpane and blankets. "It is a shame we can't stay right here, but my family wouldn't understand. Or perhaps they would," he mused.

"But your cousins," she said too quickly. "They will only be here briefly."

"Trying to get rid of me, Emily?" he asked as he pulled the sheet from the bed.

It was a playful taunt, yet she paled again, and turned that delectable body away from him to shrug into her dressing gown. He swiftly put his arms around her from behind, then cupped her breasts before she could cover them.

"You can't take everything so seriously," he admonished, knowing that although she might resist his touch mentally, she quivered beneath his caresses.

She put her hands over his, holding them still against her. "This is my life, Matthew. It's all I have, and I've had to do terrible things to protect it. It isn't easy to know that my sins have become an amusement to you."

He gripped her hands, and pulled her even tighter against him. "Forgive me."

She gave a sad laugh. "Forgive you? There is nothing to forgive. I don't understand how you can forgive *me*."

She broke away from him and fled to the dressing room.

Chapter 20

Emily took a slow bath, hoping Matthew would come in, all naked and tempting. The more they could become enraptured with each other, the better for her.

Her stomach twisted with pain at her continued betrayal, but she had no choice. She told herself that she would make him happy, keep him from ever knowing about Stanwood. She wouldn't think about love; she didn't really even know Matthew, just as he didn't know her.

But never before had she met a man she wanted to know more than him.

And now she was beginning to know his body, and the magic he was capable of making her feel.

She knew he considered her secrets an amusement. He wanted the comfort of her in his bed, with no courtship, no commitment on his part. Though such a plan was tentative at best, she had no other choice.

She was his mistress. She owed everything to

him, from the roof over her head to the clothes on her back. She owed *him*.

And she owed it to him to keep him and his family safe.

Thank goodness it was Saturday and she did not have to make excuses for why she wouldn't leave the estate and teach school. Stanwood would have to wait to get her alone.

When she emerged from the dressing room after dismissing Maria, Matthew was waiting for her in their bedroom, dressed for the day.

He looked down her body, smiling. "You look lovely today."

"Thank you." His sweet words and attention soothed her. She'd worn a green gown with yellow ribbons, because it reminded her of spring, when everything seemed fresh and full of promise.

"Are you ready to greet the family at breakfast?"

She cocked her head. "And is there something special about it?"

"Only that now that we've been intimate, people will notice."

She laughed. "They will not. Nothing has changed, as far as they're concerned, and I intend to show them that."

Smiling, he put an arm around her shoulder. "You'll see. They'll be able to tell that things are better between us."

She felt a twinge of unease. But she was used to creating an illusion, showing others what they wanted to see. She would do as she always did.

They walked together down to the breakfast room, and as if to show her that he could affect her concentration on her role, he put her against the wall and kissed her quite thoroughly, until she was limp and trembling. The fact that he couldn't keep away from her made her feel happy and relieved.

When they heard giggling, Matthew didn't release her although she stiffened, her hands pressing on his chest as they both looked up. His sisters waved and retreated into the breakfast room, leaving them alone.

Emily sighed. "You did that on purpose, as if to prove to me that people would notice us. You didn't even give me a chance to behave as I always do."

"I don't want you to behave as you always do," he said, nuzzling beneath her ear. "You don't always have to be in control, Emily, not anymore."

"How can you say that?" she whispered back, still playing reluctant. "If I'm not in control, I'll slip up; I'll make a mistake, and then where would we be? You'd lose yourself the convenience of a mistress, and I would be banished, if not find myself in jail."

He stepped back and lifted her hands to kiss the back of both. "I won't let anything bad happen to you, sweetheart."

I won't let anything bad happen to you. Even though it was all a game to him. She was a new favorite toy that he could take out and play with. She had to make sure he couldn't do without her. *She* would be in control of her fate.

He took her arm and led her into the breakfast room, where the first thing she saw was a smirking Rebecca whispering to Daniel's wife, Grace. Emily knew Matthew's prediction about being noticed would come to pass.

"So there you are," Christopher said from the head of the table.

Matthew grinned. "And where else would we be?"

"I don't know about today," Daniel said dryly, "but last night, when I wanted to ask Emily for the pleasure of a dance, we couldn't find either of you anywhere."

Emily smiled, knowing she was blushing, the perfect response. She felt Matthew looking down on her with amusement. He was supposed to behave as if nothing unusual had happened.

Matthew shrugged. "I was surprised how wearying it was to renew acquaintances with several hundred people. Emily noticed that I had overextended myself and needed to rest."

She could barely keep from rolling her eyes. Lady Rosa and the professor exchanged a pleased look.

Though everyone else smiled, Emily was quite certain that Daniel and Christopher looked at each other with silent understanding, which confused her.

Daniel pulled out a chair and said, "Matthew, you had best rest yourself and save your strength, if you're so frail."

"He's not too frail to kiss Emily," Rebecca said, "right in the hall where anyone could see."

Matthew grinned at her. "I almost swooned in my weakness, and she was holding me up."

"With her lips," Susanna said, blinking at them innocently over her spectacles.

Emily laughed along with everyone else, playing her part. She'd spent a long time inhabiting the guise of Emily the Wife. It fit her like a glove now.

"If you are so frail, Matthew," she said, "perhaps I should fix you a plate at the sideboard."

"I'll manage with your help," he said.

He swung his heavy arm around her shoulder and let her lead him to the sideboard to a chorus of chuckles.

"You would never make a good actor," she said under her breath.

He leaned down to whisper in her ear, "Who is acting?"

She felt pleased at her triumph, but instead of showing it, gave in to an eye roll.

When they were seated at the table with brimming plates, Matthew turned to Daniel. "And why do I need my strength today?"

"My sister has a dubious plan," Christopher said, looking at Elizabeth.

She grinned. "I proposed an archery contest, so I could show off my new skills."

To Emily's surprise, Matthew shuddered. "You mean so you can find a new target to wound."

Elizabeth pouted prettily. "You have been gone too long. I am much better at it. Just ask Abigail, my teacher."

Abigail smiled. "She *is* much improved, but her brother hasn't given her the chance to prove it." She eyed her husband speculatively.

As everyone discussed the idea, Emily could only think of being outside, right in the open, where Stanwood could spy on them all.

Matthew watched Emily leaving the breakfast room with his sisters. He meant to follow, but he saw Reggie watching him thoughtfully. Catching Reggie's arm, he pulled him across the corridor to a little parlor, away from his cousins' excellent hearing.

He shut the door and turned around to find his friend still regarding him with interest.

"Do I look like a laboratory specimen, that you study me so?" Matthew asked dryly.

Reggie grinned. "You look . . . happy."

"I'm always happy."

"Then *particularly* happy."

"And you won't come right out and ask why?"

Reggie tilted his head. "Why would I demand answers of you? You owe me nothing."

"You have been my confidant in all this," Matthew said, lowering his voice as he walked toward his friend. "It's only right that you know that Emily and I talked about everything last night."

"Everything?" Reggie said, eyes widening.

"Even my false amnesia. I was right, you know. She was a desperate girl, unable to support herself. She didn't think she was harming anyone by coming for help. And she wasn't the one who created the fiction that she was my wife."

Reggie smiled. "And now she's very grateful."

That caused Matthew to pause, but he shook off the strange feeling. "We're both grateful."

"Then enjoy yourself, Matthew. You deserve it. I hope it lasts as long as you wish it to."

How long was that? Matthew wondered.

It was a mild, early autumn morning, so Emily and the other ladies were comfortable wearing shawls. The servants had set up a target against a bale of hay on the vast lawn outside the east wing of Madingley Court. Emily thought the target too near the woods, but all seemed to think their aim wouldn't be a problem.

The women chose bows, and Emily found herself standing beside Susanna, who looked at her bow dubiously.

"Is there a problem?" Emily asked.

"Only that I was never good at this. I didn't see the need to aim a pointy stick at a target, not when the countryside was there for me to draw."

Emily smiled. "It was the one sport I had a chance to compete with against my brothers. I practiced almost every fine day."

A large hand settled on her shoulder, and she tamped down her start of fear.

Matthew said, "You never told me you were an expert at this, Emily."

"It never came up."

"And *I* wouldn't have brought it up," he countered, "because I, too, had better things to do than aim a pointy stick at a target."

"Like what?" she asked, looking up at him.

That was a mistake, for the sun caught the red glints in his auburn hair, and his smile was merry and wicked. She knew she kept blushing, because every time she looked at him, she thought of him naked, and remembered the things he'd done to her with his mouth. Heavens, how did married people ever become used to this?

"Fencing is the manly sport," Matthew said with mock solemnity.

"You'll have to teach him, Emily," Susanna said,

elbowing her. "It's an embarrassment when one's brother can be bested by ladies."

"I think it appropriate that we can best him," Emily said.

"Then this will be the only time," Matthew insisted.

Susanna giggled, then turned and called out to the rest of their family and friends that Emily intended to teach Matthew archery.

Lieutenant Lawton was there, Emily saw, watching them too closely. Had Matthew confided in him yet again? Did the lieutenant know she'd complained about him to Matthew? She didn't want to intrude on their friendship—especially if Lieutenant Lawton might resent her. If he was the one working with Stanwood, his anger could make everything worse.

When they stood alone, she said to Matthew, "So you truly cannot shoot an arrow. You're not making this up?"

He grinned. "You mean like I made up all the other things for you to teach me?"

She gave an exaggerated sigh. "The layout of the Madingley grounds—I cannot believe I fell for that! How to kiss—please. I pitied you and felt guilty all at the same time."

Softly, he caressed her cheek with the back of his fingers. "And now you're angry at me for the deceptions."

She met his eyes. "It isn't right for me to be angry, so I won't be."

"You can just make unwanted emotions go away?"

She said nothing for a moment, for she knew it wasn't that easy. "You claim you're not angry with me, that you've forgiven me. Perhaps *you* haven't really succeeded in making your emotions go away."

She walked toward the archery targets before he could respond. Soon, the men were discarding their coats and rolling up their sleeves, taunting each other with their prowess, even Matthew, though he boasted about skills he thought would be easy to acquire.

She could not help noticing that Mr. Derby was watching Susanna, his expression unusually somber. Susanna glanced at him occasionally, seeming hesitant, even contrite, but she never went to him. Emily didn't interfere, knowing she'd done enough—at least as far as Mr. Derby was concerned.

Approaching the gathering of men, Emily put her fists on her hips and said, "Matthew, you cannot continue to boast when you have nothing with which to back it up. Come with me, please."

The older people, sitting beneath the shade of a pavilion, laughed and cheered her on. Matthew followed her as if chastised, then insisted she explain every skill in detail. She didn't know the true extent of his ignorance, or if he was hiding it with playfulness, but she went along with it all, entertaining the crowd.

She hadn't realized that standing so close to his back, adjusting his arms as he aimed the bow, would take such concentration on her part. It was too easy to forget what she was doing, to stare at the veins in his bare lower arms, so different from hers, to want to smooth her hands across the broad width of his back. She wanted to run her fingers through his hair, to put her arms around his waist.

Oh, she was so ensnared by her desire for him.

When at last one of his arrows hit the edge of the target, she announced his training a success and retreated from him to get her breath back. He looked over his shoulder at her, his grin saying he knew exactly what she was doing, what she was thinking.

How hard was it going to be to keep things hidden from a man who wanted to know her far too well?

She tried to focus on the contest, smiling with the others when every arrow Susanna shot went wide into the woods. Elizabeth was the queen of the day, showing off her new skills. Emily listened with amusement as the family related the various people Elizabeth had almost shot with her first attempts years before. Emily played down her own skills, allowing Elizabeth to win. When Matthew looked at her knowingly, she tossed her head in a saucy manner.

Without thinking of the consequences, she volunteered to find Susanna's arrows. The trees soon enclosed her, cooling the air, making her regret discarding her shawl. The happy voices faded.

And then she heard a branch crack behind her.

She froze. No one else had said they were assisting her. Had someone changed their mind? Lieutenant Lawton? Mr. Derby? Even one of the servants?

"Hello?" she called. When no one answered, she added, more quietly, "Are you looking for arrows?"

The breeze rose, and so did the hairs on the back of her neck. Someone was out there, too close.

Had Stanwood been so brazen as to enter the Madingley grounds?

Though she had only one arrow in hand, she knew she was finished hunting. She wanted the safety of numbers again. But she knew someone was behind her, so she couldn't return that way.

Heart pounding, she started moving swiftly ahead and to the left. She had the advantage of knowing the paths, for she'd walked and ridden through these woods on her way across the estate.

"Emily."

She heard someone call her name behind her, a man's voice almost whispering—but not Matthew. Who was it?

She started to run, gripping the arrow tight, knowing it was her only weapon. Branches brushed her arms and her face, but she couldn't afford to slow down, knowing that she had to run an even longer distance to find safety.

As the contest was halted for refreshments, Matthew approached his parents and aunts. They were watching their children fondly, talking among themselves when he sat down.

The dowager duchess, his aunt Isabella, said, "I never thought I would see all three young men married before their sisters. Matthew, I thought you might be the last one of all the cousins."

He smiled and looked toward his sisters, who were sharing a bowl of grapes. It was getting far too easy to pretend that he was a husband in truth.

"And when we received that letter saying you'd married," his mother added, "in *India* of all places, or so we assumed, why, we didn't know what to think."

He shrugged and lifted both hands playfully.

"Do you remember anything yet from early in your marriage?" Aunt Isabella asked.

Matthew shot a glance at his mother, who didn't even blush.

"We thought it best to inform the family, Matthew," Lady Rosa said. "They should know everything."

He smiled at the dowager duchess. "No, Aunt Isabella, the details of my marriage still elude me. But I find I don't care anymore."

"That is obvious," she said with amusement. "You seem very happy to be home with Emily. It is not surprising that you've fallen in love with that sweet girl all over again. Perhaps it even invigorates one's marriage."

Fallen in love? Was that what they all thought?

Before he could respond, he saw Emily emerging through the trees. She clutched a single arrow as she moved swiftly, then came to an abrupt halt when she reached the lawn. For a moment he thought she swayed.

He excused himself and went to her.

She gave a little start when he said her name, then smiled and held up the arrow. "I only found one."

After he took the arrow, she clasped her hands behind her back.

"Emily, why are you breathing so heavily?"

"I needed the exercise, so I walked quite vigorously."

"Or you were trying to escape?" he asked with perception.

She met his gaze swiftly. "Escape who?"

"I don't know." He put his arm around her. "There's no reason for you to feel guilty or to avoid everyone. Our secrets are our own."

She nodded, lips pressed together. "I'll try to do better, Matthew," she said softly.

Chapter 21

After dinner that night there was much excitement as all the young ladies decided to play the piano and sing. Matthew was grateful when Christopher and Daniel pulled him away as Professor Leland entered the drawing room ahead of them.

"What are we doing?" Matthew asked, laughing, when he was led into the library.

Christopher shut the door. "Since we're leaving tomorrow, Daniel and I felt the need for a final discussion."

"You certainly don't need to leave your home," Matthew countered. "Surely most of the *ton* are not in London at this time of the year."

"You need time with your wife and family," Christopher said. "The rest of us would be in the way."

Daniel pushed Matthew into a chair. "So what has changed?" he demanded, smirking. "Besides the fact that you bedded Emily last night."

Matthew only arched a brow. "That is between me and my wife."

"Your *wife*?" Christopher said in a low voice, coming to sit beside Daniel on the sofa opposite Matthew. "Listen to yourself!"

Matthew sighed even as he smiled. "I've been pretending it for a week now; it's hard to break the habit."

"You don't seem to be able to break the habit of *Emily*, either," Daniel said shrewdly.

"She told me the truth," Matthew said.

Christopher straightened in obvious surprise. "She did? Of her own volition?"

"Well . . . first I told her I didn't have amnesia, and that I knew she wasn't my wife."

Daniel cocked his head. "After you slept with her, I bet. I'm impressed at what a rake you've become."

Christopher shot Daniel a frown. "I'm not impressed. Matthew, you took her to bed under false pretenses."

"I didn't force her; it was a very mutual decision."

"But she still thought you believed her to be your wife," Christopher said with a touch of anger. "What was she supposed to do?"

"I gave her a choice." Matthew was surprised at how defensive he suddenly felt. "She said yes."

"She knew what she was getting into, once you returned," Daniel said.

At least he had *someone* on his side, he thought.

Christopher sagged back on the couch, closing his eyes. "I am worried about you, Matthew. I don't see how you can escape this mess easily. But you say she knows the truth now?"

"And she agreed to await my decision about how to resolve it. She's just what I knew she was—a desperate woman with no one else to turn to."

"And she's still desperate, and still has no one else to turn to," Christopher said. "Don't you see?"

Matthew forced himself to consider Christopher's point. "You're trying to say she's still trapped—I know that. But I'm trapped, too. She started the lies, and I don't know how to stop them." He hesitated. "Maybe I don't want to stop them."

"What?" Christopher demanded.

Daniel just laughed.

"Maybe this is exactly the kind of marriage I want, where we both know what to expect."

"And you can't be hurt?" Daniel said softly.

Matthew arched a brow in surprise. *Daniel* was talking about *feelings*? Marriage really *had* changed him.

"It's not about being hurt," Matthew said easily, when they both continued to study him.

"What did your real wife do to you?" Christopher asked, sympathy in his voice.

That was something he was resolved to never tell anyone. "Emily is different than other women I've met in Society," he said. "She works hard at her teaching, and I think it's because she's trying to give something back for the help she's received from the family."

"Listen to yourself!" Christopher said, shaking his head. He took a deep breath. "I can't tell you what you're feeling or what you should do; you'll have to discover that on your own. But I can tell you that women are proud. Emily isn't going to accept this fake marriage for long."

"She already did, before I ever told her the truth."

"But you've changed the rules now," Daniel interjected. "It will matter." He paused, then said shrewdly, "I can see you're different since returning from India. You're no longer so controlled, so repressed."

"It's a good feeling," Matthew said.

"It can be a deceptive feeling," Daniel added. "Don't be misled."

Christopher stood up and looked at Daniel. "We'd better go. Abigail tells me that your wife brought your violin. Aren't you and your mother performing together tonight?" he asked with a smirk.

Matthew sat still as he watched them leave, feeling uncomfortable and not knowing what to do about it.

When he and Emily retired that night, she threw herself into his arms with eagerness. Their lovemaking was passionate and thrilling, and even though he was exhausted, he wanted her again more than he thought possible. But she fell asleep with her back to him, perched on the far edge of the bed.

After eating breakfast together and attending church as one big family, Daniel, Christopher, and their families left for London. Matthew stood under the portico, arm lifted as he gave a final wave goodbye. One by one the others drifted inside, until only Emily remained with him.

"You will miss them," she said. "Perhaps you should have gone to London with them. I'm so busy here, I wouldn't have minded."

He smiled down at her. "I wouldn't think after last night's performance that you wanted to rid yourself of me."

She smiled and slid her arm around his waist.

"What do you have planned for today?" he continued. "Come riding with me?"

"No."

She spoke so swiftly that he was surprised.

Wearing a chagrined smile, she said, "I promised your sisters I would paint with them in the conservatory today."

"Susanna can't paint without you?"

"We're going to discuss the plants as well. My students are studying a little botany, and it will help me to prepare. Susanna said I could show her paintings to the children." She touched his arm, smiling, and disappeared inside.

Matthew soon found himself roaming their bedroom, feeling . . . restless. He didn't want to think about Christopher's warnings, but he couldn't help it. He reflected that he hadn't changed the rules in this game Emily had begun. He simply knew the truth now. She didn't have to lie to him anymore.

Her wardrobe door was open, and he found himself absently touching gown after gown, remembering her in each, amazed that she could be so demure—and so arousing—all at the same time.

But Emily still had to lie; and so did he, if he wanted to keep his family blissfully ignorant.

And though he'd told her there would be no baby, he couldn't guarantee it, especially not if he continued to bed her morning and night.

A gown caught on something heavy, and without thinking about it, he reached inside to free the delicate fabric. A portmanteau had been pushed to the back, and to his surprise it felt bulky. After all this time, surely she'd unpacked.

He opened it to find a stash of sewing projects, samples as well as completed articles, all packed carefully between sheets of thin paper.

He remembered Emily saying that she was an excellent seamstress, and even he could see the skill in the few pieces he looked at. Then why hide her work?

He felt another chill of memory. She'd said that she had meant from the beginning to support herself. The bag was full now; he recalled seeing her embroidering the handkerchief at the top just a day or two ago. Why hide it away—unless she planned to leave him after all?

Leave him? That would be foolish on her part, when she was safe and comfortable right here. He'd promised to take care of her. Surely he was misreading the situation; she just hadn't had time, since everything had changed between them, to unpack this bag of samples.

But before dinner he found himself knocking on Susanna's door. When she let him in, he smiled at the paint spattered across the skirt of her old gown. There were sketchbooks scattered across her desk, table, and chairs. The room smelled of paint, even though she didn't paint here, and he wondered if the laundrywomen moaned when confronted with her paint-stained garments.

"What is it, Matthew?" she asked distractedly, looking back and forth between two gowns she'd laid out on the bed. "I have to change for dinner. We're *both* cutting it too close."

Then he was distracted by the work he saw displayed on the open sketchbooks. Several were of Emily, maybe even done today, for she was smiling against the backdrop of the conservatory.

From behind him Susanna said, "She's been gracious enough to pose for me often during the year. I must admit, brother, that I have seen a new vibrancy in her since your return. It is very obvious that she loves you."

He thought he detected a hint of sadness in her voice, but couldn't focus on it. He already knew Emily was an excellent actress, and would be able to fool anyone into thinking she loved him. But then he remembered her passion and eagerness last night, and the way she'd kissed him so tenderly. He didn't want to think about love; it wasn't part of what they were doing together.

But it hurt him to think of her wanting to leave him.

"I'm getting to know her all over again, of course," he began thoughtfully. "I've noticed how beautiful her sewing is."

Susanna choked on a laugh, and he turned to face her.

"Her sewing? You really must be in love with her to notice something like that."

Not in love, but too curious and worried. "I feel like I want to remember everything about her. Is sewing important to her? Should I be taking her to London, escorting her from one dressmaker's shop to the next?"

"She does that quite regularly," Susanna said with a laugh. "It is her favorite shopping trip, to see the new styles, and talk to each dressmaker. When we're in town, it is a weekly occurrence. Dear brother, don't tell me you want to take over for me on those trips? That would be devotion above and beyond a husband's duty."

Matthew laughed, leaving her to prepare for dinner, but his amusement faded as he walked back to his room. Could Emily be planning to leave him? And how could he blame her? He'd taken her as his mistress, without the security of a commitment. And she'd had no say in it, believing that her lies would condemn her in the end.

He didn't want her to feel bad with him. He realized that her pain mattered to him. He wanted her to be happy, to be content.

Could he be falling in love with her?

Just knowing that she was somewhere in the house made him want to be with her. He enjoyed the lively way she talked back to him, her consideration of his family and the hurt she might cause them. And knowing that he would be with her in the night, making love, made his day that much better.

Maybe this *was* love—on *his* part.

What if Emily actually did plan to leave him?

* * *

The next day, Emily sent a note to Mr. Smythe, the village curate, asking if he would mind teaching the children during the coming week. She couldn't risk leaving the estate, not when she suspected that Arthur Stanwood had been chasing her through the woods. He'd almost caught her; she'd heard his panting breath as he ran behind her, the branches crackling. When she felt him tug at a lock of her hair that had come loose, she'd slashed behind her with the arrow, not even breaking stride. She'd hit something, but hadn't turned her head to see if she'd wounded him.

Just as she'd reached the lawn, she slowed to a walk, and only then looked back. But she saw nothing, and didn't linger to explore.

Why would Stanwood chase her? He'd said he would contact her about his blackmail. Maybe she angered him by not making herself available in the village. She hadn't wanted to risk being alone with him where she couldn't be seen.

Matthew and his father had gone for the day, and she was glad, for the more Matthew could focus on his family's business ventures, the less time he'd have to contemplate what she might be keeping from him. She and his sisters and mother were to meet the men at Cambridge that evening for a special lecture the professor was giving, open to the public. It had been her idea that they attend as a family; Lady Rosa acquiesced with pleasure. Susanna, Rebecca, and Emily had exchanged surprised glances behind Lady Rosa's back. Much as the Lelands' relationship had improved, an anatomy lecture would surely bring back bitter memories.

Yet Emily was so used to being out doing things, that remaining at the house felt constricting to her. She decided by the afternoon that a walk about the grounds—nowhere near the woods—couldn't hurt.

The day was overcast and chilly, and she hugged her shawl about her shoulders. Gardeners worked in the various beds, and servants moved back and forth between the outbuildings and the house. As she was walking the gravel drive, a wagon came around the far side of the mansion, obviously leaving the kitchen courtyard. She moved to the side, so the driver could easily pass her.

As the wagon slowed, she looked up to give a pleasant nod—only to see Arthur Stanwood smiling in triumph down at her from the driver's seat. He was wearing plain garments and a cap pulled down to his brow. While she stood gaping up at him, he touched the cap respectfully.

"Afternoon, Mrs. Leland." He lowered his voice, "Or should I say—Miss Grey?"

"What are you doing here?" she hissed, her shock forgotten as she looked all about her. The servants continued to work, and no one gave them more than a glance. "Meeting your spy?" she demanded.

"I just delivered a load of coal for the kitchen," he said, ignoring her second question. "There are so many supplies needed for an estate this size."

"So you've ingratiated yourself with someone in the village, too?"

Wearing a smile, he looked about and asked, "Where are the captain's lovely sisters? I enjoyed watching them yesterday. Such fine forms as they shot their arrows."

She clenched her fists, her body rigid with anger and fear. But she had to hold fast to her purpose and dissuade him.

He laughed softly, and then his smile faded. "The only way you can keep me away is to raise a hue and a cry, Emily. And then everyone will want to know what's wrong. And you'll have to tell them. Do you want this lovely family to know what a criminal you are? You didn't seem to yesterday. It was a shame you wouldn't talk to me."

"I wasn't sure talking was all you wanted from me," she said. So he *was* the one who'd chased her.

His expression changed and he glared down at her. "I'll do anything I want to you. And you will take it. It wasn't I who created this mess you're in, but why shouldn't I take advantage of it? What arrangements have you made to get your pretty hands on a substantial amount of money?"

"I already told you that I have no access to money," she said coldly. "I have been given no jewels or precious gifts, not even a wedding band. This plan of yours will not work!"

"Find a way."

"I cannot. Matthew has confronted me. He knows I'm not his wife. Why would he give me money when he's searching for the best way to rid himself of me?"

"Even if you're telling the truth about his knowledge of your lies, I don't believe he wants you gone, or he would have sent you away immediately. No, my dear Emily, he is obviously enamored of you. Have you been granting him your favors, the ones you wouldn't give me?"

She didn't know what answer would pacify him.

"Well?" he demanded, his voice louder.

"Be quiet!" She looked frantically around her. "It won't help you to be caught."

"Thank you for pretending to think of me, Emily, but I know it is only selfish concern on your part. If I'm caught, you'll have to explain your association with me. You'll have to tell him what you did for me. And then your lies—and your security—will be over. You can't want that. No, it is clear to me that Leland continues to want you, at least in his bed. And he'll pay. You have to find a way to make it happen. I will contact you again in four days, not a moment longer. I want ten thousand pounds."

She gasped. "But his father is a professor! They don't have such money."

He grinned. "How will you know until you ask? Find it, steal it, I don't care. If the duchess has jewels, help yourself to those. Surely she won't miss a few." Straightening up, he touched his cap once again. "Good day, Miss Grey. It has been a pleasure."

Chapter 22

That night, Matthew led Lady Rosa, his sisters, and Emily into the lecture hall at Christ's College to hear his father speak on the uses of the newly redesigned microscope to the anatomist. They sat in the back, for women weren't usually admitted, regardless of the public nature of the speech. But they stood out anyway, because there were less than a couple dozen people in attendance—including them.

Matthew leaned over to whisper in Lady Rosa's ear. "It's a shame they didn't publicize the event better." He'd been hoping she would see how well-respected the professor's work was.

She shook her head. "Sadly, the only university programs that seem valuable are mathematics and the classics. People don't realize the importance of the sciences in this modern world of ours. It is a good thing your father has his important research, for he only has six or seven students studying beneath him right now."

Matthew simply blinked at her, too surprised to speak.

She cleared her throat and lifted her chin. "I am not ignorant on the subject of my husband's work. Now be quiet, so that I can listen."

Matthew sat back and saw Emily watching him, wearing a little smile.

The professor spoke on subject matter that often sounded like another language to Matthew, but his obvious enthusiasm made him a good speaker. Several students asked questions, and the discussion went on for quite some time.

Matthew glanced past Emily to his sisters, wondering at their reactions. Susanna, of course, was an unofficial scholar herself, but Rebecca might very well be yawning.

He frowned. Rebecca wasn't yawning at all. Her face was pale, her eyes red-rimmed. She was trying to watch their father, but her head would droop forward until she straightened herself.

He put his hand on his mother's arm, and when she looked at him, he inclined his head toward Rebecca. Lady Rosa's eyes widened in alarm.

"I thought she was seldom ill anymore," Matthew said softly.

"She has had nothing more serious than a cold

in many years," his mother said grimly. "You and Susanna stay here and wait for your father. I will take Emily home to help me with Rebecca."

Not Susanna? Matthew thought in surprise. But then Susanna was the one who would appreciate the lecture most, and perhaps Emily was the better nurse. Emily was already holding Rebecca's arm, whispering gently to her. Rebecca nodded, cast a wan smile at Matthew, and allowed the two women to assist her from the hall.

Susanna slid closer to Matthew. "I didn't even realize she was ill," she said, watching the door close behind them.

"I, too, noticed nothing. I'm certain she'll be fine," he said in a reassuring voice. "Father will be done soon, and we can return with him."

The professor's gaze was focused on the door his daughter had just been helped through. If he was distracted as he continued to answer questions, he did a decent job trying to pretend otherwise. A half hour later he called an end to the evening, gathered his books and papers, and walked quickly, his academic gown fluttering behind him, to meet Matthew and Susanna in the back.

By the time they arrived at Madingley Court, the physician had already been sent for, and Rebecca lay in bed with her eyes closed, her face damp with perspiration. Her chest shuddered with an occasional deep cough.

Matthew stood near the door while Professor Leland rushed to the bedside. Emily came to stand beside Matthew, and the touch of her arm against his was somehow reassuring.

"How is she?" he whispered.

She shrugged and spoke softly. "Feverish, but not terribly. She is quite lucid, thank God, and she says her body aches. Apparently she awoke this morning feeling unwell but hoped it would go away. She hated being so weak when she was young."

"This is only one illness. Surely it does not constitute a return to her childhood infirmities."

"I hope not," Emily said solemnly. "I'll go see if Lady Rosa needs fresh water."

Matthew helplessly watched Emily as she moved with competence about the room, assisting in any way she could. Susanna seemed nervous, as if hiding her fear, but Emily had a soothing way about her that inspired peace of mind.

When the physician had come and gone, claiming that there was little to do but wait for the fever to break, Matthew persuaded Lady Rosa to sit with him in the corner and eat from the tray of food brought by a maid. Emily took a distraught Susanna out of the room for a while.

Together, Matthew and his mother ate in silence, watching the professor calmly talk to the unconscious Rebecca, while wiping her face and arms with a wet cloth.

Lady Rosa began to talk. "Your father has always cared so much for you children."

"I know," Matthew said softly.

"What other man would be here, so involved in his sick daughter's care? And I have been making him suffer all these years."

"Mother—"

"No, there is nothing you need to say. The past has been dead for many years in everyone's eyes but my own. No more."

He ate in silence then, watching his parents cast uncertain but longing glances at each other. If it wasn't for the fact that his sister was ill, he would have felt relieved by the change that had blossomed between them while he was gone. Through much struggle, they'd gone beyond a painful marriage to something that strengthened each of them.

It was a long night, and everyone took their turn keeping Rebecca company, talking to her when she awoke, giving her sips of water and spoonfuls of broth. Matthew made sure he was there when Emily was, because he enjoyed watching her with his sister, her serenity, her firm belief that Rebecca would be well.

And she was right. By morning the fever had broken. He and Emily were with her, and they sent for his parents. Matthew helped Rebecca sit up a little higher in bed, and she crossly slapped his hands away.

"I am not an invalid," she said in a weak voice, then coughed.

Lady Rosa and Professor Leland hurried into the room, and when they saw her, their faces burst with smiles. Matthew hid his own when Rebecca groaned as if in disgust.

"You didn't need to act like I was going to die," she said, arms folded beneath her breasts.

Matthew suspected it was to hide the trembling of her hands.

"It was just a little fever!" she continued. "Everyone gets them now and then. Part of a simple cold. You all overreacted."

And perhaps she was right, Matthew thought, but how could she blame them after her history? But he kept that thought to himself so she wouldn't turn on him.

Lady Rosa kissed her on the brow, then took a deep breath. "It seems we are not needed here, Randolph," she said with equanimity to her husband. "If anyone does need us, we will be at the cottage with much to discuss."

And then they left the room, leaving behind a surprised silence.

Susanna rushed through the door. "What did I miss? Mama and Papa were walking arm in arm!"

Matthew put his arm around Emily. "I'm not quite sure what happened, but I do believe they want to be alone together at the cottage where they fell in love. To talk," he added, for the benefit of innocent ears.

Rebecca and Susanna looked at one another and gave identical snorts.

As Susanna went to Rebecca's bedside, Matthew looked down at Emily, who wore a pleasantly serene expression.

He said, "You look rather proud of yourself."

"I knew with some effort their relationship could be repaired," she said, lips twitching against a broader smile.

"And it's that easy to repair relationships?" he asked softly.

Her smile faded away, and he regretted his words.

Emily excused herself and returned to her bedroom. It had been a long night, and she knew she should sleep. But now that her worries about Rebecca had abated, her thoughts kept roiling in her mind, tormenting her with memories of Stanwood and his threats and his unknown spy.

She was no closer now to solving her problem. She couldn't imagine going to the duchess's private bedchamber and ransacking it to steal something valuable. It made her ill to even think about it.

The only thing of value that she owned was in a little box on her dressing table. She sat down before the mirror and opened it to stare at the beautiful necklace given to her by the Lelands at Christmas the previous year. It was made of tiny pearls, so she was certain it had some value, but hardly ten thousand pounds' worth.

On his way to breakfast—which took priority over sleep—Matthew stopped in the entrance hall to go through the mail. There were several letters for him, most with flowery writing signifying another invitation to celebrate his return.

But one letter seemed different than the others, his name crudely spelled out, and with only one *t* in *Matthew*. He opened it up and read:

Captain Leland,

I know the truth about you and Emily Grey. I no longer trust her to get the money she's been assigned to, so it is up to you. I require ten thousand pounds or I will expose your false marriage. Give it to Emily. She will soon know where to reach me.

There was no signature. For a long minute Matthew gaped at the letter, rereading it twice, as if the words would miraculously change. Even after everything he and Emily had shared with each other, her lies had continued, and she was involved in a blackmail plot against his family. His head reeled at the very thought, while fury twisted his gut.

How many more times would his intuition prove false?

Breathing heavily, he walked into the great hall and sank into a chair beneath a display of centuries' worth of swords. They glinted in the sunlight above his head, and he wanted to rip one off the wall, find this bastard and—

And what? He didn't even know the man's name!

But Emily did.

Dazed, he thought of her so sweetly tending to his sister, all the while planning to . . . blackmail him for money? He blinked, his head beginning to clear. It didn't make sense.

And suddenly he couldn't believe it of her, not after everything he'd learned, everything they'd shared. His assessment of her was *not* wrong. She was a woman thrust unprepared into tragedy, who'd done what she had to do in order to survive. And if this unknown man was telling the truth, then he had been putting even more pressure on her to blackmail Matthew. And Emily hadn't succumbed, hadn't come begging for money.

She hadn't begged for his trust or his help, either, and that frustrated and saddened him.

But he hadn't proved worthy of her trust, he realized with deep regret. He hadn't tried to solve the problem of their supposed marriage, only used it for his own pleasure. Was that how his first wife had felt, that she couldn't come to him with the truth, couldn't ask for his help?

When Emily heard the door open behind her, she quickly closed the jewelry box and rose to her feet. Matthew walked around the bed and stopped to look at her.

She couldn't read his expression at all, and that panicked her. "Is it Rebecca?"

"No, as far as I know she's feeling better."

"Thank God." She put a hand to her chest and closed her eyes. But when Matthew said nothing else, she at last looked at him. "What is it? Just tell me."

"I will, but it is a shame that you just couldn't tell *me*."

She stared at him with incomprehension. He held out a piece of paper, and she took it, bending her head to read.

The blood drained from her face so quickly she had to put a hand on the chair behind her to steady herself. Stanwood had gone behind her back, told Matthew everything, made it seem like she was involved. Her eyes hurt suppressing tears as she met Matthew's questioning gaze.

"I would never help him plan to extort money from you and your family!"

"So you knew about it?" he asked.

She closed her eyes for a moment. "Yes. He came

to me with his threats several days ago, and I tried to find a way to outwit him. But there is nothing I can do, for he has the truth of my lies on his side. I wanted to protect you, had hoped—" She broke off. "You think the worst of me, don't you? You think he's telling the truth. I continued to lie to you, and that is unforgivable."

When he caught her arm, she was ready for his condemnation. His family was all that was important to him, and she'd brought a murderer down on them.

But his touch gentled, and he took her other arm, giving her a little shake.

"Emily, look at me," he said in a low, urgent voice.

After seeing passion and humor in his eyes, it would kill her to see it replaced by hatred. But she had no choice; she owed him her courage. She straightened and looked into his face.

When she saw tenderness in his gaze, her breath left her in a rush.

"I believe you," he said softly, holding her arms so she couldn't flee. "Do you hear me? Whoever this man is, he's a scoundrel. I don't believe you were helping him to blackmail me."

Her breath returned in a rush. "You believe me?"

His eyes tinged with sadness, he murmured, "I just wish you could have trusted me with all of it. This man—Stanwood?—has been terrorizing you, yet you kept it all to yourself. I would have helped you, Emily. I know in the beginning I only sought my own amusement, but I swear to you, when I took you to bed, I never thought it a lark. It was almost as if . . . we were married, in some strange way."

"Matthew, all I wanted was a marriage to you, even if it wasn't in truth. But I was wrong. Married people shouldn't lie to each other like we did."

He nodded. "And that's my fault, that I made you feel like you had to keep this from me."

She straightened and stepped away from him.

Matthew felt the rejection like a slap.

"Ever since my family died," she said solemnly, "I've always had to handle everything myself. But I wasn't brought up to be independent. I never had to make decisions for myself unless it involved what book to read, what gown to have made, or what party to attend. My father and brothers protected me from everything, but they couldn't protect me from their own deaths."

She stood erect, trying to be so strong. He desperately wanted to hold her, to protect her, but she held herself apart.

"I was incompetent, and so very uneducated," she said.

He knew that was why she studied so hard, to better herself, as well as help the students who'd had no one to champion them before she'd arrived. She looked toward the window, as if she couldn't bear the sight of him.

"Do you know how it felt to be the poor relation no one wanted? Not only did I have no family, I did not even know where I would sleep after my cousin took the house, but for a kind neighbor temporarily taking me in. But she had no room for me, either." And then her hot gaze met his again. "I came so far down in life that I had to work as a chambermaid cleaning rooms at an inn owned by Stanwood, because sewing garments did not bring in enough rent money. Men regularly propositioned me because I was powerless, helpless."

Matthew's throat was tight with emotions he'd never confronted before. He couldn't imagine how frightened and alone Emily had been. He would never let anything harm her again.

"Was it Stanwood who hurt you?"

"He tried," she said. "Oh, at first he simply watched me, and I felt the threat of what he truly wanted of me. The only way to hold him back was to do . . . other things he wanted. I stole for him, Matthew. I truly am a criminal, in more ways than one. Twice I took money from a bedchamber I'd cleaned. But I wouldn't keep doing it. And when I refused, he put me against a wall to finish what he'd started."

Matthew's entire body was stiff with fury and weakness.

"I wouldn't let him make me helpless," she insisted with heated anger. "My brothers had taught me where to kick a man. Then I ran from him to Mr. Tillman, who so desperately wanted me to escape, pretending to be your wife. And then Stanwood found me—" She closed her eyes, and one tear escaped. "He murdered that poor old man, frail with sickness, right in front of me." Her breathing caught. "He held a pillow over his face and I fought him, pulling at his arms, but he threw me back."

"Emily . . ." He whispered her name, feeling his own helplessness. He realized he was like Stanwood and those men at the inn who'd propositioned her, used her. How was he supposed to make things better between them? And he desperately wanted to, because his family was right, he'd fallen in love with her. But if he told her that now, she wouldn't believe him. He had to prove himself to her. He wanted a real marriage, and everything that went with it.

Chapter 23

Emily watched Matthew reach toward her, then stop, his face full of confusion and pain.

"I don't want secrets between us, Emily," he said softly.

"There are always secrets, Matthew. We don't know how to trust each other."

"But I trust you," he said, putting his arms around her. "I haven't told you everything, but I want to now."

She remained silent, looking up at him, taking shelter in his embrace for the brief time allotted to her.

"My wife was named Rahema, and as you can see from her name, she was a native woman."

Her lips parted in amazement, and her own problems faded for a moment. "She wasn't British?"

Shaking his head, he pulled her with him until they were seated in two chairs before the warm hearth. Bracing his elbows on his knees, he reached for her hands and held them.

"She was at the mission when I was brought in from the jungle, wounded. She nursed me, and we became lovers. I soon realized she was ill and might not survive. I felt such . . . tenderness toward her, such gratitude." He looked down at their joined hands. "I did love her. So to provide for her, I married her."

"I'm glad you did," she said softly.

He gave a faint smile. "You would never condemn me for doing something outside the boundaries of Society. I never even thought about the scandal, should it become known. I was just like the rest of my family."

"You loved her, Matthew, and you wanted what was best for her."

"She told me she'd been baptized an Anglican, which was important for a legal marriage. Neither of us thought she'd live long, and I just wanted her to have some peace. Surprisingly, she recovered, and even moved with me to my next post. That's when I sent the vague letter to my parents telling them I'd married, so they'd have time to become used to the idea before I presented them with a native bride."

She winced. "Your family thought that letter was preparing them for me."

He smiled. "Glad to be of help." Their smiles faded and he gave her a searching glance. "I thought Rahema was happy with me, but I never saw the truth."

She took a deep breath, squeezing his hands. "She was lying to you?" And then he'd come home to find another woman doing the same thing to him. Emily was surprised he hadn't been more angry with her from the beginning.

"After she died, I discovered she'd never become a Christian. Hell, that probably means we weren't even married according to English law. She'd used me to support family she never told me about. My money wasn't enough. She was so desperate, she exploited the things I told her about my assignments to betray our army."

"Oh, Matthew!" His name was an involuntary cry.

"Men died because of her—because of me. And I never knew any of this until she was dead." His eyes were distant as he relived the memories of his past.

"And then you came home and found me," she whispered. "And now I've betrayed you, too."

He clutched her hands tighter. "I enjoyed every moment of our game. And you haven't betrayed me. I know you aren't involved in Stanwood's plots. You've been caught in circumstances you've been powerless against, and it's made me realize that Rahema was, too. I cannot forgive what she did, but I understand now that she was trying to survive the only way she knew how." His eyes grew sad. "And she didn't think she could trust me enough to tell me the truth. She must not have thought I could help her."

"You don't know what it's like to have no one," she said softly. "It . . . changes you. You've always had your family."

He sat forward on his chair, looking meaningfully into her eyes. "There won't be a scandal for Stanwood to reveal, because we're going to Scotland to be married, to Gretna Green, where we don't need banns read or a special license."

She gaped at him, hope unfurling like a blossom after winter. "Married?"

He grinned. "Yes. The pretend marriage will be real, and will solve all our problems. We're good together, Emily. We can be happy."

But he didn't say he loved her, and didn't ask for her love in return. She'd told herself all along that love didn't matter. If she was the only one in love, then so be it.

She thought about foiling Stanwood, and remembered that he wasn't working alone. If their marriage made Stanwood powerless, it could also dissuade whoever was helping him. Telling Matthew would only make him question his friends, when they were only trying to protect him from her.

"We leave tomorrow," Matthew said. "I know just what to say to my family."

* * *

That night, Emily could not sleep. She knew Matthew thought the evening had been a success. He'd told his family they were going on a honeymoon to Scotland, and everyone was happy that they'd have time alone. She'd tried to relax, to tell herself she was getting everything she wanted: a husband, a protector, security.

But she kept looking at Matthew, and her feeling of unease grew into dread. Lieutenant Lawton and Mr. Derby had both expressed their good wishes, but all she could think was: which one was lying? Who would do something drastic, feeling that they had to protect Matthew from her?

It would never end, she knew. One of them would eventually talk to Matthew, furthering his doubts about her. Right now she was an exciting game; he'd said so himself. That couldn't last. He'd grow bored with her, and then it would be too late—they'd be married, and Matthew would regret it.

Not long ago that wouldn't have mattered to her. She'd only wanted safety.

But Stanwood was a desperate man. What would he do if he could no longer blackmail Matthew and her?

She'd fallen in love with Matthew, and the thought of him unhappy—or hurt—because of her, was too much to bear.

Very carefully she slid from the bed and tiptoed to the dressing room, not letting herself look at him, for fear she'd change her mind. She donned a day dress and cloak, packed a change of clothing and some necessities in a portmanteau, and calmly went out into the corridor.

"Emily?"

She gave a start of fear at the loud whisper, turned around and saw Susanna at her bedroom door, carrying a candle, a shawl wrapped over her nightgown. They gaped at each other.

Susanna marched toward her, glaring at the portmanteau, and then taking in her clothing. "What are you doing?" she demanded. "You and my brother cannot possibly be leaving in the middle of the night!"

Emily set down the portmanteau. "But we are. Go back to bed and don't tell anyone. It will be a surprise!"

Susanna stiffened. "I don't believe you. I just had a strange feeling all evening that something was wrong. You didn't seem yourself. I'll see what Matthew has to say."

When she touched the doorknob, Emily put a hand on her arm. "No, don't."

Susanna studied her so thoroughly that Emily felt like a specimen under the professor's microscope.

"Don't?" Susanna repeated. "Why shouldn't

I disturb him? Shouldn't he know that his wife is leaving in the middle of the night?"

She tried to think of a lie—she was always so good at them. But nothing could excuse this behavior. She thought of everything Susanna had gone through, how close their friendship had become—and she couldn't continue to lie.

Emily stiffened her shoulders. "I'm not Matthew's wife."

Susanna only blinked at her from behind her spectacles.

"Did you hear me?" Emily hissed. "I'm not his wife, so you have to let me go!"

Susanna leaned in toward her. "What are you saying?"

"How can I be any clearer?" Emily groaned and closed her eyes for a moment, stunned at how difficult it was to say the truth. "I was never his wife. It was all a lie. I thought he had died, so I used his name to save myself."

"But. . . . but . . ." Susanna just continued to blink at her owlishly.

Emily expected her to gasp or scream or cry. She wanted to cry herself, never imagining how painful it would be to have this wonderful family know the truth about her.

"Does Matthew know?" Susanna demanded when she'd pulled herself together.

Emily nodded tiredly. "From the beginning. The

whole amnesia story was his way to delay hurting his family while he investigated me."

Susanna gasped. "How did he even think of such a thing! And you didn't know he was lying?"

"Not until last night."

Susanna's brow wrinkled. "But since then you've announced a honeymoon."

"I won't go. It will be too dangerous for him."

"Too dangerous for him?" Susanna echoed, baffled.

"He thinks—he thinks if he marries me in truth, everything will work out." Though she tried hard to keep her emotions from escalating, her eyes started to sting, and she had to wipe them with the back of her hand.

"Well, of course he wants to marry you," Susanna said.

Now it was Emily's turn to blink at her through her tears. "I lied to him—I lied to you all!"

"And now you're going to run away to protect him? What about taking risks, as you told me?"

"I—I— This is different! Matthew deserves someone better than me."

"I don't know all the details, but you would never have done something like this without a good reason."

"Susanna, you don't even know me," Emily whispered.

"What balderdash. Of course I know you.

You've been like a sister to me. You've helped educate the village children. And you love my brother."

Emily hugged herself. "You don't understand. There's a man blackmailing me. Matthew thinks he can protect me, but what if—what if—"

"Do you trust him?"

"Of course."

"You've done something more daring than any woman I know. And now you're trying to protect Matthew, rather than letting him do the same for you. Let *him* take the risk now, Emily. I can tell he loves you. I wish I knew everything you've been through—and you must promise to tell me—but for now, I will only say that this must be true love, since the both of you are trying so hard to protect each other."

"But Susanna, there are things he doesn't know yet, things that might hurt him. How can I tell him that—"

"Because you must." She gripped Emily's hands. "You may think this is crazy, but I admire you. Don't skulk away now. Prove to me that the love you feel is important enough to fight for. Prove to me that I should look for such a love, too."

Emily bit her lip. "You're right, I know you're right. I'm just so frightened for him, for all of you."

"Go back in there and talk to him. And don't

worry about what you've told me. I vow never to repeat anything unless you tell me to."

Emily's tears began afresh, and she tried to blink them away, whispering, "Susanna, I love him so. He's become everything to me. Feeling this way is . . . wonderful and terrifying at the same time. But it makes life worthwhile."

Susanna sniffed even as she smiled. "Go to him."

Matthew awoke to darkness and lay still, listening to Emily breathe. He should have been happy; they were going to outwit Stanwood. But instead he'd grown more uncomfortable as the evening progressed. He'd told himself that he was just worried, that they'd be able to return in time to meet Stanwood and prove they were married. Let Stanwood threaten to tell the world their story; Emily could no longer be hurt. For Society's ears, Matthew could turn the whole thing into a romantic escapade with a happy ending, if he had to.

Emily would always be at his side. And he'd make sure she knew she was safe and loved.

He heard the flare of a candle lighting and opened his eyes. Emily was walking toward the bed from the hearth. He frowned up at her as she set the candleholder on the bedside table. She was fully dressed in a day gown, and her cloak was thrown over the back of a chair. A portmanteau rested beside the desk, and he wondered if it contained her sewing samples.

"You're not leaving," he said softly, firmly.

"No, I'm not."

That stopped him.

"But I was going to."

"Emily—"

"Just listen. I was, but then I saw Susanna in the hall, and we had a talk. She knows almost everything now, Matthew."

"I'll make her understand."

"She says she already does. I don't think she needs our help anymore, because she was helping me." To his surprise, twin tears etched glistening lines down her cheeks. "I was going to leave because I couldn't let you put yourself in danger. Stanwood killed a man, and he might try to kill you or your family."

"We'll take care of him," Matthew said, sitting up and swinging his feet over the side of the bed.

"But there are things you need to know."

He realized that she would have risked her life by leaving, rather than let any harm come to him or his family. Tenderness washed through him. He wanted to counter with his love for her, beg her to love him in return, but she didn't yet trust him; he saw that now. The only way she would allow herself any kind of trust was if he could put her safely out of Stanwood's reach.

"Then tell me, Emily. I can understand why you felt you couldn't tell me before, since I've been lying to you."

She rolled her eyes. "My lies were worse! But this isn't a challenge about whose lies top the others." She sighed. "I think someone within the household is working with Stanwood."

He stiffened. "You think he put a man in here?"

"Perhaps, but I truly think someone is trying to protect you from me. The first blackmail note I received from Stanwood came in the post, but the second was left here in this room. The notes only arrived after you—and your friends—returned home."

"And after the *Times* article."

"Yes, but . . . it would make sense if someone was trying to help you. Your friend Lieutenant Lawton would naturally want to see me away from you. He's from Southampton, just like Stanwood."

Matthew shook his head. "He has no reason to go behind my back and help Stanwood."

"But . . . he's been so secretive about where he goes every day."

"And that is his business. I trust him."

"What about Mr. Derby?"

"Peter? Who's barely been out of Cambridgeshire his whole life?"

"He felt humiliated when I rejected him last

spring. And he somehow thinks I believe him undeserving of Susanna."

"These are valid motives," he said quietly, "but if Stanwood is being helped, it could as well be any one of dozens of servants. We'll remain vigilant, I promise you."

She nodded, but he watched her twist her hands together, and her eyes darted to the door.

"Emily, don't leave me," he said, his voice husky with emotion.

She closed her eyes.

"Together we can best Stanwood." He stood up, reaching out to cup her face with both hands. Her trembling was nearly his undoing. "Can you please try to trust me? I know you've only had yourself for so long, but you have me now. I want to marry you."

He leaned down and kissed her, softly at first, pressing his lips against her mouth, her cheeks, her eyelids, and then her mouth again. "Emily, sweetheart."

Her name was a heartfelt groan from deep in his chest, and finally she flung her arms around him.

"I won't leave you," she said against his lips. "Make me feel safe, Matthew, please. Make me forget."

He undressed her gently, and showed her with his body every feeling he didn't dare express aloud. He caressed and pleasured her until she cried out his name. When he sank into her, it was as if he was a part of her. He had no concern for preventing conception—he wanted lots of babies with his Emily.

This time she stayed contentedly in his arms, sleeping the sleep of the exhausted.

He gladly drew her beneath the covers and into his embrace. She rested her head against his shoulder, her arm across his chest. After kissing the top of her head, he murmured, "Sleep."

Though it took a while, at last her breathing slowed, the stiffness went out of her muscles, and she relaxed into sleep.

Arthur Stanwood lay naked in bed the next night, well sated by the woman at his side. She talked too much, and normally he wouldn't have tolerated that, but in this case she was helping him immensely.

"Tell me more about Madingley Court," he said, knowing that Emily's maid, Maria, needed only a little prodding to keep talking.

She rattled on about life in a palace, and the lives of the servants. He let her go on a bit, running his hands through her hair, soothing her.

When she took a breath, he said, "I've missed you these last few days. I haven't been able to come up to the house on an errand."

She smiled up at him, curling herself provocatively against his side. "I've missed ye, too, though they've kept me so busy I could barely think!"

The first unease crept into his mind. "Why?"

"I've told ye about the young Mrs. Leland, and the captain comin' back from the dead. Things was awkward between 'em for a while, but love has blossomed again."

He laughed. "And that keeps you busy?"

"When they're leavin' on a honeymoon, it does."

He stiffened, and she yelped when his hand tangled in her hair.

"Sorry, love," he said through his teeth, forcing a smile. "So they're leaving?"

"Already left, they have. This mornin'."

Gone. Stanwood had thought Emily completely cowed, and instead she'd slipped away from him. He remembered his unexpected guest that afternoon, who blackened his eyes and bruised his ribs, giving him one more chance to pay the money he owed. One more chance, before the man made sure that he never enjoyed life again.

"And what romantic place is the captain taking his wife?" he asked.

Maria sighed. "Somewhere in Scotland. He dearly loves her, he does."

Stanwood sat up, knowing they already had a day's journey on him. Maria gave him a wanton smile and reached up to him. He came down over her—and put his hands around her neck. He couldn't leave behind a witness to his interest. As she struggled silently, he ignored her, making his plans.

Emily was not going to escape.

Chapter 24

E mily stood still while Matthew hooked up her gown. Over her shoulder she could see his distraction, the way he kept looking to the window. They were on the second floor of a nondescript inn, the same as the previous night. No one had accosted them, no one had lurked in the shadows. She at last had begun to think that Matthew's plan might work, that they'd eluded Stanwood and anyone else he'd coerced into helping him.

She smiled. "We've been journeying two days. We'll meet the train by midday. You can relax now."

He kissed her nose. His easy affection and sweet gestures still amazed her.

"You know the train doesn't continue all the way to Scotland. We'll have to finish our journey to Gretna Green in a hired carriage."

"I won't mind," she said, thinking of all the ways Matthew had kept her occupied in their private, enclosed carriage.

He grinned, then sighed. "I must meet the coachman and footmen to see about the next change of horses. Will you wait here for me?"

"Of course. I have my sewing to keep my mind and fingers occupied."

He looked at her portmanteau as if it were the enemy. He'd already confessed his suspicion that she wanted to leave when he found her sewing projects. She laughed and pushed him toward the door.

A short time later she had just finished putting on her stockings and was searching for the shoes she'd kicked off last night when the door opened.

She was bending over, looking beneath the table. "Matthew, have you seen my shoes?"

A hand covered her mouth and an arm snaked around her waist hard, pulling her upright and backward against a man's body.

She heard Stanwood's voice in her ear. "Find your shoes quickly, or you leave without them."

Oh God, Oh God, raced through her mind, and fear shot a burning path down her body. His hand smelled like leather, and he was so close to covering her nose that she panicked about taking a deep breath. Arching, she tried to inhale, pulled at his hand. He would get nothing if he killed her, she thought as she reeled with dizziness.

But he repositioned his hand, and she took a deep, satisfying breath through her nose.

"Can't have you dying, now can we, my love? Not after I questioned every posting boy between here and Cambridge. You made me work hard to find you, and I will make you suffer for it."

She groaned as she sagged against him. After each stage, the posting boys took the rented horses back to the previous inn, while the carriage was outfitted with new horses—and new posting boys.

She started to struggle again, hoping to delay Stanwood until Matthew's return. Again he pulled her hard against him, arching her neck back painfully.

"You are coming with me now. You cry out, and your *husband* is dead. I have a man with his rifle trained on your Captain Leland as we speak. I won't mind at all going to his family with my demands after he's dead. They might be even easier to threaten than you."

She'd been right all along, she thought with despair. Stanwood had help. Yet how could one of Matthew's friends or servants aim a rifle at *Matthew*? It didn't make sense.

Once they were out of the room, she thought, there would be more people, and the chance to escape him. She nodded quickly, letting her hands fall to her side as she pretended to acquiesce.

He let go of her mouth and spun her about, roughly holding her face until she was forced to look at him.

"I will show you true pain if you cross me," he hissed at her, drops of spittle landing on her face.

She almost gagged, but was even more frightened by the look of panic he wore. His calm confidence had turned ragged, and that made him even more dangerous. He let her don her shoes, then took her arm and hauled her to the door.

In the corridor, Stanwood urged Emily to the left, toward the servants' stairs in back, away from the front of the inn. Still holding her by the arm, he forced her down the stairs ahead of him, so quickly that she stumbled and would have fallen the rest of the way if he hadn't caught her.

In the kitchen courtyard, she looked about, hoping that the inn's stable yard was nearby. But Stanwood urged her around a corner and to the far side of the inn, away from the road and people who could help her.

Away from Matthew.

The ground sloped gradually down toward a river, roaring fast beneath the bridge after the previous day's rain. The grounds were wide-open, deserted, and Stanwood would be able to take her anywhere, with no witnesses. She had to run.

Using the wet grass to her advantage, she pretended to slip, using all of her weight in a hard fall. Stanwood was knocked off balance, and as he bent over, she drove her elbow back into his groin, a trick she'd learned from her brothers.

He groaned harshly, letting go of her so suddenly that this time she did hit the ground. But she was up and running a moment later. She risked one look over her shoulder and saw that Stanwood was not far behind her.

And he was between her and the inn.

Matthew opened the door to their bedchamber, only to find it empty.

"Emily?" he called, wondering if she still needed a moment of privacy behind the changing screen.

But there was no answer.

He'd told her to wait here. They hadn't made a move these past two days without consulting each other. A sick feeling of dread tightened his chest.

He ran back down the stairs to the ground floor, searching the many public rooms, but she wasn't there. He pushed past several people to get out the front door, only to find the coachman standing beside the carriage, the footmen talking together near the back.

"Did my wife come out here?" he demanded.

The coachman's eyes widened. "No, Captain. I haven't seen her."

"She's missing," Matthew ground out, then went back into the inn.

The young, plump maid who'd served them dinner the previous night was walking swiftly across the entrance room, and skidded to a stop when she saw him.

"Captain Leland, I've been lookin' for ye everywhere. I saw your wife bein' pushed down the servants' stair not a quarter hour ago. I thought perhaps 'twas your man, but he handled her so roughly—"

She broke off when Matthew cursed. "Did you see where they went?"

"Outside, Captain," she said, wringing her hands.

Matthew turned and strode back through the front doors again. With that kind of head start, Stanwood could have pushed her into a carriage and been down the road already. Fear tasted bitter in his mouth, jumbling his thoughts. He couldn't lose her, not when he'd sworn to protect her, when he loved her. She was alone with a madman, frightened for her very life—and he had once again proven himself unable to help her.

As he stepped outside, he heard, "Matthew!"

Peter Derby ran toward him, his arm bound in a makeshift sling, blood staining his coat.

"Peter?"

Peter's face was ashen as he stumbled to a halt. "It's Stanwood," he said, gasping. "I've been following him. He's here."

"I know."

Peter gaped at him, lines of exhaustion etched across his forehead. "So you know about him—and Emily?"

"I do. Do you know where he has her?"

"No. Then it seems I'm too late."

Grimly, Matthew said, "Did you help him?"

"I'm sorry, Matthew," Peter said, collapsing onto a bench. "I—saw her receive the blackmail note, and I was able to read it. I didn't know what to do."

"You could have come to me," Matthew said grimly, his eyes searching the yard.

"I tried to stop him," Peter said, holding his wounded arm. "When I saw what kind of man he was, when I discovered that he'd killed Emily's maid—"

"Maria?" Matthew interrupted.

Peter nodded, his eyes bleak.

"What happened next?"

"He shot me when I tried to stop him. I tried to reach you before he did—"

"He just took her. He can't be far. Wait here, Peter." He spoke as forcefully as he would to a soldier under his command.

Emily ran as fast as she could down the grassy slope, slipping, sliding. Her breath wheezed in and out of her lungs with her fear.

On the far side of the river she could see cottages set back from the road. If she could just cross the bridge and reach them—

Her legs pounded across the gravel as she hit the flat of the road. She risked one glance over her shoulder—and Stanwood was there, just coming down the hill, limping, but strengthening as he began to gain on her.

The low bridge had stone walls less than the height of her hips, nothing more than a barrier to keep a coach or wagon from going over into the river. Before she reached the other side, he caught her, grabbing her by the arm, jarring her to a stop so suddenly that she fell hard against the half wall, the stone smacking her painfully in the hips.

He held her bent backward over the wall, his lean face red with fury as he gripped her by the shoulders. She could hear the roar of the water below, feel the spray as water hit the bridge abutment.

"If you *ever* disobey me again, I will silence you like I did your vicar!" he shouted into her face.

He shook her so hard she bit her lip and tasted blood.

"I'm a dead man without you, and if I have to die, I'll take you with me!"

Panicked, she choked out a scream, and he backhanded her across the face, flinging her sideways so her ribs slammed hard into the wall. The pain of his blow rang through her head, and the breath was knocked from her lungs. Desperate, knowing she could very well die, she came upright fast, slamming into him so hard she knocked him sideways, off balance. His lower body hit the half wall, his arms flailed and he fell over it, just managing to catch the crumbling stone edge with one hand.

His shriek was piercing. "I can't swim! Oh God, I can't swim!"

Hands on the lip of the wall, she stared over at Stanwood, his lower legs already dangling in the churning river that pulled at him. His free arm waved frantically as he tried to find another hold.

Emily understood desperation all too well—she couldn't just watch him die. She gripped his wrist where he held onto the wall, knowing that if he let go, she wouldn't be able to prevent his fall.

"Stop flailing!" she cried.

Leaning over the wall, she desperately held onto him, while the water spray soaked them both. She looked over her shoulder—

And saw Matthew running down the hill.

"Mathew!" she screamed.

He pounded across the bridge, and without hesitating or questioning or gloating over their enemy's downfall, grabbed hold of Stanwood's free arm, taking over for her. In that moment, everything inside her eased and lightened with gladness and love.

But Stanwood was beyond terror, kicking and screaming as he begged for his life.

"Stop moving!" Matthew shouted.

Emily cried out as Stanwood lost his grip on the edge of the wall. He lurched downward, held only by Matthew, who used two hands but was no match for the pull of the river, which now swallowed Stanwood up to his thighs. Their wet skin seemed to slide against each other. Matthew cursed and tried to brace his hips against the wall.

Then Stanwood fell, his scream silenced by the water.

Leaning over the wall, Emily and Matthew gaped as he surfaced once, flailing in the powerful current, then went under for the last time.

"Should we go for help?" she cried, clutching Matthew's arm.

He shook his head, his breathing labored as he said, "He'll be dead in a moment, long before a boat could be put to water."

She buried her face against his chest, shuddering, and he took her into his arms.

"If only I'd arrived earlier," he said roughly into

her hair. "But at least there's someone who can answer our questions."

She lifted her head to stare up at him. "Who?"

"Peter Derby." Matthew gave her a grim smile. "You were right all along."

Emily felt no triumph, only sadness. It was over; Stanwood was dead, and he couldn't hurt them anymore. But what about Mr. Derby?

She and Matthew walked slowly back up the hill to the inn, arms about each other. In the yard outside the front door, she saw Mr. Derby sitting on a bench, his face white with strain. When he looked up and saw them, he hung his head in relief.

"Thank God you're all right," he murmured when they approached him.

"You're damn lucky she is," Matthew ground out.

Emily squeezed his waist, then released him to stand on her own. "Matthew, it's all right. He was trying to protect you all, and was even wounded doing so. I cannot blame him for that."

"I know I should have come to you, Matthew," Peter said.

"Instead you left Stanwood's note for me?" Emily asked.

He nodded. "When I . . . realized that you weren't what everyone thought, I was so angry at

being fooled. I thought that you, a criminal"—
he winced—"were laughing at me, laughing at us
all."

Matthew took a menacing step forward. "How
dare you—"

"Matthew!" Emily cried, taking hold of his arm.
"How can you blame Mr. Derby? I *was* lying to
you, using your family."

"You were desperate to survive when you had
nothing else," Matthew insisted.

"I know desperation," Mr. Derby whispered.
"I cannot blame you, Emily. I have spent so long
wondering what I was going to do. I have little of
my own, and it has haunted me, so much so that I
became obsessed with my future. Matthew, when
you returned, I saw that you'd become so successful,
your life had gotten so much bigger, while mine had
only gotten smaller. And then I realized what Emily
was doing to the Lelands, that I could do everyone
a favor by exposing her."

"But you *didn't* expose me," Emily said in
surprise.

He shook his head, his expression bitter. "I followed you, and I saw Stanwood doing the same.
I confronted him; I just wanted to talk to him, to
understand—"

"And then he forced you to help him," she said
softly.

"God help me, but no. I went there meaning to get the truth from him, and instead he made me see what a laughingstock you were making of a noble family, that you deserved to pay for what you'd done."

"He can make people believe and do anything."

"And then he offered me a share of the money." Mr. Derby's expression turned bitter. "I told myself all along that I wouldn't take it, but . . . I don't know what I would have done in the end. I took that note to Madingley Court for him. I didn't know what was going to happen, but Matthew, you only seemed happier as each day passed. I questioned my choices constantly. At last I challenged Stanwood, and he got the best of me."

"He had a gun," Emily said. "And you tried to help us. You have my gratitude." She stared with concern at his arm. "Is your wound still bleeding? You must see a doctor."

"It looks worse than it is," he said. "I deserve what I got for being fool enough to think I should handle everything on my own, that I knew better than you did, Matthew. I ask your forgiveness, although I would understand if you cannot grant it."

"Of course you have our forgiveness," Emily said before Matthew could speak.

She felt Matthew's arm squeeze her shoulders.

"I do understand," Matthew said. "You made a

bad choice, Peter. But what about your choices from now on?"

Mr. Derby closed his eyes for a moment, leaning his head back against the wall. "I don't know. I've made a mess of things."

"You need to find a life of your own. Cambridgeshire might be too small for you, as it was for me. Go to London, Peter. Come talk to me there. I can help you find something to do with your life that doesn't make you feel beholden to your brother. I know people in the military and in business. Let me help you."

Mr. Derby nodded and sighed. "It's good of you to offer, Matthew. I need to think about what I've done—what I want to do. I promise to never reveal your secrets."

"Let's have the innkeeper send for a doctor," Emily said, looking between the two men with relief. She was not surprised at Matthew's generosity. He'd forgiven her, and she'd committed a much graver sin than Mr. Derby had.

In their room, the coal grate gave off welcome heat, and Emily sat near it, dressed in a dry gown but still shivering.

Matthew was preparing her cup of tea with the cream and sugar just the way she liked it. When had he learned that? she wondered, feeling dazed.

He put the cup and saucer beside her, then gently turned her face into the light coming through the window and examined her cheek.

His face darkened. "He bruised you. My God, if only I'd arrived earlier—"

"Matthew, please." She took his hand and held it against her face. "You've said that ten times. Everything is all right."

He gave a tired nod. "Because of you, my little survivor. It still amazes me that you were able to knock him from the bridge."

"Desperation will do that to a person," she said wryly.

He sobered. "You'll never know desperation again, I swear it."

She looked into his warm hazel eyes, so changeable, no longer unreadable to her. She found herself tongue-tied, hesitant, not knowing what he intended, now that he no longer needed to marry her. Did they have a marriage worth saving, or did he mean to just let it go?

To her surprise, he dropped to his knees in front of her and took both her hands in his. "Emily, I almost lost you."

Her lips began to tremble even as tears stung her eyes. "But you didn't, Matthew. I'm here."

"I love you," he said, his voice husky with emotion.

She inhaled, feeling shaky with wonder and dawning happiness. "I love you, too."

"I want to go to Gretna Green and marry you for real. It wasn't just an excuse to escape a madman's plot. I've never met anyone who had to fight so hard to save herself—and I'm including soldiers."

She giggled through her tears.

He didn't smile, his expression so solemn. "I thought I left England to escape the restrictions put on me by my family. But really, I was escaping myself, the man I'd let myself become. So repressed, so controlled, worried about the decisions I'd make. I changed myself, but then I made the mistake of not thinking about the consequences of what I did. It's one thing to do as I wish, as long as no one is hurt. But people got hurt. I didn't look deeply enough at Rahema, just saw what I wanted to. And then when I returned and discovered you here with my family, again I didn't think—I just did as I wanted, just told everyone I had amnesia. I compounded one lie with another, risking everything."

"I gave you no choice! You were trying not to hurt your family. Don't blame yourself for that. In India you married the woman you loved. How could you have foreseen the consequences that would develop?" She cupped his cheek. "I love you, Matthew. I love you for giving me the chance to prove myself. I love you for wanting to help Susanna—and for accepting that she has to do some things on her own."

He closed his eyes and kissed her palm. "Nothing

will stand in the way of our happiness. I grew up thinking marriage was painful, that each day was only something to be gotten through. I thought my life had to be more exciting—but each moment with you is that for me."

"Matthew, up until now I've been a challenge to you. What happens when you see me day in and day out? You'll know everything about me. You might regret being tied to me for eternity."

He grinned. "We'll live our own adventure in marriage. I'll never tire of learning everything about you."

Her face was hot with embarrassment and a love that seemed to want to burst from her. But she forced herself to take it slowly. "Susanna knows about me," she said. "What about the rest of your family, Matthew? Will you tell them the truth of how I came to be married to you? Honesty is so important in a relationship. I vow to you you'll always have that from me."

He leaned forward to kiss her gently. "Thank you. But how we met and fell in love is our secret. I will speak with Susanna. I am lucky to have you, however unorthodox our courtship."

"But I'm not afraid of the truth any longer, Matthew. They're your family, and I don't want a lie to wedge a wall between you and them. They're like a gift to me from you, and I treasure them and your relationship with them."

He smiled tenderly. "Then every year on our anniversary, we'll reconsider our secret. Perhaps for now I want just the two of us to savor our unusual love story."

"That is so romantic," she said, chuckling, even as she wiped the tears from her cheeks. "You have made me feel so safe, Matthew, and it's been a long time since I've felt that way. And even my guilt is gone, for after all, if I wouldn't have become your wife, marrying a stranger, we would never have found each other!"

They shared laughter and kisses, holding each other close, and she knew at last that she would never have to let him go. She felt secure in Matthew's love, secure in the world she'd created for herself. Now all they had to do was get married— for real.

Epilogue

She'd had more than her share of weddings, Emily thought, walking beside her dear husband toward the main drawing room of Madingley Court. She had a false wedding that brought her into the life of Matthew Leland, where she found love and security beyond her wildest hopes. She had their secret wedding in Scotland, where they made their relationship legal and pledged themselves to each other forever.

And now he was giving her a gift, a secret that he refused to reveal. And since he was a man who did things on impulse, who surprised and delighted her every moment of each day they were together, she didn't know what to expect.

He grinned at her one last time before he threw open the drawing room doors.

She gasped. His entire family had arrived without her even knowing it. The Lelands, the Cabots, and the Throckmortens were gathered together, all smiling at each other and at her. Peter Derby had gone to London, but Lieutenant Lawton was there, escorting Lady Hollybush, the widow he'd been courting in secret because he was worried she was too far above him. From the lady's adoring expression, Emily didn't think the lieutenant had anything to worry about.

"What is going on?" she asked as Matthew took her hand and drew her forward. She looked helplessly at Lady Rosa, who was openly crying in the professor's arms. Susanna and Rebecca were holding hands.

"Since I don't remember our first marriage," Matthew began, giving her a secret smile that no one could see but her, "and my family wasn't a part of it, I wanted to celebrate it again with everyone I love."

Emily's eyes started to sting. "But—"

"No protests," he said. "You are special to me, Emily. I want everyone here to know it. I don't remember falling in love with you the first time—"

She winced.

"—but it must be a sort of magic, a destiny, because it happened all over again. Weddings are about family, creating a new family within the ones already established. I wanted you to know that you will always have me, and all of my family. We're yours now."

Tears blurred her eyes and fell down her cheeks.

"Oh, Matthew," she whispered. "I love you so much."

He put his arms around her. "Good, because the vicar is here." Lowering his voice, he said, "Marry me, Emily, and not because you want to make things right. Marry *me*."

"I will—I do. Oh Matthew!" She threw herself into his arms, his strong body her shelter. She was so blessed. How many women could marry the man they loved—several times! Everyone clapped and cheered, even as she thanked God for giving her a husband, a new family, and love.

Unforgettable, enthralling love stories,
sparkling with passion and adventure
from Romance's bestselling authors

NEVER DARE A DUKE   *by Gayle Callen*
978-0-06-123506-1

SIMPLY IRRESISTIBLE   *by Rachel Gibson*
978-0-380-79007-4

A PERFECT DARKNESS   *by Jaime Rush*
978-0-06-169035-8

YOU'RE THE ONE THAT I HAUNT   *by Terri Garey*
978-0-06-158203-5

SECRET LIFE OF A VAMPIRE   *by Kerrelyn Sparks*
978-0-06-166785-5

FORBIDDEN NIGHTS WITH A VAMPIRE *by Kerrelyn Sparks*
978-0-06-166784-8

ONE RECKLESS SUMMER   *by Toni Blake*
978-0-06-142989-7

DESIRE UNTAMED   *by Pamela Palmer*
978-0-06-166751-0

OBSESSION UNTAMED   *by Pamela Palmer*
978-0-06-166752-7

PASSION UNTAMED   *by Pamela Palmer*
978-0-06-166753-4

AVON

978-0-06-143438-9

978-0-06-164836-6

978-0-06-164837-3

978-0-06-170628-8

978-0-06-171570-9

978-0-06-154778-2

At Avon Books, we know your passion for romance—once you finish one of our novels, you find yourself wanting more.

May we tempt you with . . .

- **Excerpts** from our upcoming releases.

- Entertaining **extras**, including authors' personal photo albums and book lists.

- Behind-the-scenes **scoop** on your favorite characters and series.

- **Sweepstakes** for the chance to win free books, romantic getaways, and other fun prizes.

- Writing **tips** from our authors and editors.

- **Blog** with our authors and find out why they love to write romance.

- **Exclusive content** that's not contained within the pages of our novels.

Join us at
www.avonbooks.com

AVON

An Imprint of HarperCollinsPublishers
www.avonromance.com